THE GREAT
DEBATE

Also by T. L. TEDROW

Missouri Homestead
Children of Promise
Good Neighbors
Home to the Prairie
The World's Fair
Mountain Miracle

BOOK 7

THE GREAT DEBATE

T. L. TEDROW

SCHOLASTIC INC.
New York Toronto London Auckland Sydney

Illustrations by Dennas Davis

ISBN 0-590-22657-6

12 11 10 9 8 7 6 5 4 3 2 1   5 6 7 8 9/9 0/0

Printed in the U.S.A.   40

First Scholastic printing, March 1995

To my pretty wife Carla and our younguns,
C.T., Tyler, Tara and Travis.

May we never forget the magic of childhood dreams which
is really what being young at heart is all about.

And to my good friends at Thomas Nelson,
for making these dreams come true.

CONTENTS

FOREWORD

Laura Ingalls Wilder is known and loved for her pioneer books and the heartwarming television series based on them. Though much has been written about the old West, it was Laura Ingalls Wilder who brought the frontier to life for millions of young readers.

The American West offered a fresh start to anyone brave enough to face the challenges. These people tamed the frontier, crossing the prairie in wagons carrying furniture, seeds, and children, looking for a place to build a new life. They went west to raise families, build farms and towns, churches and businesses. They went knowing they would face hardship and danger, but that those who survived could build a future for their children.

Laura Ingalls's adventures did not stop after she married Almanzo Wilder. She went on to become a pioneer journalist in Mansfield, Missouri, where for sixteen years she was a columnist for the weekly paper, *Missouri Ruralist*.

Laura Ingalls Wilder, a self-taught journalist, always spoke her mind. She worked for women's rights, lamented the consequences of war, and observed the march of progress as cars, planes, radios, and new inventions changed America forever.

While this book is a fictional account of Laura's exploits, it retains the historical integrity of her columns, diary, family background, personal beliefs, and the general history of the times in which she lived. However, any references to specific events, real people, or real places are intended only to give the fiction a setting in historical reality. Names, characters, and incidents are either the product of my imagination or are used fictitiously, and their resemblance, if any, to real-life counterparts is purely coincidental.

T. L. TEDROW

CHAPTER 1

PRAIRIE MEMORIES

Laura sat by herself on the train to St. Louis, staring out the window. She watched the Missouri countryside flash by with vacant eyes. Her mind was on the suffragist rally she was going to address.

Laura's articles on women's rights had attracted the attention of Ellen Boyle, the hauntingly beautiful Irish woman who was a leader in the campaign for women's voting rights in America. Ellen had invited Laura to speak at the St. Louis rally.

Laura nervously twisted the button on her blouse, lost in worry. *Ellen Boyle will be there. So will Susan B. Anthony. I've got only a prairie education. I learned to read and write at home. These women are probably college educated. I hope I don't embarrass them. I hope Ellen accepts my invitation to come to Mansfield and speak.*

Laura had slept badly since receiving the invitation to address the rally. At first she was elated. Then the worry set in. *I'll be on stage before a large crowd of strangers. Ellen wrote that I should expect a hostile crowd. What will I do if they heckle me?*

Her fears and worries had upset the balance of life at Apple Hill Farm. *I've been so on edge. I've been really snappy at Manly,* she fretted. *I'll have to make it up to him when I get home.*

Manly, Laura's husband of twenty years, had not been in favor of Laura going to St. Louis. He asked her once to reconsider, but Laura said it was something she had to do. From that moment on, he avoided all discussion of the rally and women getting the right to vote.

Manly had driven her to the train station in silence. *He didn't want me to come, but he didn't try to stop me,* Laura thought. *He just went quiet on me. I guess he was expressing his feelings through his silence.*

She shook her head. *I tried to make him understand, but he's only worried about what the men of Mansfield think. He bears a lot in silence. I know they are probably giving him a hard time.*

I wish he'd talk to me about it, but he always shrugs it off. "Honeybee, I married you for better or worse," he says. I wonder which he feels it is now?

Laura wanted to think of something else. She reached into her purse and took out the article she'd found on Sacagawea, the brave young Indian woman who led the Lewis and Clark expedition. The article had inspired her to begin a fund-raising drive to build a statue in honor of Sacagawea.

As she reread it, Laura was again moved. *Sacagawea was so young, so brave, heading off across the wilderness with a newborn baby on her back. Without her guidance, without Sacagawea, Lewis and Clark would have failed in their expedition to open up America.*

Laura thought about the statue she wanted to build. She thought about the painting she planned to show at the rally, an artist rendering of the beautiful Indian woman with the baby strapped on her back, pointing the way for Lewis and Clark. She thought about her plan to ask Ellen Boyle to come to Mansfield to help raise funds for the statue. Then she thought about the snide and whispered criticisms that had been thrown at her around town.

Women deserve the right to vote, she thought, as another small town passed by. *If women don't stand together on this issue, our chance to vote may never come again.*

Laura was lost in a sea of contradictions. The only four states that had granted women the right to vote before 1900 were Western states—Wyoming, Colorado, Idaho, and Utah—yet the women's suffrage movement had originated in the East.

Why do men have such attitudes? Why were they willing to

accept our efforts to tame the prairies and now won't let us vote? Are we just babymakers and cooks, just pieces of furniture to move around and discard at will? We have minds with our bodies. We're not cattle.

I've got to get my mind off this, Laura thought. Then she did what she used to do back on the prairie: she took out her diary pad and began writing.

Sometimes, just writing about crossing the prairies is soothing. It takes me back to a place and time where, as a young girl, I didn't have to worry about politics. We were more concerned with eating and finding a place to build a home.

I remember writing on my lap with the wind rocking the wagon across the plains, Ma knitting, and Pa singing out a song. He'd hug Ma and say, "This is the way life's supposed to be: a man and his woman together with their kids, ridin' across the prairie, makin' their own way."

Laura put her pencil down. *Is that the way it's supposed to be? Is what I'm doing at odds with Pa's beliefs?*

She closed her eyes and thought about what her father would say. About how he would feel on her speaking out. She smiled as she thought, *Pa would be for me doing this. He always said that Ma was his partner in life.*

Laura nodded off asleep at peace with herself. *The women's rights rally in St. Louis will be the biggest crowd I've ever spoken to. But if Sacagawea could cross America without a map, I can stand up and speak out for all the women who have followed behind her. Manly will just have to understand.*

CHAPTER 2

ELLEN BOYLE

Ellen Boyle looked over the crowd of men assembled in downtown St. Louis, Missouri. It was a hostile crowd that waited for her to take the podium.

With her beauty and strong convictions, Ellen attracted crowds wherever she went. Her flowing auburn hair and disarming smile both dazzled and infuriated male audiences.

"Don't bother to speak!" shouted a burly man from the edge of the podium.

His dockworker friend agreed. "Yeah, women ain't never goin' to get the right to vote as long as men are controllin' things!"

"Ellen, you're too pretty to be standin' up there," shouted a lawyer. "Come with me and I'll take you to dinner."

Ellen winked. "Sign that voting petition and I might consider it." The men around the lawyer slapped him on the back.

She leaned over and said to Page O'Mally, her assistant, "I've spoken to crowds and I've spoken my mind to the walls of my room. But this will be the first time that I've spoken to a bunch of river rats."

"Ellen, hush," Page said. "That's an insulting term along the Mississippi."

"You are what you are," Ellen said, shaking her head.

Ellen had been through dozens of rallies like this. *Some men come to listen, some to heckle, and some to just cause trouble.* She had already pinpointed the trouble-makers. It was a protective habit she had gotten into. Even though it was a warm June 1, 1906, she shivered at their cold stares.

Ellen watched as Susan B. Anthony finished speaking. Susan, from Rochester, New York, was the most famous fighter for women's rights in the land. She looked to Ellen as she walked from the podium. "It's a bad crowd," she said.

"But it's better than the one we just had in Boston," Ellen answered.

"It's a big mountain we're trying to climb."

"It's either climb or fall off. There's no middle ground in this fight." Ellen stared intently at Susan, who nodded in agreement.

Susan pointed with a nod of her head toward Laura Ingalls Wilder who sat apprehensively on the stage. "She looks like she might faint."

"I don't think she's ever been up against the likes of this before," Ellen said.

"She writes for what paper?" Susan asked.

"The *Mansfield Monitor,* or something like that. I read her articles and invited her to speak."

"Think she can handle it?" Susan asked.

"We'll soon see," Ellen said with a smile.

Susan started to say something but was drowned out by hecklers. "Go home! Take care of your husbands, if you got 'em!" jeered a sidewalk vendor.

"Yeah, you women suffragists ain't welcome here," shouted another man in the crowd.

Susan shook her head. "Boston or St. Louis, it doesn't seem to matter where you are with this issue." She walked over to Laura. "It's your turn, deary. Good luck."

Laura looked at the note cards in her hand. "Now I know how the Christians felt when the lions were roaring."

"At least after the lions ate they went to sleep. These men are something else," Susan said.

"Are you girls speakin' or gabbin'?" shouted a butcher, wiping his hands on his apron. "Some of us have to get back to work."

Ellen called over to the two women. "Mrs. Wilder, if you're goin' to speak, come on. This crowd is not one to wait." She looked across the stage at Laura. *She looks nervous, like a fish out of water. I hope she can handle this.*

"Hey, Ellen," the lawyer shouted, "how come you're not married? Can't you find a man?"

Ellen instinctively fingered the locket under her blouse and started to speak, but Page O'Mally shouted out, "She hasn't got time for that nonsense. She's married to the cause."

"Sounds lonely to me," the lawyer said.

Sometimes it is, thought Ellen. *Sometimes it really is.*

She desperately wanted to open the locket and look at the picture of the moment in time before she married the cause. When she was going to marry one certain man.

As Laura Ingalls Wilder took the podium, Ellen turned her focus back to the cause she'd championed since leaving Ireland—since leaving the man she loved.

CHAPTER 3

SPEAKING OUT

Laura took a deep breath trying to calm her nervousness. The train had been delayed for several hours, and she had rushed by cab to the rally. To make matters worse, when she stepped up onto the platform with Ellen Boyle and Susan B. Anthony, she had dropped her speech notes.

This unruly gathering was a long way from the polite library groups she usually spoke to back in Mansfield, as president of the local Good Government Club.

Mansfield, she thought. *My writings have divided the town, even divided my own house. But standing up for my rights is something I've got to do. I couldn't live with myself any other way.*

Laura's articles advocating women's having the immediate right to vote *had* stirred up the town. Andrew Jackson Summers, Laura's boss and editor openly opposed her, and she'd begun to notice that the male merchants of the town were treating her coldly.

Then Laura came up with idea to build a statue of Sacagawea in Mansfield, so everyone could remember and appreciate the sacrifices that women had made in building America. Thinking that everyone would gladly contribute toward funding the statue, she'd been surprised to find stiff resistance in Mansfield. Laura and her friends had only been able to raise less than a third of the money needed to pay the artist.

And so she had come to St. Louis to invite Ellen Boyle to Mansfield to speak at a women's fund-raising rally. It seemed a good idea at the library meeting back in Mansfield, but that was before Laura faced this crowd.

The only way to change opinion is through discussion, to build a consensus, to get community agreement, she thought. But this crowd was not a community looking for a consensus. It seemed more like a pack of hounds that had cornered a fox.

"My name is—"

"Speak louder, we can't hear you," shouted a cobbler.

"Sorry," Laura said, blushing. "My name is—"

"I said we can't hear you," the cobbler shouted again.

Ellen quipped from the side of the stage. "Ignore him, that's just a tactic to throw you off balance."

Laura closed her eyes for a moment, then began again. "My name is Laura Ingalls Wilder, and I'm a writer for the *Mansfield Monitor.* I've come to ask your support for the statue we want to build in Mansfield, to recognize the achievements of women in America."

Laura gripped the podium and tapped on the life-sized sketch of the statue she wanted to see placed in Mansfield's town square. The crowd moved closer to view the beautiful buckskin-clad figure with a baby on her back, seeming to point the way on the issue.

"This statue that we, the women of Missouri, are raising our hard-earned money to build, will honor the memory of Sacagawea and the pioneer mothers of the West," Laura said, looking at the hostile faces confronting her.

A few men in the crowd hooted, but most kept quiet, letting her speak. "This is an opportunity to hail the liberty that is dawning for the women of this great land. It symbolizes the opportunity for the wise, patriotic, and chivalrous free men of America to welcome their wives, mothers, and sisters as equals; to give them the voting rights they so deserve and have earned."

"The only thing you women have opened is your mouths," another lawyer shouted at the stage.

It was a cold, curious, and critical crowd facing Laura. She had never spoken for women's rights outside of Mansfield. She didn't know what lay ahead.

Ellen did. She had seen crowds like this from Boston to Denver. Men who might have all the manners in the world suddenly turned crazy at the thought of their wives voting. *There's no middle ground in America,* she thought, brushing back her auburn hair with her fingers. She ignored the wolf whistles from some of the men. *We either win or lose it all on this issue.*

Ellen kept an eye on the reaction of the crowd as Laura described the heroics of the young Shoshone Indian woman who had blazed the trail for Lewis and Clark on their journey west from Missouri, one hundred years earlier. But the men mocked her speech, never grasping the significance of the woman who was being honored.

"This woman was a slave to another Indian tribe before she gained her freedom," Laura said, pointing her finger at the crowd. "And it was as a free woman that she agreed to help lead Lewis and Clark through the wilderness of this land. She carried on her back her small baby boy, fathered by a French-Canadian trapper."

"You can dump her squaw statue in the river," a drunken dock loader jeered at Laura.

"Trust me, the river rats *have* crawled out," Ellen whispered to Page O'Mally.

Page nodded. "This is turning ugly," she said, as a barrage of peanuts hit the stage.

Laura cleared the peanuts from her notes and looked up as the butcher shouted, "What you want to honor a half-breed baby-maker for?"

Some of the men looked at each other. "A half-breed?" shouted a deck hand from the edge of the stage. "We're honoring a half-breed's momma?"

Laura's eyes burned. "A mother? Yes, Sacagawea was a mother. She had married a French-Canadian and had a child of mixed blood, which I think symbolizes America, a land of people from all over the world."

"Get out of here," laughed the lawyer. The group around him began to jeer.

"You men should be ashamed of yourselves. This woman helped stretch our empire to the Pacific."

"Come on lady, she was just an Indian," shouted a tourist with his harried wife in tow.

"Just an Indian?" Laura said, shaking her head. "In honoring Sacagawea, we pay homage to thousands of uncrowned heroines who made possible the achievements of America's great men!"

The tourist laughed. "You ought to tell jokes on stage."

"She just wants to close our saloons," the whiskey vendor shouted to the crowd. "She's another one of them temperance fanatics."

"Is that what you want to do?" asked the butcher. "Deny us hard-working men the chance to buy a cold one after work?"

Laura shook her head. "I am here to speak about the statue we are building and women having the right to vote. Not about men having the right to drink themselves to death."

"I need a drink after listening to you," the whiskey vendor shouted, downing a glass. "Anyone else want a half-price shot?"

A dozen men cheered, lining up in front of the whiskey cart. "Go home and cook for your husband," a dry goods store owner shouted to Laura.

Ellen walked up and whispered to Laura, "Don't let them get to you. They just want to fluster you so they can have a good laugh at your expense."

Laura wanted to scream out her anger but couldn't. "I've journeyed across the prairies, carrying my own load," she said to Ellen. "This isn't fair."

"Life's not fair," Ellen said.

"There they go, gabbin' again," shouted the butcher, "just like a bunch of hens!"

"You've got a bit farther to go to convince this crowd," Ellen said, lightly touching Laura's shoulder.

And it looks like I've got a bit farther to go before I am an equal citizen of the United States, Laura thought.

Laura had made her decision to stand with the women on the frontlines on this issue. The choice was to accept things as they were or speak out. To Laura, there was no choice.

Having to ask for the right to vote seemed absurd to Laura. She had been raised in the West, which was the first area of America that was full of promise for women.

It isn't fair, Laura thought. *We had to fight off Indians, endure disease, starvation, and an aching sense of loneliness on the endless, barren prairies. It was the women of the prairies who pressed for schools, churches, enforcing the law, and driving out the bad elements. We opened up and changed America. And now we can't vote on its future.*

The audience began to boo. "Cat got your tongue, lady?" the tourist shouted.

Ellen looked worried. "Are you all right?" she asked quietly from the side.

"Maybe she's scared," Susan Anthony said. "It happens to the best of us."

"I'm all right," Laura said, shrugging off her mood. She raised her hands and shouted, "If it hadn't been for the endeavors of countless women, the West would never have been won."

"Two bits for a head shot," a man said, carrying a box through the crowd.

Ellen noticed some of the unruly men reaching into the box. "Here it comes," she said to Susan, ducking as a barrage of rotten eggs hit the stage. Laura didn't flinch as they hit her dress and splattered around her.

Laura picked up an egg which hadn't broken and hurled it back. "You're as rotten as the eggs you throw," she shouted.

An apple hit the side of Laura's head, dazing her for a moment. A mean-spirited laughter swept through the crowd as Laura held on to the podium for balance.

Ellen stepped up beside her. "Sit down, Mrs. Wilder. Let me have a go at them."

She helped Laura to her chair and came back to the podium, kicking eggshells from around her feet. Ellen stood ramrod straight and eyed the men. An egg sailed toward her and she ducked, as if it was just an everyday occurrence.

The improvised bandstand was barely larger than a packing crate, but Ellen's presence made it seem like the grandest stage in the country. She waved to the few women in the crowd.

"Thank you for coming, ladies," she said, nodding to their cheers. "I hope that none of these rude louts are your husbands."

"Go home!" shouted the butcher.

"Yeah, good-bye, sis!" a gigantic dockworker said with a laugh. Then he turned and shouted, "Pass me an egg, quick!"

"Just ignore the bullies," Ellen said to her followers, "and pass the petitions around."

"Nobody sign them," a burly black man shouted. "Women got too much power now."

"They do?" Ellen said, with mock indignation. "I don't think so."

"You ain't never met my wife," he said, playfully patting the woman beside him.

"How soon we forget when we couldn't vote, when we weren't free to choose our destiny," Ellen said. The black man suddenly looked embarrassed.

"You don't know the importance of the ballot. You take it for granted," Ellen said from the podium above the mumbling of the crowd.

"Yes, we do," the men chorused back at her.

"And that's why we don't want women votin' for president," a balding deckhand jeered.

The hostility warmed Ellen to the confrontation. "Do you men really think it would be possible for women to make a worse mess of politics than you have?"

"Yes, yes!" the men cried out, slapping each other on the back.

The butcher said, "We'd end up having an army of beauticians instead of soldiers."

"Maybe it would be better to have beauticians armed with curling irons than waste our money on weapons of death and destruction."

Suffragettes moved through the crowd asking for signatures on the petition urging the United States Congress to open the way to voting rights for women. Some of the men signed it, then left quickly to avoid any heckling from the vocal opponents.

"Isn't it time to pass an equal suffrage amendment to the Constitution?" Ellen asked quietly during a lull in the crowd.

"Why should we?" the butcher cried out.

"Because it is the just thing to do!" Ellen snapped back, looking him in the eyes. "The women's suffrage amendment, to give one-half the people of this great country the right to vote, was first introduced into the U.S. Senate in 1868 and to the House of Representatives in 1869. It hasn't been passed yet."

Some of the crowd laughed and joked among themselves.

After pausing for a moment, she held up her hands and the crowd quieted down. "What we ask is simple. Shouldn't the same arguments made for extending suffrage to white men, to native-born citizens, to those without property and education, and to foreigners, be offered to women?"

"Go home and clean your house!" a workman shouted.

Ellen shook her head. "A moment ago a black gentleman made fun of women's having the right to vote. The Republican party enfranchised a million black men in the South after the Civil War, giving them the right to vote, but excluded black women." She looked at the black man's wife who looked straight back at her.

"This fundamental principle of democracy—the equality of all citizens of the republic—should be incorporated into the Constitution to give women the same rights as men."

A teenage boy standing with a rowdy bunch of classmates, threw a tomato. One of his friends grabbed the petition and literature from one of Ellen's followers and tossed it all into the air.

A minister in the crowd held up his Bible. "It says in the Bible that man does not originate from woman, but woman from man; that women were created for man's sake."

"Leave the Bible out of this," Ellen shouted.

Another egg spattered at Ellen's feet and a man reached up and tried to pull her down. "Get off the stage, you witch!"

"Keep your hands off her!" Laura shouted, coming to Ellen's defense. Another apple hit Laura's back. She picked it up and flung it back, hitting the man she thought had thrown it.

The crowd surged forward, trying to get closer to the action. The petition-carrying women tried without success to form a line to block the crowd who pushed against the stage, rocking it back and forth.

Shouts, screams, glass breaking—it was out of control. Laura started toward the edge of the stage but a group of men pushed her back.

The last thing Laura remembered was falling as the stage overturned and police whistles sounded from all directions. After that it was all darkness.

CHAPTER 4

JAILBIRDS

When Laura regained consciousness, Ellen was nursing a nasty bruise on Laura's forehead.

"Where am I?" Laura mumbled, trying to sit up.

"Take it easy," Ellen smiled, "you're going no place fast."

Laura blinked and looked around, recognizing the faces of some of the women from the rally. Then she saw the bars. "Jail?" she asked. "What happened?"

Ellen laughed. "What happened? Why, you missed the biggest fight since San Juan Hill!" The women in the cell laughed.

"But why were *we* arrested? They started it."

"I don't know why they hauled you off with us," Ellen said. "You were out cold."

"Someone told the police you were one of us," Page said.

"Said you were a radical, so they dragged you along with us," another woman added.

Ellen smiled. "That you are."

Laura sat up, a bit dazed, and touched her forehead. "Ouch, that hurts."

"It looks as bad as it feels, Mrs. Wilder," Ellen said.

"Please call me Laura," she said, wincing at the pain. "What laws did we violate?"

"They have you charged with distrubing the peace and assault," Ellen said.

"Assault?" Laura asked.

"You hit a man with that apple you threw," Ellen said, laughing.

Laura groaned. "What am I going to tell my husband?"

Ellen saw the look of concern in Laura's eyes. "This your first time being jailed?" Laura nodded. "Well, when you fight for your rights, it's going to happen."

"It's either jail or accept being second-class citizens forever," Page said.

Laura looked around, then at Ellen. "I came to ask you to come to speak in Mansfield, to help us raise money for our statue."

Ellen smiled. "You'd still want me to come after what happened?"

"Now more than ever," Laura said, grimmacing at the pain above her eye.

"When?" Ellen asked. "I can't come this week. I've got to help some women strike against a sweat shop tyrant."

"I was hoping you could come the fifteenth of the month. It's a celebration in our town and we'll have a big turnout."

"What's the celebration?"

Laura looked down, embarrassed. "Mule Day," she said softly.

"Mule Day!" Ellen laughed. "What's that?"

"Sounds like a joke," one of the women smirked.

"It's no joke," Laura said defensively. "The farmers show their mules, and the town has a bake sale and general get-together."

"You want me to speak to a mule celebration?" Ellen asked, making a face.

"Mules are just beasts of burden," said one of the jailed women. The others laughed.

Ellen rubbed her chin. "Beasts of burden? Isn't that what some of the men called us yesterday? I like the sound of it."

Laura watched Ellen carefully, worried that she was about to get herself into more hot water.

Ellen continued. "That will be the subject of my talk at your Mule Day. How women have been the beasts of burden for men throughout history."

"I like it," said one of the women, and the other women nodded.

"How we have been used for toil, raising children with no appreciation," Ellen said to them, rousing them on.

"That's a fact," said another woman.

Ellen stood up and said loudly, "How we will no longer be taken for granted. That we must be given the right to vote, to help shape our own destiny!"

The women in the cell clapped and cheered but stopped when the jailer banged on the bar with his stick. "You jailbirds shut up in there!"

Ellen laughed. "Jailbirds? You big buzzard, come in here without that stick and we'll show you what these birds are made of."

The jailer sneered. "You act more like men than women. I pity the poor saps who're married to you. And besides," he said, turning away, "you smell like a bunch of rotten eggs." The jailer walked away with the jeers of the women echoing behind him.

Ellen nodded to Laura. "I'll be coming to your Mule Day, Laura. I've read the articles you wrote about women's rights. I wouldn't miss this for anything."

Ellen paused then asked, "What was that you wrote last week? 'If politics is not what it should be, if there are unjust laws, then it is the responsibility of women—all women—to confront the men and tell them to give us our basic rights. We can clean up the unfinished business of bringing equality to America if we stand together.' "

Laura blushed. "I guess I got carried away—"

Ellen stopped her. "Carried away? I wish you'd written more!"

"How much money are you trying to raise for the statue?" Page asked.

"We've raised two hundred dollars from the women of Mansfield, but we need about twelve hundred dollars more."

"That's fourteen hundred dollars!" Ellen exclaimed. "That's a small fortune."

"Yes, but it's just a pittance to what it should be. I wish we could raise enough money to put one in every state," Laura said boldly.

"Be that as it may," Ellen said with a smile, "what you're doing is a grand start."

"Who's makin' the statue—a man?" asked one of the women in the cell.

"No," Laura said, "there's a famous female artist in the Ozarks named Mae Jefferson."

"Is that the same one as M. Jefferson, the sculptor written about in the *St. Louis Post-Dispatch* yesterday?" Ellen asked. "It didn't say she was a female."

"I've never met her," Laura said, "but it's my understanding that she goes by her first initial so she can get work." Laura looked down for a moment. "I didn't know M. Jefferson was a female until her agent told me."

"I think it adds more meaning to what you're trying to accomplish," Ellen said. "I'd like to meet this M. Jefferson when I come to town."

"I don't know if I can arrange that. She's a recluse who lives in the hills," Laura said.

Ellen nodded. "Well, see if you can arrange for her to come hear me speak. She sounds like one of us."

"Anybody in there named Wilder?" the jailer shouted, rapping on the bars with his stick.

Laura looked up. "I'm Laura Ingalls Wilder."

The jailer looked down at the piece of paper in his hand. "Yeah, you're the one," he said, unlocking the cell door.

"Where are you taking me?" Laura asked, panicking for a moment.

"Man claiming he's your husband has arranged to pay your fine."

"How did my husband know I was in here?" Laura asked, relieved. She straightened out her dress.

Ellen put her arm around Laura. "Susan Anthony managed to keep herself from being arrested. She was worried about your going to a hospital, so she found your address in your wallet and sent a telegram to your husband."

Laura shook her head. "A telegram from Susan B. Anthony will be the talk of Mansfield by nightfall."

Ellen laughed. "Make the best of it! Wear it on your arm like a badge of honor."

"Come on, lady," the jailer said, "I ain't got all day."

"Is my husband here?" she asked.

"Naw, but he's on the phone."

"My goodness, why didn't you tell me?" Laura exclaimed. She walked out of the cell without saying good-bye, then remembered her comrades and turned. "Is there something I can do for all of you?"

"Susan's working things out. We should all be out by morning," Ellen said.

"Then you'll come to Mansfield on the fifteenth?"

Ellen laughed. "I wouldn't miss your Mule Day if you paid me. And speaking of pay, I'll come under certain conditions."

"What are they?" Laura asked, suddenly worried that Ellen would charge a fee to speak, something Laura hadn't anticipated.

"You pay my way, put me up, and feed me. Then give me a spoon of your town."

"A spoon?" Laura asked.

"A commemorative spoon of Mansfield," Ellen said. "I've been collecting them from coast to coast, wherever I speak."

"That's right," Page said, "Ellen has spoons from San Francisco to New York."

"Yeah," said another, "you ought to see what she's got in her suitcase back at the hotel."

"Ladies," Ellen said, blushing. "It's just something I collect." She looked at Laura. "So if you agree to my terms, I'll be there."

Laura didn't want to tell her that Mansfield was so small that it didn't have any commemorative spoons. "I'll agree to it."

"Lady, come on. Your husband's on the phone," the jailer shouted.

"He can wait a moment," Laura said. The jailed women hooted in support, and Laura blushed.

Ellen laughed. "And if you can find me a black-cat-and-witch spoon from Salem, Massachusetts, then I'll be forever beholden to you."

"Witch spoon?" Laura asked.

"They call it the Salem spoon. The first one ever made in this country," Ellen said. "My collection won't be complete without one."

"Lady, the phone. Or do you want to stay in jail?" the jailer asked, shaking his head.

"I'm coming," Laura said. She looked at the other women and then at Ellen. "I'm proud to have met you all."

"This will give you something to write about," Ellen said. "Now get on to the phone before your husband hangs up on you. He must be a good man for posting your bail and standing up for you."

Ellen watched Laura walk through the cell doors, wondering what it would be like to have a man care enough about her to stand with her on the issues. For a brief moment, she longed for the happy days in Ireland, when she had a young man who would have done anything for her.

Ellen sighed. *He loved me. He wanted to marry me.* She looked at the other women around her. *But now I'm married to the movement. I've spent years speaking out for the women of America, but I haven't had time to do anything for myself. I'd like to stop for a while, take a rest. But who'll take my place?*

In her mind she saw the green fields of Ireland. Riding into the wind with Thomas, her auburn hair flying free, their laughter a testament to the happiness of their world. *What would my life have been like if I'd said yes, if I'd married him? I wonder where Thomas is right now?*

Ellen rested her head against the cell bars. *He's probably a thousand miles away, ma:ried, with a house full of children. Oh, Thomas, the woman who has you is lucky indeed.*

She slipped the locket out from under her blouse and snapped it open. In the picture, a woman twenty years younger stood next to a handsome boy-man. She smiled again. *There was fire between us, there was. My mother worried that we were going to elope, that the fire of waiting to be married would consume us.*

She closed the locket up and looked through the bars. *It almost did. Sometimes I wish it had.*

CHAPTER 5

LONG-DISTANCE CHILL

Manly waited on the phone, rereading Laura's article from the previous day. It was on the front page of the *Mansfield Monitor,* and he'd heard about it from every man in town.

A Woman's Duty
By Laura Ingalls Wilder

Women can no longer hide behind their husbands and fathers and brothers by saying, "I don't pay any attention to politics. That's men's business." We've not paid attention for so long that we've let men make a mess of things—things we're paying for through taxes, broken families, and growing unrest in our cities.

Women have a duty to think for themselves. We must no longer hide our feelings and beliefs behind the silence imposed by society, religion, and unconstitutional laws passed by men for men.

Women cannot simply agree with men for no reason at all. This country has had a string of wars, labor problems, and hungry people that attest to the fallacy of the blind leading the blind.

We women know in our hearts, though we have been reluctant to admit it, that men are not infallible. They do make mistakes and can have wrong ideas.

Just because we took marriage vows to love, honor, and obey, doesn't mean we took vows to hide, cower, and not think for ourselves. A woman's duty is to herself—to do what is right. And what is right is for all women to demand the right to vote.

That is every woman's duty.

Manly shook his head. *She's really gone off and done it this time.* He looked at his watch. *Where is she? This call is costin' a fortune!*

"Hello, Manly? Are you there, Manly?" Laura asked loudly over the noise on the line. Several policemen in the room looked up so Laura lowered her voice. "Are you there, Manly?"

Manly dropped the paper. "Laura? Laura? What in tarnation's goin' on up there? Are you all right?" Manly asked through the static.

"I'm all right. Just a bruise on my head and . . ." The static cut her off.

Manly shouted over the line noise. "From the telegram, I thought you'd been hurt bad. I was worried, Laura."

Laura felt her forehead and winced. "I'm fine. Just bumped my head when I fell off the stage." There was silence on the line. "Did you hear me?"

"I heard you," Manly said stiffly. "First I was worried, and then I couldn't understand what you were doin' in jail."

"There was a lot of pushing and shoving at the rally, Manly."

"They told me you'd been arrested for disturbin' the peace and assault. Assault? What happened?"

"I threw an apple back at a man who threw it at me," Laura said, igorning the shaking heads of the policemen around her.

"And hit him in the head," Manly said.

"It just happened. You had to be there," Laura said defensively.

"But the policeman said there was a riot and a whole bunch of you women were thrown in the pokey."

"That's right, but we didn't start it." Laura paused, waiting for a reaction from Manly, but there was none. "The men caused the riot."

"Jailbirds are always innocent," a policeman in the room said to the old officer next to him.

"They all say they didn't do nothin', don't they," the officer said, rolling his eyes.

"Did you hear me, Manly? I said the men caused the riot."

"Riot!" Manly exclaimed. "My word, woman, what else happened?"

"I'll tell you all about it when I get there. You probably shouldn't tell anyone about what happened."

"Tell anyone? Who's left to tell?" Manly huffed. "When Stephen Scales got your telegraph, he had Sarah connect us on the telephone. She listened in, and by now everyone in the county knows you're a regular convict! I asked you not to go."

"Manly!" she exclaimed. "I'm not a convict! I was just jailed and released." The policemen in the room laughed quietly among themselves.

"Then you're a jailbird no less," Manly said. "But you can read all about it when you get home," he said, in disgust.

"Read what?"

"Summers heard about it and is printin' a front-page story about you bein' tossed in jail like a common pickpocket."

"Can't you stop him?" Laura said, very distressed. "Make him wait until I get back on the train."

"Laura, Summers is probably tickled pink about all this. The way you two have been duelin' it out about women gettin' the right to vote with your columns, why, this will go a long way to provin' him right."

"Right? My getting arrested has nothing to do with women getting the right to vote." There was a silence on the line. "Manly? Manly, are you still there?"

"It's got everythin' to do with everythin'," Manly said softly. "It's men who decide if women get the right to vote, and Summers will use this to sway the undecided."

"Then you march over to his office right now and stand up to him!" Laura demanded. The policemen in the room raised their eyebrows at the way she addressed her husband.

"Hold your horses there, Geronimo," Manly said over the line. "I'm not the one in jail for assaultin' someone and I'm not goin' to march over and say nothin'. I just spent my new horse money to get you out of the pokey. You tell Summers anythin' you want, but leave me out of it."

"But, Manly, I was just—"

"I don't want to be involved," Manly said. "Now catch tomorrow morning's train to Mansfield and I'll pick you up at the station."

"Manly, I'm . . . I'm sorry."

"We'll talk about it when you get home." He clicked the phone off leaving Laura staring at the receiver.

"Somethin' wrong, lady?" the jailer asked from behind her.

"No . . . yes . . . I," she stammered, disturbed by the way the call had ended.

The jailer laughed. "Make up your mind."

"Just like a woman," the old officer said.

"Where can I get a taxi back to my hotel?"

"I'll show you to the front door. You can get one there," a kindly young policeman said.

Laura was unaware of the bold headline being typeset that very moment in the newspaper office back in Mansfield.

CHAPTER 6

NO APPRECIATION?

Andrew Jackson Summers looked at the proof sheet and smiled. "This should stir some things up," he said to himself.

Tony Loren, the typesetter, shook his head. "Sure you don't want to hold this til Laura returns?"

"Not on your life!" Summers said. "Laura's been campaignin' how women are better able to lead the world then men. Well, let's see what she has to say about this."

Tony looked at the headline again.

LAURA INGALLS WILDER ARRESTED
IN VOTING RIGHTS RIOT!
BOOKED FOR ASSAULT!

"But she was knocked unconscious and wasn't in the fight," the typesetter said in protest. "That happened to me when I was back in Italy."

"So?" Summers said, quite pleased with himself.

"So, she didn't know what was happenin'."

"She was still arrested and booked, wasn't she?" Summers said. "She was booked, just like a man."

"Yeah, but for assault *with an apple,*" Tony said. "Come on, Mr. Summers, be fair. You make it sound like she was a drunken sailor in a knock-down bar fight."

"An apple or a rock, it's all the same."

"Oh, that's ridiculous."

"He who owns the press has the last say," Summers said with a smile. "Maybe this will stop all this nonsense about women deservin' the right to vote." Summers took a sip of coffee and shook his head. "Women should stay home and take care of their children. Leave men to do men's work."

Tony was perplexed. "You mean like workin' for a newspaper and writin'?"

"Exactly!" Summers said, spinning around, happy with the turn of events.

"Then why do you have Laura write for the paper?" Tony asked.

Summers coughed, realizing he had contradicted himself. "Well, this is different. She's a writer, and people like readin' her."

The typesetter persisted. "How's it different?"

"'Cause she's different. She helps sell newspapers and doesn't have any small children at home," Summers said, getting more and more uncomfortable.

"Your explanation sounds more convenient than different," Tony said, looking at his boss.

"And I think you ought to concentrate on your job and leave the writin' and thinkin' to me, if you hear what I'm sayin'." Summers said, going back to his desk.

"You're the boss," Tony said, going back to his machine.

Summers nodded. "That I am. And I hope Laura Ingalls Wilder knows that. Now run this other piece I wrote on the bottom left of the page."

Tony read the piece and did what he was told, setting the type for Summers' article.

When Will Women Appreciate What Men Have Done For Them?
By Andrew Jackson Summers

When will the women of the world appreciate what men have done for them? Are they blind, or is this just more proof of their natural inferiority attested by the great men of the ages?

From the Bible through all the great literary works, it is a given fact that women are inferior. This is the reason men rule. When the women suffragists finally accept this fact, we can all get back to leading the normal lives that God intended.

Plato said that women were bad men reborn and the Old Testament said, "She shall be called Woman, because she was taken out of Man." Martin Luther wrote, "Girls begin to talk and to stand on their feet sooner than boys because weeds always grow up more quickly than good crops." While I'm not saying women are weeds, I guess they do need a bit of trimming down. I believe they don't appreciate what we men have done for them.

Just look at the ads in this newspaper for all the modern conveniences we've invented to make their home lives easier. Washing machines, dough kneaders, automatic milking machines, and churners. Men have given women the opportunity to press a button and let a machine do the rest. This gives them more time to work on dinner and tend to the children.

But why don't suffragettes understand and appreciate what men have done for them? Maybe we men should be a little firmer at home on the women we have spoiled. Of course, for those suffragists who are unmarried (which, I suspect is the majority), their only hope lies in finding a husband who will make them appreciate the natural order of things.

Tony shook his head as he finished setting the type. For the first time he was unsure of his views.

I've never thought about the way men treat women. Why do we take things for granted just because they've been handed down? Don't all things change with time? Are men really superior?

There were so many questions in his mind, he didn't know where to begin. But the task of sorting them out would be left to another time. He had a newspaper to get out. He had his job to think about—and supporting his wife and children.

CHAPTER 7

ADAM'S RIB

Outside of town, the frogs croaked their night songs. Rev. Youngun stopped to put his spare change in the big jar beside his desk. *Saving for a vacation to see the ocean,* he thought. *Wonder what it really looks like?*

He looked at the bills on his desk that his stipend from the church never fully covered. Sometimes, he was tempted to use the money in the change jar to pay the bills, but he never touched it. He'd promised his three children he'd take them to see the ocean. *And that's a promise I'll keep.*

A nightbird sang outside the window. He thought of his late wife, Norma, who had died of the fever. *Norma, I think you'd be proud of our children,* he thought, nodding.

Rev. Youngun looked out, pleased with the world. He had his health, three good children, and a beautiful widow named Carla Pobst whom he wanted to marry. Everything was coming together. Like his father had taught him, good things are only a matter of time and living right.

Even with scrimping and saving, he was not able to buy them the toys and clothes that other children had. But he did his best and gave them his love and affection, as he tried to be both mother and father.

He remembered giving them new pads and pencils when school started back in the fall, paid for with money he'd made from a service in Springfield. Larry, Terry, and Sherry had thanked and hugged him like it was Christmas. *I cried that night, wishing I could give them more. But I give them all I can. Sometimes my efforts come back in little ways to thank me.*

Like tonight. My guardian angel must be in the room, he said, looking over at Terry, his soon-to-be-eight-year-old, redheaded son. *She must have brushed her wings on him, that's for sure. I guess this is part of the thanks for all I've sacrificed.*

Terry was doing extra religious studies and had offered to look at picture cards of the Holy Land. Rev. Youngun couldn't help but smile as he watched Terry study the stereopticon viewcard. Beezer, their talking parrot, sat on Terry's shoulder trying to peek into the viewer.

"Terry, you don't know how proud you make me," Rev. Youngun said.

Terry kept his eyes glued to the viewer. "That's good, Pa," he said.

Beezer squawked, "My turn."

"Furget it, Beezer. I'm studyin'," Terry mumbled, glancing quickly at his father, who had gone back to reading the paper. Terry reached into the box and took out another funny card and slipped it in. *Please forgive me, Lord,* Terry thought, *but a kid's gotta have fun sometimes.*

Rev. Youngun continued reading the paper, humming happily. He'd gotten a call from Carla Pobst, who was back in Cape Girardeau. She told him she might be able to come to Mansfield for the Mule Day celebration. He could hardly think of anything else.

"My turn," Beezer squawked again.

"Hush, bird brain," Terry said.

Rev. Youngun took a deep breath. *I never thought I'd see the day that Terry would be so interested in something of value. Maybe he's changed. Maybe he's growing up, becoming a young man.*

"My turn," Beezer screeched for the third time.

Rev. Youngun's pride turned to amazement. He put the paper down. "Son, what card are you on? The walls of Jerusalem? Bethlehem?"

"My turn," Beezer said, flapping his wings.

"Yes, Pa," Terry said, not listening. He had borrowed the comic picture card series "The Horrid Mouse" from his friend, Little James, and was nearing the best part.

Rev. Youngun cleared his throat. "I asked, what card are you looking at?"

"My turn," Beezer squawked again, clawing at the viewfinder.

"Yes, Pa," Terry said, not paying any attention to what his father had asked. Things were getting exciting. The Horrid Mouse was at his nastiest, and Terry couldn't wait to get the next card in.

Rev. Youngun stood up and walked over to his son. "Terry, did you hear what I said?"

"Say your prayers!" Beezer screeched.

Beside Terry were two boxes. One was unopened, "The Holy Land Series" of viewcards. The opened box was hand-labeled, "Funnies." Rev. Youngun took the viewholder from Terry.

"Pa, what are you—" Terry gulped.

"My turn," Beezer squawked.

"Pa . . . I was just . . ." Terry stammered.

"Say your prayers," Beezer said, doing a summersault on the back of the chair.

Rev. Youngun put his eyes to the viewer. The Horrid Mouse was taking the cheese from the man's plate and was ready to jump from the table. He lowered it, looking at his son. "Is this mouse part of the Holy Land Series?"

"Maybe it's a Bethlehem church mouse," Terry said, looking down.

"You're pathetic!" Beezer squawked.

"Did I give you permission to look at these funnies cards?" Rev. Youngun asked.

"No. But you didn't say I couldn't look at Horrid Mouse," Terry said, thinking on his feet. *When in doubt, talk fast.* "Isn't he great, Pa? Here, take a look at this card," he said, holding one up. "I mean, it's like bein' there when he's grabbin' the cheese. And you should see the funnies called 'One Stick of Gum for Two.' You won't believe how funny it is!"

"You can say that again!" Beezer squawked loudly.

Terry started to repeat himself, "You won't believe how—"

Rev. Youngun stopped him. "I'm sure they're all very funny," he said, putting the viewholder and funnies card box on top of the cabinet in the parlor. Beezer flew over and climbed on top of the pictures, trying to bite them.

Rev. Youngun crossed his arms. "If you've got time to look at the funny cards, you've got time to clean your room."

"You can say that again!" Beezer screeched, flying across the room.

Rev. Youngun ducked as the bird flew overhead. "Upstairs, now!"

"Oh, Pa!" Terry cried. "Let Sherry do it. That's girls' work!"

"You're pathetic!" Beezer squawked.

Rev. Youngun held up his hand. "It's your room. You do it."

"I ain't no maid."

"It's, 'I'm not a maid,' " Rev. Youngun said, ducking again.

"That's right," Terry said, nodding his head. "I'm not a maid and neither are you. Cleaning houses is women's work."

"Young man, you will do what I say. Now get up to that pigsty of a room and clean it. It's your room and your work to do."

Terry stomped off. "Gosh, Pa. I ain't a girl!"

"Cleaning your own room has nothin' to do with being a boy or a girl."

Terry groaned. "I just wish old Adam had kept his rib bone to himself."

"What's that you said?" Rev. Youngun asked.

"I just wish Adam hadn't made Eve. You preached last Sunday that boys came from God and girls came from boys and that women are to obey men. But if they won't do our work, what good are they?" He turned and stomped up the stairs to his room.

Rev. Youngun thought about what Terry said and remembered quoting Genesis: "And the Lord God caused a deep sleep to fall upon Adam, and he slept; and he took one of his ribs, and made he a woman, and brought her unto the man."

But that wasn't what I was really saying, he thought, reflecting on Terry's interpretation of it. *I wasn't saying that women were created to be maids.*

He walked out onto the porch, reflecting on the rest of Genesis. God gave Adam the task to name and put the animals in their place and Eve was to—was to what?

The question hit him like a bolt of lightening. *What is woman?*

he wondered. *What if Carla asked me a question like that? What would I say?*

He thought back to what his father taught him, "The home is the wife's world; the world is the man's home." *Is that what I'm teaching my children? Is that why Terry thinks that Sherry should clean his room? What would Carla think about that kind of attitude?*

His only thoughts about Carla had always been about their buggy rides, romantic strolls, and the few times they'd kissed. He had never thought about how she might feel on the issue of women having the right to vote. *What do I really believe? Should women have the right to vote? Does anyone have the right to deny them the right to vote? I've never asked her opinion on anything. I just took it for granted that we thought alike, that we agreed on everything.*

He opened the desk drawer and took out the engagement ring he'd bought. It had taken almost half of his meager savings, but it was something he wanted to do. *I love her, I do. I want to marry her,* he thought, looking at her picture on his desk.

He remembered the look Lafayette Bedal gave him when he ordered the ring. "Are you gettin' married, Reverend?"

Rev. Youngun started to deny it then caught himself. "Can you keep a secret?" he asked. "I'm thinkin' 'bout askin' the widow—"

Bedal stopped him. "Carla Pobst," he laughed. "The whole town knows you're sweet on her. Heck, some of the boys at Tippy's been wagerin' on when you'd be announcin' it." Bedal leaned over and winked. "If you let me know now, I can place a small bet and I'll split it with you."

Rev. Youngun didn't know if he was serious. "I don't believe in gambling, you know that. But you'll be the first to know—along with everyone else who hears the announcement."

He leaned back in his porch chair and realized that he was thinking with his heart and not his mind. *If she wants the right to vote, I don't care. I just want her to be my wife, to love, honor, and obey me, and*—he stopped, rethinking his words. *Obey me? I love her. I'm not looking for a servant. I'm looking for a partner. I'm looking for a . . . a . . . wife.* He sighed, finding new meaning in the word.

Now all he had to do was think of when he should give her the ring. *What if she says no? My heart will break. She's got to say yes. I know she will, I hope.*

Trying to take his mind off it all, he picked up the newspaper. The women's suffragist speeches and St. Louis rally were all over the front page. He read through the story, then looked at the reprinted editorial from *The New York Times:*

> The granting of suffrage to women is repugnant to instincts that strike their roots deep in the order of nature. It runs counter to human reason, and flouts the teachings of experience and the admonitions of common sense.

This is an issue that won't go away, he thought, reflecting on the article. *This is something that will haunt men until we come face to face with it.*

He sat on the porch trying to sort things out, troubled by his thoughts and unable to forget Terry's interpretation of his sermon. By the children's bedtime, he was still working on the question of what is woman?

He looked in on Sherry, who was lying in her bed. "Ready to sleep?"

"Waitin' on the sandman," she said softly.

Rev. Youngun entered and sat on her bed. He took her hands and said, "Let's say prayers."

"Can I say them by myself first?"

"Certainly," he said, smiling at his daughter.

After she finished her prayer, Sherry asked, "Pa, are you going to marry Carla?"

"Are you, Pa?" chorused the boys from their room.

"Goodnight, boys." Rev. Youngun called out. He looked at Sherry. "I care for Carla very much."

"Are you going to get married?" she whispered.

"We'll talk about it tomorrow," he said, kissing her goodnight.

He walked softly to his room, got in his night shirt, and slipped under the covers. After saying his prayers, he took a deep breath and exhaled. *Let me have pleasant dreams, dear Lord.*

He drifted off to sleep, frogs croaking in the night. Though they weren't rich, the Younguns had a good life.

He was happy to be living on the edge of a small town where you can walk anywhere in a few minutes. Happy for the simplicity and independence of the rural life they lived.

But most of all, he was happy thinking about his last buggy ride with Carla, and of her lips. They were the pillows of his sweet dreams about those moments together. In his dreams, all his wishes were granted.

CHAPTER 8

SMOKE-FILLED ROOM

James Steadman, Wright County's top attorney, blew a smoke ring across the table. A dozen eyes watched it waft through the air until it disintegrated against the wall.

He tapped the ash from his long cigar and looked at the assembled merchants of Mansfield. They had answered the invitation to his office to discuss Laura's articles and her invitation to Ellen Boyle to come to Mansfield.

For most of them an invitation was as much as a command performance. Steadman had represented each of them in court, at the courthouse or behind the courthouse. Beyond his usually high fees, he held an unwritten I.O.U. on each of the men, for something he had done for them above and beyond the letter of the law.

Only Thomas Huleatt owed nothing to Steadman. Huleatt owned Tippy's Saloon, named for County Tipperary in Ireland where he hailed from. A handsome man who had never married, he had come out of curiosity. And he was the only man in the room who knew Ellen Boyle.

Laura's arrest and Summers' article had set the town talking. There was a general edge in the air. Sides were being drawn, mostly along gender lines. Some wives spoke out and others held back their thoughts, suffering their views in silence.

In his holdover British accent, Steadman said, "Laura Wilder's gone too far."

"I agree," said Lafayette Bedal, the French-Canadian merchant.

"It was bad enough her gettin' arrested, but now she's bringin' that Irish firebomb to speak in town." The men in the room murmured in agreement.

"It's got everyone upset," said Billy Pickle, the town's barber from Hungary. "That's what my customers are tellin' me."

"I hear she brings trouble wherever she goes," said Bedal.

"We don't need her upsetting our women in this town," Steadman said. "They're happy with things just the way they are."

The men nodded agreement and watched Steadman blow another smoke ring. No one spoke until it had faded across the room.

"You can take it from one who knows the lass," said Huleatt, "trouble follows her brash voice."

"You know this Ellen Boyle?" asked Steadman.

Huleatt nodded and paused. He'd never told anyone they had been sweethearts. About his loving her so much that her not marrying him was the reason he left Ireland. That it was the reason he never married. He didn't ever again want to lose another piece of his heart to a woman.

Steadman cleared his throat. "Thomas? You going to say something?"

"We came from the same village in Ireland. Even then she caused all kinds of trouble for the locals with her ideas that men and women were equal." He shook his head. "Equal? Can you imagine anyone believin' that?"

John Campbell, owner of the feedstore and from Scotland, laughed heartily. "The way I hear it, this whole women's votin' thing started with that Irish woman."

"She's run her mouth a good bit, I'll hand her that," Huleatt said, nodding.

"Gentlemen," Steadman said, "we've got to decide what we're going to do."

"Like what?" Pickle asked. "What can we do? She's already been invited."

Steadman sipped from his coffee cup. "I think we should tell Laura Wilder to cancel the invitation to Boyle."

Huleatt laughed. "Have you ever tried to get that Wilder woman to do anything she don't want to do? Or don't you remember her fighting the Klan and the farmers over kids not going to school?"

"Or defendin' ol' Josie when people were callin' her a witch," Bedal said.

"And don't forget the way she stirred up all the ruckus at the World's Fair protectin' that pygmy," Pickle said.

"She's a stubborn one, she is," Campbell agreed.

Pickle shook his head. "Glad I'm not married to her."

"This is not a meeting to be disrespectful to Laura," Bedal said. "She's my friend and—"

"I don't care if you're blood kin," Steadman said. "We've got a problem with her inviting this woman suffragist leader here to speak."

William Bentley, the town's wealthiest resident and owner of the logging mills, sat quietly, listening to the others. Steadman turned to him. "William, don't you have anything to say? Can't you reason with Laura Wilder?"

Huleatt laughed. "Like he did two summers back over cuttin' down trees?"

"Laura and I have had our run-ins," Bentley said, looking around the room. "She's a powerful person to oppose when she gets her mind set to something."

"What about her husband?" Pickle asked.

Huleatt laughed. "What about him? He's the quiet side of a mouse, he is."

"Well, can't someone take him aside and get him to control his wife?" Steadman asked.

"Manly's a good man, but I don't think he can or would want to," Campbell said. "I wouldn't if I were in his shoes and God bless that I'm not."

"They have a different kind of marriage," Bedal said. "He lets her—"

Steadman put up his hand to stop him. "He lets her run rough-shod over him and doesn't do anything about it," he said, stubbing out his cigar into the ashtray. "And with her having free rein over at Summers' newspaper, she's got a regular call to battle in every-thing she writes."

"It's a free press," Pickle said.

Steadman stared intently at Bentley. "Nothing's free," he said, under his breath.

Bentley shook his head at Steadman. "I know what you're thinking. It didn't work for me, but you've probably got more power over Summers than anyone with the legal notices he prints for you." The men caught the direction the conversation was going and leaned closer.

Campbell piped up. "I liked his article about women not appreciatin' what we've done for them. I made my wife read it."

"Mine too," said Pickle, not mentioning that she'd made him sleep on the sofa the night before.

Steadman looked Bentley in the eye. "You think Summers can do something to tone her down?"

"He put her arrest on the front page," Bentley said. "I never expected that."

"I thought they were good friends." Steadman said.

"He's been upset," Huleatt said. "Thinks she's getting the best of him with her articles on women voting."

"She is," murmured several of the men.

"That's right." Campbell said, "It's embarrassin'."

"And I hear he's steaming mad about her getting arrested," Bentley added, "which is why he put that piece on women being inferior right under the article on her arrest."

"He ought to be upset," Huleatt said. "It ain't right having a jailbird for a reporter."

"Right as rain," muttered Billy Pickle. "And it seems wrong for her to be raisin' money for a statue to some Indian woman and her half-breed child."

Campbell stood up. "Well," he said, "what's worse is Laura invitin' this Irish firecracker to speak during our Mule Day celebration." He paused and turned to Huleatt. "No offense intended."

Huleatt smiled. "None taken. I think it's kind of appropriate that Ellen is speakin' at our Mule Day," he said. "Even when I knew her she was as stubborn as a mule!"

The men in the room laughed. It helped Huleatt ease the pain of her memory to talk about Ellen in such a way. It made him feel he was getting even with her for hurting him so long ago.

"And the article in the *St. Louis Post-Dispatch* said Laura kicked a policeman, just like a mule," Steadman said.

"That was another woman, not Laura," Bentley said, correcting Steadman.

"Laura or someone else, they're all agitators," Steadman said. "What do you say we pour some drinks and come up with a plan?"

"Hear, hear," chorused Pickle and Campbell.

"I've got to be going," Bentley said. "My wife's sponsoring the Charity Bake Sale and Fashion Show for Mule Day this year. She's so busy she barely waits dinner for me."

"But she's at home cookin' dinner like she should be," Huleatt said, grinning, "not out stirring up trouble like Boyle."

"Sarah's at home all right," Bentley said, adjusting his hat, "but I doubt she's cookin'. Good day, gents. Keep me informed about what you decide."

After Bentley had gone, Steadman stood up and looked at the men. "Mule Day is June 15. That's less than two weeks away. Let's have a drink for the road, then you all sleep on it tonight and get back to me with your ideas."

Steadman poured Irish whiskey from the decanter on the cabinet behind his desk. He held up his glass. "Let's toast to women being good and quiet at all the right times." The men joined in Steadman's toast and finished their drinks.

As the men filed out, Steadman took Huleatt aside. "Thomas, you know this Boyle woman. Isn't there some way you can get her not to come? You know, for old time's sake?"

"She was sweet on me, but I turned her down," Huleatt said, shaking his head.

"You were sweethearts?" Steadman asked hesitantly.

"No, no. Even then she had more mouth than common sense. She wanted to marry me but I couldn't see myself tied down to a loudmouth, so I left for America. I thought I'd seen the last of her." He looked away to blink for a moment. "Broke her heart, I did," he said, blowing his breath toward his eyes to dry them.

"Have you tried to contact her since she became famous over this women's vote issue?" Steadman asked.

Huleatt controlled his emotions and turned back. "If she knew I was in Mansfield, she'd be sitting on my doorstep, asking for my hand in marriage again."

"Then you're not going to let her know you're here?"

"I'll have to think this one through," Huleatt said. "Maybe I'll think of something to keep her from speaking."

"Come up with a plan, Thomas. We've got to do something."

"Let's hope they don't get the vote," Huleatt said, hitching up his pants. "It will be the end of this great land."

Huleatt walked back to his saloon, thinking about Ellen Boyle. Thinking about the day they had their pre-engagement picture taken and the argument they'd had.

CHAPTER 9

ARGUMENT

It all came back to Thomas. The old photographer who made them stand for thirty minutes before he snapped the picture. The smell of the musty studio. The tension between Ellen and him.

"Thomas," she whispered through her teeth as the photographer fiddled with his camera. "You don't want a wife, you want another farm animal."

"That's not true," Huleatt whispered back, trying to maintain the pose. "I want a wife, just like my mother is to my father."

"But that's not for me," she said. "I want to do something. I have my dreams, you know."

"Dreams are just dreams," Huleatt said. "Reality is reality."

"Will you two be quiet?" the photographer snapped. "I'm trying to set up this picture. It'll be around for a lifetime."

"Sorry," Ellen said, then whispered again. "The reality for women is that men can dream big but women are taught only to dream of having the luck of marrying a wealthy man."

"What's wrong with that?"

"What's wrong?" she said, stepping out of her pose. "Women should be able to have dreams too."

"You moved!" shouted the photographer.

"If you'd just take the picture, we could get on with our lives," Ellen said, stepping back into position. She whispered to Huleatt, "This picture was your idea."

"My mother wanted us to have a keepsake. She believes that this picture before our marriage will—"

The photographer interrupted him. "Ready? On the count of three. One. Two. Three," he said, snapping the picture.

The flash momentarily blinded them both. Huleatt reached over and took her hand. "Please, Ellen, let's not argue. I love you. Everything will work out."

"That's what you always say."

Huleatt smiled. "But it's true. I'll be a farmer and you'll have lots of babies and—"

"You just don't see, do you, Thomas?"

"See what?" He smiled and winked. That usually calmed her down.

"That men just think that all women want is to be wives and babymakers!"

"But I'll be a good father."

Ellen took his hand. "Thomas, what I'm trying to tell you is that mothering takes more time than the fact of being a father."

"But your mother had a large family."

"She doesn't understand either," Ellen said, turning to face the window. "It's something I can't explain. I feel I have to speak out, to tell the world that women can dream. They can be more than just mothers."

"There's nothing wrong with mothers."

Ellen looked him in the eyes. "And there's nothing wrong with having dreams that can be realized—dreams that might not include being a mother at all."

"I don't understand," Huleatt said sincerely.

"And that's the problem with men, society, and . . . with us."

"Now come on, we've got to be going to my mother's house for the gathering," Huleatt said, trying to brighten the mood.

"But I haven't said I'll marry you," Ellen said, protesting lightly.

Huleatt smiled. "And you haven't said you won't. Everyone knows we're going to get married someday, so that's good enough for me. I'll wait."

Huleatt sighed as he stood on Mansfield's Main Street. *I've waited ever since. I've never found a woman quite like you.* Suddenly the anger welled up inside him as he entered his saloon. *I've suffered a lot because of you, Ellen Boyle,* he thought, storming through the bar. *It's time I got even.*

CHAPTER 10

SARAH'S WORLD

Bentley hung up his hat and pulled off his boots at the door. Sarah didn't like men wearing their boots on her oriental carpet, a rule that had upset more than one man in town.

Sarah sat in the parlor, talking on the phone and looking through a stereopiticon. Her Persian cat, Cuddles, sat on her lap. The cat's ears perked up when he saw Bentley.

"Oh, Lisa," Sarah said, laughing, "you wouldn't believe these ballroom dance scenes. They're so outdated!" Sarah giggled, looking through the viewholder at the colorful pictures.

The stereopiticon was a twelve-cent, hand-held viewholder, into which penny-each view cards were inserted. The 3-D effect had a way of pulling the viewer into the picture. It was a popular way for rural America to escape from their parlors.

Bentley tried to slip by without being noticed. The cat meowed as he tiptoed across the hall. *The last thing I want to do is spend an evening looking at fashion cards or more pictures of her wearing silly-looking dresses.*

Sarah cried out, "Lisa, you should see how this woman is dressed. Her corset is showing!"

Sarah's laugh was so loud that she startled Bentley. He didn't see Cuddles under his feet and stepped on the cat. "Sorry, Cuddles," Bentley mumbled, as the cat flew back to Sarah's lap.

Sarah looked up at her husband. "William, you're home. Just in time for dinner," she said, then returned to the phone. "Got to go,

Lisa. I'll call you tomorrow about the fashion show. It's time we brought some culture to Mansfield."

She hung the phone back on the wall and patted Cuddles. "Poor baby. Did Daddy step on you?" Cuddles meowed.

"I didn't see your cat," Bentley said, standing in the doorway.

"Not *my* cat, William, *our* cat. Cuddles loves you as much as he loves me." Sarah cooed, scratching the cat's tummy.

"I'd rather he save all his love for you," Bentley said. He secretly detested the noisy cat. "Is dinner really ready?"

"Martha's got it in the warmer. I told her you'd be late, as usual," she said, shaking her head. "Really, William, can't you ever get home on time? I work so hard to get things right on these meals."

Sarah turned away and Bentley made a face behind her back. *You work hard? You just tell old Mrs. Martha Cunningham what to cook. You've never cooked, washed dishes, or really tended to our son since we married!*

"What are you thinkin' about, William?"

"Oh, nothing. It's been a long day."

"I'm exhausted too," she said, shaking her head. "You wouldn't believe all I've been through today."

"I'm sure you must be tired. How are the bake sale and fashion show coming?" he asked, trying to change the subject.

Sarah stood up, holding Cuddles. "It's going to be just fabulous! I've got the latest fashions coming from New York, and to make the locals happy, I'm even going to sponsor the bake sale again this year."

"You signed on to sponsor the Bake Sale. They've never had a fashion show during Mule Day, and—"

Sarah interrupted him. "And that's the point. Why should we do the same thing every year? Let's bring a little culture to this town."

"But Sarah, it's Mule Day, not French Poodle Day. This is for the local farmers," Bentley said, shaking his head.

Sarah's eyes flared. "You promised you'd support me in keeping in touch with the real world when you brought me out here to the wilderness, where I have to shop by mail and—"

"And I've supported you rather well, maybe too well," Bentley said. "Are you ready to eat?"

Sarah ignored him. "Did you hear any more about that Wilder woman's arrest?"

"Just that her husband paid the fine and she's coming back on the train tomorrow."

"I was hoping they'd keep her locked up for a few days to cool her down. Everything she writes is so distressing, I have to lie down after I read it." Sarah held her hand to her forehead.

"From what I understand, she wasn't really part of what happened," Bentley said.

"I hope going to jail teaches her a lesson," Sarah said, shaking her head. "She's such a know-it-all."

"She does speak her mind," Bentley said, eyeing the cat who was eyeing him. The cat hissed at Bentley.

Sarah turned when the cat hissed again. "Cuddles, don't do that to Daddy. He loves you."

Bentley smiled insincerely. "Are you ready to eat?"

Sarah ignored him again, fluttering about the room in a tizzy. "She's an embarrassment!" Sarah declared. "She and that Irish woman, that Ellen somebody. They just don't appreciate men and what it means to be a woman."

"I guess you liked Summers' article in the paper," Bentley said. Sarah nodded.

"All these women suffragists are agitators," Sarah said, shaking her head. "They just can't leave well enough alone."

Martha Cunningham opened the kitchen door, her back bent from laboring into her seventies. "Mr. Bentley, are you ready for your dinner, sir?"

Bentley smiled. "Yes, Martha, I'm *really* hungry. Just give me a moment to wash up."

When the kitchen door closed, Sarah handed Cuddles to Bentley. "Here, hold this sweet thing while I go see if that old woman has forgotten my instructions."

The minute she turned away, Bentley made a snarling face at the cat who meowed back. Sarah heard it and turned, but saw her husband smile, patting the cat on the head. "See, Cuddles likes you."

Martha stuck her head back out. "Do you still want salads?"

"We *always* want salads," Sarah snapped. Martha closed the kitchen door. "Honestly, William, I think she's gone senile."

Bentley, who had a soft spot for the hardworking helper, shook his head. "Sarah, go easy on her. Martha works her heart out for you. She's just getting old."

"That's no excuse! This is a good job and she's lucky to have it." Sarah patted Cuddles on the head. "Martha and all these women suffragists are against everything it means to be a woman."

"How did you bring Martha in with Ellen Boyle? What's she done?" Bentley asked in exasperation.

Sarah sighed. "If they'd just understand that women were meant to have children and serve their husbands, they'd be a lot happier."

"One day you'll realize how lucky you really are," Bentley said in frustration.

"You mean because I married you? Hah! I could have had a dozen handsome men who were wealthier than you, much wealthier! I sometimes think I must have been ill when I agreed to marry you and move out to this primitive part of the country."

Bentley turned away. "Don't start in on that again. It's not too late to start over, you know."

Sarah laughed. "You'd die without me. And who'd want you after I took all your money?"

"Sarah," Bentley said, trying to control his temper, "enough's enough. Stop it. I don't want to hurt your feelings."

"Most women just don't see the way women should really be."

"The world looks different through your eyes. Not everyone sees things as you do," he said, uncomfortable with the way his views were beginning to change.

Bentley had seen things differently ever since his confrontation with Laura over saving the trees. He'd been proven wrong and for the first time had been forced to face himself, his views, and his arrogance.

He wasn't comfortable with the change and hadn't discussed it with any of his male friends. He was embarrassed. But he had listened and learned from Laura and had come to realize that women had something to say. That they had something to contribute. That they had helped build the country.

His father had taught him differently, but Bentley had come to believe that women deserved rights. Now he was a closet reader of all Laura's articles. But there was no one he could talk to without feeling foolish. He couldn't talk to his wife; she believed women should be pampered and cared for. He couldn't talk to his friends; they were locked in a mindset of the past. So he kept his thoughts to himself.

Sarah handed him the cat. "That's because they're not looking in the right direction," she said, spinning around. "Do you like my new dress?"

"Very nice. How much?"

"Enough, just enough to make me happy. And I'll make you happy," she cooed, kissing him on the cheek, "because I appreciate you."

Sarah did another twirl, sashaying around the room, then danced over and kissed him again. "Just be nice to Cuddles and I'll go straighten this dinner out." She walked off saying loudly, "Martha, did you burn the soup again?"

"I *never* burn the soup," Martha snapped from the kitchen.

"Yes you do!" Sarah chastised, and began lecturing the old cook as she walked into the kitchen.

When the door closed, the cat nipped Bentley's hand.

CHAPTER 11

WORKING WOMAN

After Sarah left the kitchen, Martha Cunningham shook her head. *That woman is so spoiled she's rotten!*

At seventy-two, Martha was past the age when most women did domestic work, but she needed the money. Her husband, David, hadn't been able to work in years, since he hurt his back in the mines in Minnesota. Now he spent all his time—and most of Martha's hard-earned money—in Tippy's Saloon.

Martha worked hard for the Bentley's. Though she disliked Sarah, who was tightfisted with the help but bought every new dress she saw, Martha adored William Bentley.

Bentley knew how hard Martha's life really was. He often slipped her extra money for groceries, clothes, and to pay for her rheumatism visits to Dr. George. He never expected to be paid back, but in her own way, she gave of herself in her devotion and attention to him. It was something that Sarah was never to find out, because as Bentley had explained, "She wouldn't understand."

Bentley also cleared up more than a few bar tabs at Tippy's for Martha's husband, who Bentley thought was far more trouble than he was worth. But Bentley kept his acts of kindness—and his opinion of Martha's husband—to himself.

Martha had the strength of her Finnish mother and the common sense of her Irish father, which allowed her to tolerate Sarah Bentley. She needed the money, so she put up with the scorn from this younger, conceited woman.

If she didn't have a pretty face and nice figure, she'd be cleanin' floors like the rest of us, Martha thought as she served Sarah's soup.

Willy, Bentley's ten-year-old son, sneaked his head around the back stairs. "What's for dinner, Martha?"

Martha had practically raised the boy from an infant, giving him the love and affection his mother didn't have time for.

She smiled. "I've got you some nice stew and a piece of pie."

Willy flew across the kitchen and hugged her. "I love you, Martha."

"And I love you," she said, smoothing the boy's hair.

Sarah called out from the dining room, "Martha, bring me another napkin, please."

Willy went to the drawer. "I'll take it."

"No, give it to me," Martha answered. "I don't want your mother gettin' on to you again for helpin' me." Willy started to speak but she covered his lips with her fingers. "Now you go on upstairs. I'll bring your dinner up."

Martha took the napkin in to Sarah. She never understood why Sarah insisted that Willy not eat with them. Martha usually paid no mind to what Sarah was saying, but her ears perked up. *She's whisperin'. I bet it's about me again.*

As she left the dining room, Martha let the kitchen door close quietly behind her, leaving just enough space to listen without being seen. "William," Sarah whispered, "do you think we pay Martha too much money?"

"Oh Sarah, don't start that again."

"But money's money, and there's always someone younger who can do a better job," Sarah said, arching her eyebrows.

Bentley looked up and saw Martha peering pitifully through the crack in the door as it slowly closed. A tear was sliding down her cheek.

"Not so loud. Martha might hear you."

"Oh, she will not! She's practically deaf," Sarah said, shaking her head.

"I think you're wrong."

"But William, don't you think that two dollars and eighty cents a week is too much to pay? Her dusting is spotty and she doesn't even do the wash."

Bentley looked up, glad that the kitchen door was now closed. "You reduced her wages seventy-five cents a week when she asked you to hire the wash out," he whispered harshly.

"And that's only fair. It's what I have to pay that woman down the street to do it," Sarah said, nodding once.

"But it's not fair that Martha be penalized at her age for not being able to do the wash with her bent hands."

"Well, keeping her on here is no bargain for me," Sarah said, her eyes starting to flare with anger.

"The woman's here six-and-a-half days a week, at your beck and call. I'd say you're getting a bargain," Bentley said, staring back.

"That's the going rate and she's better off sleeping here than in her shack with that drunk of a husband!" Sarah looked toward the kitchen. "I wonder when she's going to bring our salad?"

Martha, who had wonderful hearing and had listened to everything they'd said, carried in the salad plates.

"It's about time," Sarah said. "I thought you'd forgotten us."

"Thank you, Martha," Bentley said, not wanting to look into her eyes.

Martha nodded, then went back to the kitchen. *I work for forty cents a day,* she thought. *She spends more than that on her cat.*

Sarah looked at her husband and shook her head. "And that Laura Wilder, getting arrested like a criminal. I never thought she had manners. Maybe it's her upbringing. What do you think, William? You think it's because she's from the wrong side of the tracks?"

"Not everyone is like you, Sarah."

Martha chuckled in the kitchen. *And thank the good Lord for that!*

The main course was over. The Bentleys always had coffee before dessert, so Martha cleaned up the dishes, going over in her mind what she had to do the next day.

It's Thursday. I got to be up at six, wash, say my prayers, and be ready to serve Mr. Bentley his breakfast at seven sharp. By nine-thirty, when Mrs. Bentley gets up, I'll need to have the kitchen and dining room cleaned, and the bread ready for baking.

Then after I clean up her dishes, it'll take me two hours to clean the stairs and baths. No, that's on Friday. Tomorrow, it'll take me two hours to clean the sitting room from top to bottom.

She thought of Sarah, following behind her saying, *"Carry everything into the adjoining room. Be careful with the china, you silly old thing. Don't drop the bric-a-brac, I bought that when I was shopping in San Francisco. You wouldn't believe how much it cost."*

It made Martha tired to think about all the work. *Move the carpet, clean each slat of the blinds. Thursday is always the same.* "Wipe them clean" *the missus will say, following me every step.*

Then I've got to keep checking the bread baking in the oven, answer the phone for Mrs. Bentley, even though she's sittin' right next to it, take an hour to make her lunch and wash her dishes, and by 2:30, I'll get my first chance to have a half-hour sit-down and eat my own lunch.

Then the missus will make me clean the kitchen floor for the second time, dust the entrance way, then have a half-hour to lie down before the evening meal starts.

Martha bent her head, thinking that her life had been nothing but work. She sat down beside the sink, resting her head on her arm.

My parents never spent an hour over dinner. They worked hard just getting by. But the missus, why she'll dawdle over her dinner, not even touching it. She wastes enough food to feed the church poor and torments me if the soup's the least bit curdled. Just once I'd like to give her a piece of my mind. Why if she were here right now I'd tell her—

Sarah opened the kitchen door. "Martha, what on earth are you doing? You haven't served dessert yet and I'm really disappointed."

"It's comin' right up, Mrs. Bentley."

"Well, hurry up about it. You've already had two sit-downs today. If you're taking a third, it'll have to come out of your pay."

Martha's eyes burned as the door closed. *The rich don't just take our pay, they take our souls.*

That night, as Martha collapsed into bed, fatigued and too tired to even take a bath after more than twelve hours of work, the old woman thought of what a servant down the street had told her.

"Ain't it funny how the wealthy women are always complainin' about how tired they are from watching us work all day?"

Willy poked his head into her room. "Are you asleep yet, Martha?"

"No child, but I'll be asleep right after prayers," she said, trying to sit up.

"I just wanted to kiss you goodnight," he said.

"Goodnight, Willy," Martha said, kissing his cheek. She watched the boy slip out the door. *He's been comin' into my room for years, givin' me a goodnight kiss. What harm does it do if he kisses me and not his momma?*

Martha drifted off into sleep, not thinking about the unfairness of her life or about Laura getting arrested, and not wondering when women would get the right to vote.

She was thinking about her husband, wondering where he was. *I hope David's home by now.*

CHAPTER 12

BAD INFLUENCE

Thomas Huleatt smiled as he wiped down a rack of bar glasses. He was happy that Mule Day was approaching. *I'll sell a lot of beer this year,* he thought, trying to take his mind off Ellen Boyle. Farmer's Almanac *says it'll be a hot time around the fifteenth. Maybe I should order some more kegs, just in case.*

He frowned, thinking of Ellen Boyle. *Love,* he thought, *I don't have time for it. Ellen's turning me down was the best thing that ever happened. That's why I'm successful in business. If I'd married her, I would just be another poor sap farmer, scraping by in Ireland.*

Time has a way of magnifying hurts and changing events to fit needs, which was how Huleatt had stored away the memory of Ellen. But he always remembered Ireland just as it was: *the orange skies, the fields so green it takes your breath away, and the waves that lapped on the shore as I left saying, "Come back ye son of Ireland, you can never leave it all behind."*

Huleatt picked up the *Mansfield Monitor* and read the article about the upcoming event:

MULE DAY IS COMING!
By Andrew Jackson Summers, Editor

Hundreds of people, politicians, and maybe even Will Rogers himself, are coming on June 15th for Mansfield's annual Mule Day Cele-

bration. They're all coming to pay tribute to the mule and join in the fun.

We'll have our annual mule parade, livestock show, and street market. Sarah Bentley has graciously donated the funds to put on our first charity fashion show and bake sale. The old-timers are going to have their checkers contest, though we're all sad that old Mr. Schmidt won't be around to compete again this year.

The highlight of the day will be the mule-pulling contest. Weigh-ins will begin promptly at seven in the morning, rain or shine. First prize is a ten-dollar bill. I'm told that this year we'll be giving another ten-dollar cash prize for the mule with the biggest ears in the "The Prettiest Mule" contest!

In the afternoon, we'll have a big send-off for the dads and daughters going on the Father-Daughter horseback campout. Then everyone will stuff themselves on the four-hundred-pound roast pig, donated by Bentley Land and Timber. There will be a square dance and clogging show in the early evening, followed by the queen of mules herself, Ellen Boyle, who will speak to all those who have nothing better to do about why women should have the right to vote.

This editor hopes that Miss Boyle doesn't show up for the mule weigh-in, because the other mules wouldn't stand a chance with her known ability to sling and pull a load.

Huleatt put the paper down. Though he had told Steadman it was he who had broken Ellen's heart, that was the farthest thing from the truth. Just thinking about it brought back the hurt. And of the smell of her perfume and the feel of her lips.

All those hurts. Ellen not wanting to marry him, his father dying soon after, telling him to go to the promised land. "Forget about Ellen," he said. "Go find your dream in America."

I wonder what she looks like now? he wondered, shaking his head. *By the hair on St. Patrick's head, she was the prettiest girl in the world. Not a thing I'd have changed. Prettier than any picture, she was.*

Huleatt took a quick sip of beer. *Ellen, I wish you weren't com-*

ing to town. She'll tell everyone 'bout dumpin' me. I know she will. I wish I could show her how she hurt me.

Huleatt's gaze rested on David Cunningham nursing his nickel beer like he did every night. A plan began to form. *It's my chance to get even. I offered to marry her and she turned me down. After I told all the lads that I was going to ask her. After my mother told everyone we were going to wed.*

Huleatt remembered it all as if it were yesterday. *Made a regular fool out of me, she did. Told me that she didn't need a man to take care of her. That she wanted to change the world.*

He closed his eyes, still feeling the hurt over it all. *No woman's made a fool of me since then, since she broke my heart.* He thought he had left it all behind when he left Ireland, but it came back with intensity. But he believed Cunningham could be an unwitting accomplice in his plan to get even with Ellen.

"Hey, Cunningham, are you drinkin' that beer or prayin' to it?"

Men around the bar laughed. Cunningham looked up and shrugged. "If wishes were true, this glass would always be full."

"Aye, and we'd all be millionaires with wives who knew their place," Huleatt shouted.

"Hear, hear, I'll drink to that," chorused some of the men.

Huleatt walked to the end of the bar and leaned over to Cunningham. "You hear about that Irish she-devil comin' to town?"

"Boyle's just goin' to speak. No harm in that."

"But she's a troublemaker, don't you think?"

"It's 'bout time the Irish spoke up. It's a free country," Cunningham said.

"I'll bet her speech ain't free," Huleatt said, cleaning an ashtray. "I'll bet that Wilder woman is paying her something."

Cunningham sipped his warm beer. "My Martha said somethin' 'bout her speakin' here to raise money for a statue."

Huleatt leaned over. "An Indian statue. Did you know that's what it is?" he said.

"Which one? Geronimo? Sitting Bull?" Cunningham asked.

"No, some squaw and her half-breed baby," Huleatt said, shaking his head in anger.

Cunningham sipped again. "No harm in her speakin' is my

opinion. And no harm in them putting up a statue to an Indian girl if it's not my money."

Huleatt grabbed Cunningham's mug. "Hey," the old man said, "give me my beer back."

Huleatt teased him, waving it back and forth. "How can you drink this stuff warm?"

"It's my beer," Cunningham said quietly. "Please give it back."

Huleatt shook his head and poured the beer down the drain. "That was a mean thing to do, Thomas Huleatt," Cunningham said coldly.

"I don't like my customers drinkin' warm beer," Huleatt grinned, wiping out the glass. "Gives me place a bad reputation."

Cunningham looked at the empty mug sitting behind the bar. "That was the only nickel I had on me. So I was takin' my time."

Huleatt pulled a cold draft and set it in front of the old man. "Here you go, sport. Drink a cold one."

"I said I don't have any money," he whispered, looking down. "Please don't be embarrassin' me in front of my drinkin' friends."

Huleatt smiled. "It's on the house."

"Honest?" Cunningham asked, eyeing the beer. His fingers circled the glass nervously.

"And there's more to be comin' if you want to have some fun," Huleatt said.

Cunningham couldn't resist. He took a long sip. "That's the cool waters of paradise, goin' down my throat."

"Are you interested in having an open tab here for a while?" Huleatt asked in a conspiratorial tone.

"What do I got to do? With my bad back, I'm too old to be liftin' crates or tendin' bar."

Huleatt smiled. "You don't have to do anythin' except drink and be ready when I need you."

"For what?" Cunningham asked cautiously, taking another sip.

"Oh, I just got me a little plan in mind to welcome Miss Ellen Boyle to town, and I need some help."

"Is it against the law?" Cunningham asked, wiping the foam from his lips.

"Is having a bit of fun against the law?" Huleatt exclaimed, slapping him on the back. "Drink up, David! If you want to help me out and can keep your mouth shut, the taps are open to you."

Cunningham looked at the mug, then hoisted it up and drank it down. "It's a deal. Give me another."

Huleatt took the mug and said, "And you got to promise not to tell your old lady. Is that a promise?" he asked, leaning closer.

"I promise. Now give me another beer," Cunningham said.

Huleatt took the mug and pulled another draft. "I knew I could count on you," he said, trying to shrug off the mood that thinking about Ellen had put him in.

"Hey, Huleatt, what's it gonna take to get another beer?" one of the regulars shouted out.

"A nickel," Huleatt shouted back. He pulled the draft and placed it on the bar. He took out a cigar and struck a match. "You know what we used to say back in Ireland?"

"What?" a few of the drinkers asked, leaning forward to hear.

Huleatt looked from man to man, then said, "It's better to be without a wife for a year than without tobacco for an hour." They all laughed and fought for the chance to tell one of their own.

As the men yelled out their crude jokes, Cunningham finished his beer. He winced at Huleatt's words: "A wedding lasts a day or two, but the misery forever."

Cunningham thought about his good wife, Martha, working as a virtual indentured servant for the Bentley's, and how she only came home on Sunday afternoon to give him her money and do his wash.

Life hasn't been good for my Martha, he thought. He looked at the fresh beer in front of him. *Now I won't need her money to drink on,* he thought proudly. *She can save it, now that I'm workin' for Mr. Huleatt.*

"Hey, Cunningham," Huleatt called out, "ready for another?"

"When will you tell me what you'll be needin' me to do, boss?" he asked as the cold mug was placed before him.

"I'm workin' the details out now," Huleatt said. "Just hang around for the next week or so. Just keep doin' what you're always doin'. Drink up!"

Which is what Cunningham did until he forgot all about his hard-working wife. He drank until he blacked out.

CHAPTER 13

MANLY'S THOUGHTS

Manly put the paper down. It was time to head to the train station. The ride would give him time to reflect on the *Mansfield Monitor's* headlines about Laura's arrest and Summers' counterattack on women in general.

Laura's headstrong, there's no doubt about that, Manly thought, as he rode along to the station. *I appreciate her, and she appreciates me. She's been a partner, more partner than any man could ever have been.*

But try explainin' that to the men at Billy Pickle's Barber Shop. "We know who wears the dress in your family," they say to me. But none of 'em could ever have managed all the work that Laura did after my stroke. If I told that to Pickle, he'd just make fun of me sayin', "You like bein' married to a jailbird, Manly?"

He tried to shake his thoughts as he bumped along. He had taken the Oldsmobile because he was running late, and now he regretted it. He was suddenly overcome with questions. About his own attitudes. About the partnership he and Laura had and what other men said about how women should be.

Why am I always rushin' to be on time for her? he wondered. *Why is it me who's always bein' extra helpful? Don't men rule their homes?*

He pushed the gas pedal and sped across the Willow Creek Bridge. *Why should I be treatin' her like a partner—like my durn equal—when all she seems to do is go off hither and yon on this crusade or that without askin' me? She doesn't treat me like a partner in her writin's.*

I'm the one who suffers, not her. Women don't cause her trouble and the men of Mansfield don't want to argue much with a woman—especially one like Laura who will argue right back.

And now she's gone off and gotten herself arrested in some women's rights rally in St. Louis. He frowned. *She might as well have put a sign on my back sayin', "Kick me." Men like to laugh at another man's misery, they sure do.*

He thought back to the old farmer at the feed store that afternoon. "Mr. Wilder," he said in his thick European accent, "I'm sorry to hear about your vife, but in Poland we had a saying: 'The woman cries before the wedding and the man ever after.' Are you crying, Mr. Wilder?"

Manly took a deep breath in anger. *And Mr. Campbell couldn't help but throw in one of his Scottish proverbs. He patted me on the back in front of all the farmers and said, "In Scotland, we say, 'He that has a wife has a master.' And we know who Manly's master is, don't we, boys?"*

They all got a good laugh at my expense over that one, Manly thought, shaking his head. *Made me look like a regular village idiot.*

Manly was working himself into a rage. He'd always assumed what he and Laura had was right, no matter what anybody said. But now he wasn't so sure.

Manly shook off the anger. *Laura's been a good woman to me, that I'll swear to. But I've been a good husband, too, and put up with more than most men ever would.*

As he pulled into the train station, he looked at his reflection in the window. *Put up with? That's not really fair. She's put up with a lot from me. I lost the farms, mortgaged us into debt, and had to move us in with strangers to get back on our feet. She believed in me enough to come to Missouri with only a hundred dollars to our name.*

Manly put his hands over his eyes. *We built Apple Hill Farm together. She pulled her weight. What with my bad health since the stroke and my gimpy leg, I couldn't have done it all. Heck, she did more than half my work, and the housework and child rearin'.*

I'm a lucky man. I love this headstrong woman. The train whistle sounded and Manly looked up. *I love this woman, I do. Our marriage is our business and no one else's. I wish people would just—*

"Good evening, Mr. Manly," Chan said, tapping him on the shoulder.

Manly looked up. "Oh, hi, Mr. Chan."

"Meeting someone on the train?"

"Laura's comin' in."

"Well, say hello to her for me," Chan said, walking quietly off. At the edge of the street corner, he stopped. "Mr. Manly, in China we have a saying: For a woman to rule is for a hen to crow in the mornings. Do your hens crow, Mr. Manly?" he asked, as he walked off chuckling.

Manly was fit to be tied.

CHAPTER 14

HELLO, MANLY

"Hello, Manly," Laura said, stepping off the train. She had thought of a thousand things to say, a thousand excuses to make up, but she forgot them all when she saw him.

"That's a pretty formal howdy-do, if you ask me," he said, helping her down from the train.

"It's just . . . the phone call . . . getting arrested, why . . ." She couldn't help it, she broke down and cried in Manly's arms. Instinctively, he wrapped his arms around her.

"There, there, girl. It's all right. I ain't gonna bite your head off," Manly whispered, smoothing out her hair. A few stragglers stopped and stared. Manly frowned. "Go on, get outta here. Ain't you ever seen a woman cry for happiness?"

He noticed the bruise on her forehead. "Bet that hurts, don't it?"

Laura fumbled for a hanky with one hand and tried to cover the bruise with the other. "It's na . . . na . . . nothing."

"Let's go on home and take care of it," he said, feeling the anger and resentment dissolve in his concern for her.

Laura wiped the tears from her eyes. "I'm . . . I'm . . . ," she stammered, trying to stop the sobbing.

"Take your time," he said, putting his arm around her. "Let's go to the car."

"I know you're upset," she said, sniffing.

"Well, you certainly like to bring a lot of excitement to our marriage. It ain't every day that a man's wife makes the head-lines."

Laura laughed and cried at the same time, shaking her head. "That's not the excitement you bargained for when you married me," she said.

Manly put her bag in the back seat and opened the door for her. "For better or worse, that's the vow I took." He smiled and kissed her on the cheek.

Laura sat down and turned red-eyed toward him. "Has it been better or worse? Tell me the truth."

Manly opened the door and slid onto the seat. "Honey, I got to admit that I was hot when I learned you'd been arrested. But you were doin' what you think is right. I guess that's what counts," he said, starting up the car.

"But do you think what I'm doin' is right?"

"Let's not talk about that," he said, as he pulled the car forward, The car backfired as they headed through town.

"Tell me," she pressed. "Do you agree with what I'm doing?"

Manly stared straight ahead as he drove down Main Street. "Answer me, Manly," Laura said firmly.

"Is that an order?" he asked sarcastically, feeling the anger rise up in him again.

"You know it's not," she said, lowering her voice. "I just want to know what you think."

"It's too late askin' now."

"And what's that supposed to mean?" she asked, sitting back in her seat.

"You've never asked me before what I thought about something you were plannin' to do. It's always after the fact. You sort of treat me like a Johnny-come-lately in the brains and opinion department. That's what I think."

Laura sat back, and took a deep breath. *After the fact? Johnny-come-lately? Is that what I do?* Laura was struck by a sudden wave of insecurity.

"That's what you think?" she whispered.

"That's what I think," he said, not looking at her.

"You know I value your opinion and—"

Manly cut her off. "Please, Laura, don't go tryin' to convince me of what's the God's truth. You're a headstrong woman. I knew that goin' into our marriage. But I've gotten used to it, so let's leave it at that," he said, his eyes glued to the road.

"You mean you don't agree that women deserve the right to vote?"

"I didn't say that," he said quietly.

Laura brightened. "Then you do agree?"

"And I didn't say that," he said, shaking his head.

Laura folded her arms. "Then what did you say?" Manly drove on in silence. "I asked, what did you say then?"

"I said nothin'. You didn't ask my opinion before you went to that fist-fightin' rally, so no use askin' for it after the jail cell's been opened."

"That's a cheap shot," she said, shaking her head.

"Take it any way you want. Just leave me out of your latest crusade. I don't want to be involved."

"But you have to be involved. It involves you and all the men in this land who have to vote on this issue."

"Maybe, maybe not. But it don't mean I got to go all over creation verbalizin' what I'm thinkin'."

"And just what are you thinking?" Laura asked.

Manly coughed, stopped the car, and turned. "I'm thinkin' that this is one of them 'for worse' times and that the rest of the night ain't gonna get any better."

"But Manly, I was just—"

Manly's eyes burned with intensity. Laura had never seen him like this before. "You was just tryin' to badger me into tellin' you how I'm goin' to vote, if and when women havin' the right to vote ever makes it to the ballot in Missouri."

"No, I wasn't!"

"Yes, you was. You just won't admit it, that's all," he said, pushing down on the accelerator.

Laura fell back against the seat. "You're like all the other men!" She caught herself and stopped. "I didn't mean that. I'm sorry."

"You seem to always say what you mean, so don't change now," he said coldly.

Laura put her hand on his arm, trying to change the mood.

"I've stood by you during the hard times, Manly, when we lost the farm and—"

He shook her arm off. "Don't go bringin' up me losin' the farm again. That's old history that you've brought up one too many times."

"But I wasn't trying to."

Manly pulled into the driveway and stopped the car with a jolt. Laura started to speak, but Manly put his finger in the air for silence. "You were just tryin' to make me feel bad for messin' up and over-mortgagin' the farm back in the Dakotas. I've lived a thousand nightmares over what I did. But you know what, Laura? I can't change what happened. I can't change the past. When I brought you to Missouri, I told you that if we pulled together, it would never happen again. But, oh no, you got to keep bringin' it up like it was yesterday."

Laura was taken back by his anger. "But, Manly, I'm sorry, I was just tryin'—"

He got out of the car in a huff, slamming the door. "Manly, you come back here. That's not fair!" Laura called after him.

He stopped at the stairs and whirled around. "That was fifteen years ago. *Fifteen years ago!* It's time to put that old story to rest for good!" he said, limping off.

"I'll put what happened to rest if that's what you want. Now will you come back and talk to me?"

Manly opened the front door and turned. "If you can't put it to rest, then maybe you ought to find someone else who meets your haughty standards. I'm tired of it all. We all can't be perfect, Laura. We're not all like you." He paused. "You know, Laura, one day you're gonna remember that I'm your husband, not you're assistant!"

"What's gotten into you?" asked Laura.

The sound of the screen door slamming echoed across the orchards. Lighting bugs flew overhead while the cicadas serenaded the night. No one heard Laura's sobbing, as she sat in the dark in front of the house that she and Manly had built together.

CHAPTER 15

STUBBORN AS A MULE

Larry Youngun looked at his brother, Terry, in exasperation. They had to leave for school and were getting nowhere fast. "Let's furget it! Bell's gonna ring soon."

"Come on," Terry begged, "let's try it one more time. I don't wanna walk."

Larry tried to pull the mule out of his stall, but Crab Apple wouldn't budge. Bashful the goat and T. R. the turkey were watching with interest, until finally, T. R. nipped on Larry's pants leg.

"Get outta here, T. R.!" Larry screamed, pushing the turkey away. "Maybe we should have eaten you for Thanksgivin' after all!" The turkey flapped away, stopping to peck at the food in the horse pen.

Larry looked at Crab Apple, and shook his head. "I think we're wastin' our time enterin' *this* mule in the contest."

All Terry could think about was winning the ten-dollar prize and spending it on candy. "But Mule Day is for mules, and mules are mules," Terry said. "Please, Crabbie," he whined, rubbing the mule's ears, "come on out and pull the log."

Larry looked at their big-eared mule and shook his head. "If we can't get Crabbie to even come out of his stall, how the heck are we goin' to get him to enter the log pullin' contest?"

Terry pleaded with the stubborn mule. "Crabbie, please. Just pull it once and I'll give you some cooked carrots."

"Cooked carrots?" Larry exclaimed. "Where'd you get 'em?"

Terry showed the soggy napkin in his pocket. He unwrapped the corner. "Saved 'em from dinner last night. I hate carrots."

Bashful, their fainting goat, nudged against Terry's leg to eat the carrots. "Get off, Bashful!" Terry said, as the goat began biting on his shirt. Terry backed off as the goat jumped up, nipping at the buttons.

Maurice Springer, their black neighbor and friend, entered the back of the barn, to drop off a load of feed. He had country, common-sense smarts, and he was worldly in a small-town way. He had been there after the death of their mother, to help guide them, and the Youngun children loved him with all their hearts.

"Hi, boys," he said.

"Hello, Mr. Springer," Larry said, laughing as Terry fought to push the goat away.

"Stop!" Terry screamed as loud as he could, and Bashful fainted on the spot. "That'll teach you," Terry mumbled, looking down at the goat, laid out with his eyes open.

"Shouldn't be doin' that to Bashful," Maurice said. "No sir, scare that goat one too many times and you'll scare him to death. I'm very serious 'bout that. You mind me now, hear?"

Terry rubbed the goat's head, trying to awaken him. "He just wouldn't stop nippin' my shirt. Pa said if Bashful rips another, that we got to get rid of him."

"Yeah," Larry said, "he's better off fainted here than bein' eaten by someone else."

Larry looked at Crab Apple and pulled on his neck, but the mule wouldn't move, so he gave up. Maurice saw the depressed look on their faces and asked, "What's wrong? Sun's shinin', it ain't rainin', and the fish are bitin'. What more could you ask for on a good day?"

"Crabbie won't come out of the barn," Larry said.

"Yeah," Terry said, "he won't let us teach him."

"Teach him what?" Maurice asked.

"Teach him to pull a log," Larry said.

"So we can enter him into the Mule Day Contest," Terry said.

"You boys are crazier than a monkey sittin' in itchin' powder," Maurice said. He walked over to the stall to look at the mule, stepping over Bashful the goat, who struggled to his feet and stag-gered off bleating. "Seems as if this mule's already done learned."

"Learned what?" Terry asked.

"Learned to know better than to go outside with you two boys and ruin his mornin' pullin' on a log."

"I wish mules weren't so dumb," Larry said, kicking the dust.

"Lawd have mercy, but you're wrong, boy! Mules may be stub-born, but that's a sign of their su-per-e-or intelligence," Maurice said, scratching Crabbie's head.

"You're joshin' us," Larry said.

"God's truth," Maurice said, holding up his hand. "Most people and all horses are dumber than the average mule."

"That ain't so. Is it?" Terry asked, looking back at the mule.

Maurcie smiled. "Certainly, certainly it is. Why, if a horse gets tangled up in barbed wire, it will panic and near tear it's leg off in the barbs. But a mule, why if he gets tangled, he'll just stand there without movin' until someone comes and cuts him out of the wire."

"Don't sound so smart to me," Terry said.

"What you mean?" Maurice asked.

"Why'd the mule want to go get tangled up in barbed wire anyway?" Terry said, shrugging his shoulders.

Larry shoved Terry. "That's a dumb thing to say."

"No dumber than you are," Terry said, shoving back. In the blink of an eye, the brothers were tangled together like a giant, squirming insect with eight limbs.

"Boy, boys," Maurice said, stepping between them. "Let's not go to fightin'. You're brothers."

"And that can't be helped," Terry said, stepping back with his fist cocked.

"I'm goin' to bean you," Larry said, holding up his fist.

"I said stop it!" Maurice snapped. "Ain't like you two to be goin' at each other."

"He took my candy stick from under my pillow," Larry said, giving his little brother the evil eye.

"Did not!" Terry said.

"Liar!" Larry said, cocking his fist again.

"Hold it, hold it!" Maurice said. He looked at Larry. "Ain't nice to be callin' your own brother a liar. You got proof he took your candy stick?"

Larry put his face up to Terry's. "Proof's in his stomach. That's where the proof is."

"If it happened, I was sleep eatin' again," Terry said, trying to look innocent. "But since I don't remember and there ain't no proof, I ain't guilty."

"See!" Larry said, jumping on him. "He took it! He said he was sleep eatin' again!"

Maurice grabbed their collars and held them apart. "Ain't school startin' soon?"

"Yeah, but I ain't walkin' with him," Larry growled.

"And I ain't walkin' with him neither," snapped Terry.

Maurice let go of their collars and set them apart. "Then how you goin' to get there? Fly?" Maurice asked, walking back toward the barn door.

"I'm gonna wait for him to leave first. Don't trust him," Terry said, "He might 'tack me when you leave."

"We're goin' to be late then fursure," Larry said, "'cause I ain't walkin' ahead of you. You might hit me with a hocker or somethin'."

"You boys want a ride?" Maurice asked. "I'm goin' that way to drop off a load of feed to old C. J. Hyde."

The boys had found a way out of their standoff. "Thanks, Mr. Springer," they said in unison, and they picked up their booksacks and climbed onto the wagon.

CHAPTER 16

WHERE DO MULES COME FROM?

Dangit the dog tried to jump onto the back of Maurice's wagon, but Larry pushed him off. "Stay home, Dangit. Teacher said she'll call the dogcatcher next time you sneak in and eat all the lunches."

Dangit sat on the ground and howled. Maurice picked up the reins, then said, "Let's get outta here 'fore that fool dog wakes the dead." He pulled around the corner of the barn. "Why ain't school over yet? It's June. Summertime. Time for fishin' and goin' to the swimmin' hole."

"We got to make up for the snow days we missed in the blizzard last December," Larry said.

"Ought to be 'gainst the law, keepin' kids in school past last day," Terry said, grumbling.

Maurice clicked the reins and laughed. "And what would you be doin' if you weren't in school?"

"I'd be out doin' somethin' important, like swimmin' and eatin' apples from the Wilder's trees."

"You boys been sneakin' onto Apple Hill Farm again?" Maurice asked suspiciously.

"No sir, not this year," Terry said, adding *yet* in his mind.

Maurice shook his head. "You best be sayin' an extra prayer tonight, 'cause I think that you'll be sneakin' and snitchin' apples real soon. You boys are enough to worry the warts off a toad."

The boys laughed and Maurice hugged them. He remembered what it was like to be a boy.

"See them two mules there," Maurice said, pointing to the team pulling his wagon.

"You mean Nell and Sally?" Larry asked.

Maurice nodded. "Them two," he said. "See how short their ears are?"

"They're shorter than Crabbie's," Terry said.

"Well, a good mule trader will tell you that big ears are good and bigger ears are better. That's how they set value on a mule."

Terry frowned. "What's ears got to do with pullin' a plow?"

"Nothin'," Maurice said. "Which is why Nell and Sally only cost me two dollars each. Their ears are about half as long as they ought to be, but they pull twice as hard. So I figure I got me an even deal." He paused and coughed. " 'Course, I can't be enterin' 'em into the prettiest mule contest."

"Prettiest mule contest? What's that?" Larry asked.

"Read in the paper that this year they're givin' ten bucks for the mule with the longest ears. That lets Nell and Sally out," Maurice said.

"Crabbie's got long ears," Terry said. "Think he'll win?"

"You got to get him out of the stall first," Maurice said. " 'Course there are probably mules with a lot longer ears, so I advise you to just enter him into the pullin' contest."

"We need somethin' to make him move," said Larry, shaking his head.

"Tell you what," Maurice said. "If you can't get Crabbie to get out and pull somethin', next time I'm around I'll tell you the secret." He winked at the boys and clicked the reins.

"The secret?" Larry whispered.

"Tell us!" Terry shouted.

"Nope, I ain't tellin' nothin'. You keep tryin' to get Crab Apple to come on out and pull. But if nothin' else works, I'll let you in on the secret that my granddaddy told me. It's a way to get a mule to run faster than a cat up a tree."

Terry looked at the short-eared mules and scratched his head. "Where do mules come from?"

"From other mules, stupid," Larry said, shoving his brother again. In a blink they were wrestling in the wagon.

"Look who's callin' stupid, stupid," Maurice said, pulling the boys apart for the third time. "Any more of that and you both'll be walkin'."

"Don't mules come from mules?" Larry asked.

"Mules don't come from other mules," Maurice said, guiding the wagon across the Willow Creek bridge.

"Then where do they come from?" Larry asked, as the wagon click-clacked across the wooden beams.

Maurice sighed. *How do I explain this?* he wondered. *Ain't my place to be tellin' them about the birds and bees.*

He decided that the only way to answer the question was to evade the question. He took a deep breath and began. "You know how the first two mules came to these United States?"

The two boys shook their heads.

"They were sent to George Washington, our first President, by the king of Spain," Maurice said, nodding proudly. "Uh huh, that's how it all started."

"You mean," Larry said, "that those two mules are where your two mules came from?"

"Well, not exactly," Maurice said.

Terry persisted. "Where, *exactly,* do mules come from?" he asked.

"Mules can't have other mules 'cause . . . 'cause the boy mules can't make other mules." He saw that he had sufficiently confused the boys and jumped at the chance to change the subject. "Now, I best be hurryin' you along to school. Don't want you to be late."

Terry put his hand on Maurice's arm. "I still don't understand. If boy mules can't make other mules, then how do mules make other mules?"

"They don't," Maurice said. *Boy, have I stepped in a mess of trouble this time,* he thought.

"You ain't makin' a lick of sense," Larry said.

"Okay," Maurice began, "it's like this. You take a jack and a—"
Terry interrupted. "A what?"

"A jack," Maurice said again. Terry started to speak, but Maurice put his hand up for silence. "Let me finish now, will ya?" he said, shaking his head. "A jack is a male donkey. You take a jack and a female horse, and that's where mules come from."

"Is that where mule deers come from?" Larry asked.

"No, that ain't got nothin' to do with it. Mule deers are just deers with a mule name." He giddiyapped Nell and Sally. "Come on, girls, let's get goin'. This talk is over."

As they turned off the main road and headed to the school, Maurice stopped. "We forgot to bring Sherry. Ain't she goin' to school?"

"She and Pa went off horse back ridin' again," Larry said, looking dejected. "Pa's ridin' her to school."

"What's wrong with that?" Maurice asked.

"He ain't takin' us on the campout," Terry said, whining.

"Campout?"

"Yeah, the father-daughter campout after Mule Day," Larry said.

Maurice shook his head. "What you so upset for? You wouldn't want to go camp with a bunch of girls, now would ya?"

"But Pa's never taken us campin'!" Larry frowned. "We'd like to go campin', but no sir, he's always too busy doin' his church work and all."

"Why don't you boys go off campin' by yourself some time?" Maurice asked, moving the wagon forward.

"In the woods . . . alone?" Terry asked, wide-eyed.

"What you worried about?" Maurice laughed. "Think a bear's goin' to eat you?"

"He might," Terry said, crossing his arms.

"Bears don't want to eat no scrawny redheaded kid. You got nothin' to worry about." Maurice laughed and tosseled Terry's hair. "'Course, I forgot 'bout the freckle monster."

"Freckle monster?" Terry exclaimed, rubbing his fingers across the spray of freckles that covered his nose and cheeks.

"Naw," Maurice said, enjoying the suspense, "he wouldn't want to eat you either. You'd give him in-die-ges-tion."

"Still wish there was a father-son campout," Larry said, pouting.

"And we can't enter the bakin' contest!" Terry exclaimed.

"Got to be a girl to enter," Larry said.

"You mean the Mule Day's cookie and pie contest?" Maurice asked.

"Yup. It's for girls only," Terry said, nodding once.

Maurice shook his head. "I can't imagine you two boys wearin' an apron and cookin' like a girl. Why you want to enter that for?"

"'Cause you get to eat a lot of cookies," Terry said.

Larry nodded. "And pies."

"But only girls get all the luck," Terry moaned, shakin' his head. "Campouts, cookies, pies. It ain't fair!"

"Life's not fair, you got to remember that," Maurice said in his best calming voice. "And boys get to do a lot of things that girls don't, that's a fact.

"Like what?" Terry asked.

"Well," Maurice paused, "like football."

"Missouri Poole plays football," Larry said, thinking about the Ozark mountain girl who could do anything boys did and said she was going to marry him one day.

"Well, you know what I mean," Maurice said, giddiyapping the mules forward.

Terry shook his head. "I wish they'd stick to cookin' and house cleanin'. That's the way things are supposed to be."

"Things change. Things change in this old world," Maurice said.

"Wish I had some more change," Terry said.

"What's that?" Maurice asked.

"Wish I had me some more change to buy candy with. My stash is empty."

"You should have seen him last night, Mr. Springer. He only had one piece of candy left and he ate it like it was the last piece of food in the world," Larry said. "That's when you stole my candy stick, didn't you, you stinker!"

"Did not!" Terry exclaimed.

"Where'd you get the dime you got?" Maurice asked.

"Earned it," Terry answered.

"You what? Speak louder, boy," Maurice said. *This I gotta hear. Terry ain't never done a lick of payin' work in his life.*

"I earned it," Terry said louder.

"Fibber!" Larry said, jostling him. Larry tapped Maurice on the arm. "He traded Sweettooth his lucky penny for that dime."

"Why'd Sweet do that?" Maurice said. "You got the better of him that time. You made nine cents on the deal."

"He always pulls one on Sweet," Larry said.

"He wanted my wishin' penny!" Terry exclaimed.

"Wishin' penny? Thought it was your lucky penny?" Maurice said.

Before Terry could answer, Larry spoke up. "Terry told him that if he learned how to rub the penny the lucky way, that his wish would come true."

"Did he get his wish?" Maurice asked.

Terry blushed. "He ain't learned to rub it right."

"Will he ever?" Maurice asked, looking Terry in the eye.

"Not my fault," Terry whispered. "Not my fault he don't know how to rub it the lucky way."

"Why don't you show him?" Maurice asked.

"That wasn't part of the deal," Terry said weakly.

"Son," Maurice said, patting him on the shoulder, "you might be able to take advantage of some people, but it's gonna come back on you."

"How?" Terry asked.

"Let your conscience be your guide, but I think you ought to have an honest-injun talk with yourself 'bout givin' that dime back to Sweet."

"Then I'd have only a penny. That's not enough money to resupply my candy stash."

"You could come work for me after school," Maurice said.

"Doin' what?" Terry asked suspiciously.

"Barn work. Shoveling manure. That sort of thing. Honest work," he said, eyeing Terry to drive home the point.

"That's not the kind of work I'm best at," said Terry. "I don't want to work for a living."

Maurice tosseled his hair. "Just be a boy for now. I ain't never met anyone who growed up and became what they said they'd be at your age."

"Really?" Larry asked.

"Really," Maurice said, rubbing his back. "If you don't remember anythin' else I've ever told you, just remember this: Growin' up is like gettin' the fun washed out of your life. So you got to close your eyes and hide a bit of magic in your mind, where no one else can see it, and never lose it. That's the only way you can keep the sparkle and laughter. Otherwise, life's not a whole bunch of worth doin'."

The Youngun boys thought they understood, hugging onto the man who seemed to bridge the world between childhood and the unknown for them.

"I'm not goin' to ever grow up," Terry whispered, snuggled against Maurice.

"Me neither," Larry said.

Maurice smiled and rubbed their heads. "Just don't grow up too soon. You got the best that life's ever gonna give you right now."

CHAPTER 17

FOR BETTER OR WORSE

It was the first time that it had happened in over twenty years of marriage. Laura was so bothered by it that she had hardly slept a wink and stood on the porch, trying to sort things out.

Manly slept on the couch, she thought, feeling a headache coming on. *He's never done that, not even during the hard times.*

She walked back into the house to the parlor and pulled out her memory book. In the year marked "1885," she turned to August and read a faded newspaper clipping.

Married. WILDER-INGALLS—At the residence of the officiating clergyman, Rev. E. Brown, August 25, 1885. Mr. Almanzo J. Wilder and Miss Laura Ingalls, both of DeSmet. Thus two more of our respected young people have united in the journey of life. May their voyage be pleasant, their joys be many, and their sorrows few.

Beside the clipping was a diary note she'd written.

On that morning, at half-past ten o'clock, Manly came to the house, and we drove away in the buggy for the last time in the old way. I was leaving the little girl in me behind, terrified at the things Ma had told me about marriage. We were at Mr. Brown's at eleven and were married at once, with Ida Brown and Elmer McConnell as witnesses.

> *Mr. Brown had promised me he wouldn't use the word "obey" in the ceremony and he kept his word. I told Manly before I married him that if he was looking for a wife to obey his every wish and command, he shouldn't marry me. He should get an old dog instead. I told him that if he wanted me to love and honor him, I would, but not obey. I'm nobody's servant and never will be.*
>
> *At half-past eleven we left Mr. Brown's and drove home to dinner, which Ma had waiting for us. Then with good wishes from the folks and a few tears, we drove over the road we had traveled so many times before, across the Big Slough, around the corner by Pearson's livery barn, through DeSmet, and then out two miles north to the new house and the tree claim, where Manly had taken my trunk the day before. We rode as husband and wife. Partners in life. For better or worse.*

She reread the line from the newspaper. "May their voyage be pleasant, their joys be many, and their sorrows few." *But we started with sorrows, didn't we, Manly?* she thought. Laura closed the book, walked back to the porch, and stood in the doorway, staring out at the Ozarks. A lifetime of wagons, prairie traveling, and little cabins flashed before her.

For a moment, she could hear Pa's fiddle songs, stitching the stars together with the endless sea of prairie grass. *Why can't the good times go on forever? Why must two people who have been through what we've been through have such a rift? Is it my fault? Is obeying a part of the marriage vows I should have said?*

The first years of their marriage rushed through her mind. *We tried working that tree claim, we sure did. Those were years of sunshine and shadow, almost all darkness,* she thought, feeling her eyes well up.

Manly tried, but things just went against us. He couldn't help the weather or the uncertain harvests. I was young, used to the security that Pa provided, knowing that a home was always waiting for me.

She tried to put the thoughts of losing the farm, having their house burn down, and being saddled by mortgage debt out of her mind. *Lord, please let me think happy thoughts.*

Going back into the parlor, she opened the memory book and looked through her notes and mementoes of that first year of marriage. *I was pregnant that next spring.* Laura smiled. *Manly was in a hurry about everything. "We're gonna be rich soon," he said every night. "You won't have to work after this harvest." But I kept working, doing the cooking, washing, and all the chores.*

She had written a diary note in her book.

> *I have learned to do all kinds of farm work with machinery. Yesterday, I rode the binder, driving six horses like a man.*

Laura thought for a moment about her horse, about the surprised looks she got from the townfolk when she galloped through. On the next page was a picture of her sitting on the horse, smiling like she owned the world. Below it was written,

> *Oh, how I love to ride! I do not wish to appear conceited, but I can break my own ponies. Of course, they were not bad, but they were broncos. Nevertheless, I'm the only woman in the territory who's done it.*

Laura smiled at the conceit of youth and the freedom that life on the prairie offered. *Here I was pregnant and wanting to prove to the world that nothing could hold me back. Riding horses up until I delivered. Baby Rose. I named her after the beautiful prairie flowers I've always loved. She had big blue eyes and golden hair. She was fat as a tub of butter and laughed at everything.*

She remembered how Manly would carry Rose everywhere, telling Laura that all her dreams would soon come true. "I'm goin' to make you proud of me, Laura. Just you wait and see. We'll be rich soon, girl, that we will!"

But it didn't happen that way, did it, Manly?

Closing her eyes, she could remember Manly telling her, "The rich get their ice in the summer and the poor get their ice in the winter. It all evens out, Laura."

You were so full of hope, weren't you, Manly?

Laura remembered Pa warning Manly that he shouldn't go into debt to buy a harvesting machine. He had come out to see their farm and tried to caution Manly against thinking that the easy way was the best way.

"Swing a cuttin' cradle yourself," Pa said. "It'll cut wheat and oaks and the only thing you'll spend is your sweat."

Manly laughed. "Pa Ingalls, that's just old fashioned."

"Manly, don't buy anythin' that you can't pay for in full. Debt's for fools and corrupt governments. I've learned the hard way. I know."

Laura had pleaded with Manly to listen to her father, but it was like talking to the wall. *Debt is for fools. You were so right, Pa.*

But Manly wouldn't listen. In his mind, the golden future was as certain as the sunshine.

You put us in debt over our heads, Manly, that's what ruined us, Laura thought, shaking her head. *You had to have a sulky plow, then a mowing machine, then a hay rake, and then a binder. You had to have it all because you could just make easy payments with interest on them. All you had to do was mortgage the horses, then mortgage the cows, then mortgage the machinery we owned outright. Then you mortgaged the house without telling me. Oh, Manly, you mortgaged our future away. You almost mortgaged my heart away.*

Then came the hail storm that destroyed the crops, followed by the mortgage notes being called, taxes due, doctor bills, and medicine. Then all the trees died in the drought and we couldn't prove we were living on a tree claim. Oh, Manly, it went from bad to worse.

Laura tried to block the thoughts, but she saw the barn and haystacks in flames. She saw the house burning and felt the intense pain of her hair and scalp being singed in the fire, as she tried to save their meager possessions.

The cry of a newborn chilled her soul. It seemed she was again holding her baby boy in her arms. *He looked just like you, Manly. He was the son you wanted.* But the baby died after twelve days and now lay in an unnamed grave back in the Dakotas.

For a moment, she was dreaming, floating above the rafters of their little shack. She saw herself, lying next to Manly, both nearly dead from diptheria.

"I've got to get up," Manly barely whispered. "I've got man's work to do."

"Stay, don't get up," Laura groaned, reaching out weakly for his arm.

In her dream, Laura wanted to shout out, "Don't go, Manly, don't go!" But the words wouldn't come.

Tears streamed down her face as she watched Manly struggle from the sickbed, forcing himself to work their farm. She saw him drop from the stroke, lying there partially paralyzed. His face was covered with mud, his speech . . .

In a flash it was months later. She had nursed Manly back to health, doing all the housework and farmwork herself to keep them going. She was as thin as a rail from not eating. Worry lines creased her face. She struggled to raise the money to pay the bills and to raise her husband back up so he could walk again.

But Manly had worked the hardest. He wouldn't give up. She saw him below her, crawling across the cabin floor, pulling himself along, trying to build up his strength. Not wanting help. Falling against the doorframe. Pulling himself across the ground to the outhouse.

"If I don't do it myself, I'm never gonna be able to do it," he said, shaking her loose.

"But I want to help, Manly. Let me help."

"You're doin' enough already. You're doin' everythin'. Let me do this on my own, please," he said, looking at her with imploring eyes.

But the doctor had said to let Laura help him and he'd walk faster, so Manly finally relented when he was able to stand on his own feet again.

"Laura, I can't even lift my feet over the door frame," he said, holding on to her arm as she walked him outside.

"It'll just take time. That's what the doctor said."

"But I can't even move my hands. I feel so useless. There's so much man's work to be done."

"It can wait. I'll do it for you."

All he could do was drop his head. "I feel like half a man, sometimes."

"But I'm all your wife. You and I are . . . we're partners, Manly. For better or worse. Isn't that what we said?"

You made yourself walk again, didn't you, Manly? You taught yourself inch by inch how to walk, use your hands, and stand upright. You even got rid of that cane, though you should still use it.

Laura stood up and walked to the porch. *Oh, Manly, what's happening to us? We shouldn't sleep apart!*

From behind her, she heard the familiar shuffling of Manly's feet. The dragging limp from the stroke. She wanted to turn, reach out and hug him, ask for forgiveness, but something held her back.

"You remember this, Laura?" Manly asked quietly.

She turned. Manly was holding the Christmas present that they had picked out to give each other on the first Christmas of their marriage. Inscribed on it was,

Give us this day our daily bread

"Of course I remember it. We got it from the Montgomery Ward catalog. It was all we could afford."

Manly nodded. "Sometimes I think we forget what bad times were really like," he said, walking up to her. "Ain't no reason for us to be sleepin' apart like a couple of strangers."

"But you stormed off and—" she caught herself and stopped. "And I embarrased you by getting arrested."

"And you talk too much." He smiled and hugged her. He pressed his lips against hers, lifting her up into the air. "Let's not sleep apart ever again, all right?"

"All right," she whispered, kissing him back. "And now you'll tell me what you think and how you'll vote," she asked playfully.

Manly stiffened and pulled back. "Can't you leave well enough alone? I waited for you to come apologize for hurtin' my feelin's but no, it's always me who has to meet you more than halfway."

"That's not true."

"It most certainly is," he said, picking up his hat.

"Where are you going now?" she asked.

"Today's the day of your monthly women's votin' meeting. I'm going to Billy Pickle's to get a haircut so I don't have to be henpecked no more, if that's okay with you, *sir,*" he said, handing her the inscribed plate.

"What do you want me to do with this?" she asked, feeling weak again.

"Hang it back up or change the wording."

"Change the wording?" she asked.

"Yeah," he said, opening the door. "It should read, 'Give Laura her say and her own way.'"

"And what's that supposed to mean?" she called after him as he limped down the porch stairs.

"Whatever you want it to mean. You seem to make all the decisions around this house anyway."

For the second time in half a day, tears streamed down Laura's face.

CHAPTER 18

SWEAT SHOP STRIKE

Ellen Boyle's assistant, Page O'Mally, looked at the line of policemen carrying nightsticks, lining the entrance to the decrepit garment factory. "This is not our cause," she said emphatically.

Ellen shook her head. "It's all one and the same. They hire the women cheap because the women can't vote."

"But the women here need the work," Page said, frazzled with worry over the confrontation that was certain to come.

"And that's why they take advantage of them," Ellen answered. With her sun-reddened cheeks, flowing white dress, and vibrant eyes, even the policemen couldn't take their eyes off of her.

"I bet they've got half the grandmothers in the tenements doing piecework; probably have children doing it too," Ellen said. "Come on, it's time."

As Ellen neared the front of the picket line, she whispered to Page, "Where are all the women who promised to show up?"

"Fifty said they'd walk the line," Page said, looking at the twenty women carrying signs.

Ellen laughed grimly. "We should give the coppers each a sign. There must be fifty of them, at least."

A beefy police officer stepped in front. "If you cross onto factory property, we're goin' to arrest the lot of you."

"And why are you protecting these sweat shop owners?" Ellen demanded, putting on her thickest Irish brogue.

Her beauty made him blush. "We're not."

"Don't you know that they've built their fortunes on the backs of the weak? On the sweat and toil of children?" Ellen asked, the fire building in her eyes.

"I'm here to enforce the law, not argue politics with you," the officer said. "Now, why don't you ladies go home and quit playin' these games?"

"Games!" Ellen cried out. "You call the working conditions in this shirtwaist factory a game?" The picketing women cheered her on. "Do you know what the conditions are like in there?" Ellen shouted.

The policeman matched her. "I know what the law says, and the law says that if you cross onto their property, that I'm to arrest each and every one of you."

"There are over three hundred women working in there, crammed together, with hardly any light. The snippers are paid a dollar fifty a week, no matter how many hours they're forced to work. They don't get overtime or supper money," Ellen said more to the crowd than to the officer.

"We give 'em apple pie sometimes," a man shouted from behind the factory fence.

"You're so generous I'm in shock," Ellen said, mocking the man.

"And we pay the cutters six bucks a week!" the man called out.

Ellen laughed scornfully. "And what's that for? Seventy, eighty hours?" She turned to the women on the picket line. "Who is he, anyway?"

"That's the man who runs the factory," one of the women said.

Ellen glared at him. "Why don't you pay these women a decent wage? Are you that tight with a penny that you'd starve their children?"

The manager laughed. "See that sign?" he said, pointing to the board over the entrance. The sign read,

IF YOU DON'T COME IN ON SUNDAY, DON'T COME IN ON MONDAY!

"There's a thousand women waitin' to take the place of the strikers," he shouted. "It's you who's starvin' their children."

Ellen looked at the sign again. "You've got the Christian spirit, that you do," she said scornfully.

The man shook his head. "Those women were lucky to have a job. Which is something you ought to get," he said, and he turned to leave.

Ellen closed her eyes, thinking back to the Triangle Shirtwaist Factory in New York where she had worked as a young immigrant. It was a sweat shop that did piecework—the small run items and special stitching—for the other factories.

I was too young to be listened to, she thought. *I came to America to help women but ended up needing help myself. But I learned a lot. That I did.*

The conditions were squalid. Four hundred women working on two floors, though barely enough space for half that number. No sprinklers, no open windows. Just fetid, stinking air and the mean bosses.

She remembered the monotony of the work. She and her eight-year-old sister, Pauline, worked twelve-hour days. *She was just a little lass, sitting in the corner with her scissors, waiting to cut the threads off. They sat like a kindergarten class, the group of them, working their little fingers off, doing the same thing from seven-thirty in the morning till nine at night.*

She shook the memory off and looked toward the factory. Frightened eyes—of women and children—stared back at her from a hundred windows. "How many children are working in there?" she cried out. "Call out your names."

The policeman said, "There are child labor laws on the books, don't you worry about that."

Ellen looked up toward the windows as little voices, calling out a potpourri of names, sounded out like birds in the wind. "They may be on the books," Ellen said grimly, "but you're not enforcing them."

The policeman turned. "It must be a trick you've planned."

"Trick? No trick," Ellen said coldly. A dozen little girls screamed out their names at the same time, followed by the slap of belts as they were beaten away from the windows. Ellen looked into the officer's eyes. "Those are the names of the powerless, of the lost childhoods that are wasting behind those walls."

"I ain't gonna listen to your agitator tricks," he said firmly.

Ellen looked up and saw the hand of a young girl waving to her. The face behind the hand smiled. "Either that girl's a midget or she's all of seven years old."

The policeman laughed. "You're dreamin'. The only one thinkin' of breakin' the law is you and this band of hussies you got followin' you." He turned to the picketers. "I suggest you put those signs down and go back to work before you lose your jobs."

"We've already lost 'em," snapped one of the women.

"It was your doin'," he said, shaking his head.

As the little girl's hand slid back behind the window, Ellen remembered how it was in New York. *Sure, there are laws on the books, but they aren't enforced. The bosses always get tipped off by the coppers when the inspectors are coming. That's why they pay the bribes.*

For a moment, she was back there, sitting at her machine, watching her sister. Pauline was sitting in the corner with the other young children who should have been in school.

Mr. Shulman, the factory owner, ran down the aisle shouting, "Quick, get into the boxes!"

They stuffed the children into the boxes with the finished shirts and then piled shirts on top to hide them. The inspector stood beside the boxes, saying loudly, "Good, you've got no children working here. And the Mayor appreciates your contributions."

We weren't human beings! Mr. Shulman treated us like we were animals! Ellen's eyes welled up at the memory of it all.

"No singing!" Shulman screamed at Pauline and the other bored children, as they snipped the threads away. *Aye, she loved to sing, Pauline did. But they wouldn't let her.*

"No talking!" the floor bosses yelled.

If you were found talking, even in the bathroom, you'd be fired. If you spent more time on the pot than they thought was necessary, even if you were sick, you lost a half day's pay and were sent home.

Now Ellen took a deep breath and looked around. "What are we marching for?" she shouted out, her auburn hair flying as she turned from side to side.

"Good conditions!" chorused the picketing women.

"What do we demand?" Ellen shouted, her cheeks a deep rose color in anger.

"Fair wages!" the women responded.

"And what will we do?"

"Strike!" they all shouted, pressing forward.

"Stand back, get back!" the police officer shouted. "Men, prepare to stand firm." The line of police officers pressed together.

Ellen and the women advanced and the officer shouted, "One step, march." The line of policemen moved forward like a machine.

Ellen held up her hands. "Into the factory, free these slaves!"

The officer raised his nightstick. "Two steps, march!" The line of policemen moved ahead, bumping right into the women.

It was no match but the women did their best to break the lines. "Let us in!" Ellen demanded. "There are women and children being oppressed in there."

"Back off," the officer shouted. "This is my last warning."

"And I warn you that we won't be stopped! You can beat us but we won't be denied our rights" Ellen shouted back.

"Women will not be denied," the strikers shouted in unison, and it was all over except for the arrests.

The officers encircled the women, trampling their signs, roughing up the resisters. Paddy wagons appeared from behind the factory and the women were shoved inside.

The factory manager came out, smiling. "Good work. We can't have agitators hurting the morale of my workers."

"Thank you, sir. I'm sorry for all the trouble they caused you," the officer said.

"No trouble. Actually, they may have done us a favor," he said, pointing to twelve women being evicted through the factory gates. "We found out who the traitors were. Caught them talking about the strike, we did."

Ellen looked out at the women. Among them was the little girl who had waved to her. *You're lucky to be out of there. Maybe I've saved your life.*

In the paddy wagon on the way to jail, Ellen thought back to the factory she'd worked in. *Everyone was smoking around the shirts.*

And the fire escapes were locked, to keep us from sittin' on the stairs durin' lunch, from gettin' some fresh air.

She shivered at the worst memory of all—the fire. *There were four hundred and twenty of us workin'. We'd been there twelve hours but the boss man wanted us to work till midnight.*

The smell of the burning walls came back to her and she was back in the factory. "Pauline, where are you Pauline?" The smell of smoke was in the air.

The women on the floor panicked. *We went to the fire escape doors but they were locked! Then we flowed as a group toward the elevators, but they were shut off.*

"Pauline, Pauline!" Ellen shouted. But her little sister was nowhere to be seen.

The flames licked in through the ceiling and pandemonium broke loose. "It's the end of the world!" an old Italian lady screamed. Ellen tried to grab her as she fainted, but it was too late. The frightened women trampled the woman beneath them.

The flames seemed to race down the walls, reaching out for everyone. *I've got to get out. I've got to save myself.* Ellen whimpered, her heart pounding. *But where's Pauline?*

"Where are the children?" she screamed to the floor lady who monitored the toilets.

"They already got down."

"Oh, thank God," Ellen sighed. A huge, fiery beam crushed the floor lady, killing her instantly.

Ellen raced to the windows and looked down. It was five stories to the ground. A screaming woman's body fell by outside, her skirt on fire. Everyone stopped short, watching until she hit the pavement below.

A woman next to Ellen started crying. Then another jumper passed by, then another. The women around Ellen went into hysterics.

"Why are they jumping?" Ellen sceamed out.

"It's that or burn," shouted another of the floor ladies. "Some are bound to survive the jump."

"If they land on someone else, they might survive," said one of Ellen's line workers who had kept her head.

In the fire and smoke, someone shouted for them to make a

rope of shirts, and soon a hundred hands were tying them together.

"Hurry, hurry girls!" shouted an aging Jewish grandmother. "We haven't got much time!"

Ellen was pushed forward and was out the window behind another girl from the packing line. *I was one of the first down the shirt rope—one of the lucky ones.*

When she got to the ground, she looked up at the screaming women above her. The shirt rope broke under the weight of two of Ellen's friends. She watched them twirl like pinwheels until the pavement stopped their lives.

Ellen asked everyone where the children were, and finally, Mr. Shulman looked at her and shook his head. "The children are on the eighth floor."

"Eighth floor? Why aren't they down here?"

"I was worried that the inspectors might see them comin' out in the fire," he said, looking down. "I didn't want to be fined. I thought they'd have the fire out in no time and everyone would go back to work."

"You locked the fire escapes, that's what you did!" Ellen screamed, trying to claw his eyes out. A policeman grabbed Ellen and held her until she calmed down.

By the next morning, the charred bodies of one hundred and forty-six women and children were laid out on the street like trash. Some of these women were the same ones who had tried to get Ellen to join them in a strike the year before for decent wages, better sanitary working conditions, and basic safety precautions.

But I didn't join them. I was worried about keeping my job.

The image of the charred body of her eight-year-old sister hung in her mind, searing like a knife in her insides. *That's why we must have the right to vote,* Ellen thought, clenching her jaw. *So we can stop this. So that the thousands of Paulines can live.*

CHAPTER 19

WELCOMING COMMITTEE

Laura answered the ringing phone in the kitchen. "Hello."

"Laura, this is Summers. Thought you might like to know that your friend Ellen Boyle got herself arrested again."

"She did?" Laura said, unable to hide the concern in her voice. "What happened?"

Summers snickered. "She was leadin' a bunch of women against a factory. Tried to tear the place apart is the way I heard it."

"What exactly did you hear, Andrew?" Laura asked, now suspicious and impatient.

"You can read about it in the paper if you're goin' to use that tone of voice on me."

Summers had never spoken to Laura with that kind of anger. Laura took a deep breath and slowly counted to five. Then she asked again. "What exactly did you hear?"

"My friend at the *St. Louis Post-Dispatch* said that Boyle and some of her kind instigated a riot at a job-payin' factory and roughed up the police who were tryin' to protect private property."

"Oh, come on, Andrew! You're goin' to tell me with a straight face that some women roughed up the St. Louis police?"

"Some of them women suffragists are pretty mean and tough. Heck, from what I hear they all look like lumberjacks and . . .

er, well . . . I guess you know what they look like, you gettin' arrested with them and all."

"They're just women. We're just women, Andrew. No different than your wife."

"Now hold your horses there! My wife's not one of you."

"I didn't say she was. But now that you mention it, she is coming over today to our Good Government Club meeting."

"She didn't tell me!" Summers sputtered over the phone.

Laura chuckled. "Maybe she doesn't tell you everything. Or maybe you don't ask what she's really thinking."

"Ask? Why should I ask her what I already know?"

"You shouldn't take a woman for granted, Andrew," Laura said. "That's a big mistake." Laura heard a knock on the door. "Got to go now. Thanks for calling." She hung up before he could respond.

With Laura's arrest making the front page, over twenty women showed up for the meeting at Apple Hill Farm. Except for Sarah Bentley and Alexandria Steadman—who were always invited but never showed up—everyone from Darlene Summers to the judge's wife was there.

"Ladies," Laura said, calling the meeting in her living room to order, "I want to thank each of you for coming."

"May I ask a question?" Darlene Summers asked. "It's something we're dying to know."

"And what's that?" Laura said with a sigh, knowing what was coming.

"What was it like in jail?" she asked. The women laughed good-naturedly.

Laura blushed. "It's not someplace I'd like to go back to, if that's any help."

"Were you put in with the men?" Alice Bedal asked, thinking she was going to get something to gossip about.

"Did anybody try to . . . to . . . get fresh with you in there?" Carol Campbell stammered.

"Ladies, ladies. Jail is no garden party, and it's certainly not a tea dance. But the police, as rough as they were, separated the women from the men. No, no one got fresh or anything like that," Laura said.

The first half of the meeting was spent discussing what happened in St. Louis, Laura's impression of Ellen Boyle, and the invitation for Ellen to address the Mule Day crowd. The rest of the meeting was about the statue of Sacagawea that the club was raising money to build.

"How much money have we raised to date?" Laura asked Alice Bedal, the treasurer of the group.

Alice looked at her notes. "Four hundred and forty dollars and thirty-one cents."

The women in the room applauded. "We're making progress," Laura said, nodding to them. "Carol, will you read your report on your trip to Jefferson City?"

Carol Campbell stood up. "Alice Bedal and I went to the State House to call on the governor and present him with the Mansfield petition, asking him to endorse the Woman's Suffrage Bill. He said he would try to bring it before a special session of the legislature, but was unsure when it would convene."

"That's what he said last year," Darlene Summers said sarcastically.

"Get your husband to write an editorial in favor of a special session," Eulla Mae Springer said.

"That's right," chorused several of the women in the room.

"I've got about as much chance of that as making it snow in July," Darlene said, shaking her head.

Laura held up her hands. "Ladies, ladies, we can't hold Darlene responsible for what her husband writes." She looked at Carol. "Would you continue, please?"

"After our meeting with the governor, we called on various members of the legislature, many of whom had worked to keep the suffrage bill off the calendar. The main opposition to passage is a few thick-skinned Democrats, but the better Democrats are for us. The Republicans have conceded that the bill will ultimately pass and are now behind us."

"Yes, yes," said several of the women as they broke into applause.

After their enthusiasm died down, a vote was taken, empowering Laura to meet with Mae Jefferson, the sculptor. "We want to know how the statue is progressing," Carol Campbell said.

"Tell her that we intend to pay the balance after you give her what we've raised," Alice Bedal said.

Laura hadn't told anyone—not even Manly—that she had signed a personal note guaranteeing the full amount if the club couldn't raise it. *I should have told Manly,* she thought, suddenly feeling guilty. *I've berated him for over fifteen years about the secret mortgage he took on our Dakota home. Why did I feel I didn't have to tell him?*

"I don't think we'll have a problem with the artist," Laura said. "I just hope she finishes the statue before the Fourth of July."

"I thought she was waiting for the balance of the money." Carol Campbell said. "Isn't that how our contract reads? She won't finish until she's paid in full?"

Laura nodded. "Yes, that's how it reads, but she has faith in us," she said, looking over the room. "Now, if there isn't any more new business to discuss, I motion that we adjourn this meeting. Do I have a second?"

Darlene Summers raised her hand. "Second."

"All in favor, say aye," Laura said.

"Aye," chorused the women.

Laura smiled. "Meeting's adjourned. Just make sure that you tell everyone, and I mean *everyone,* to come hear Ellen Boyle speak."

"I just hope we don't have trouble," Alice Bedal said, as she passed by Laura on her way out the door.

"Trouble? In Mansfield?" Laura laughed nervously.

"It could happen anywhere," Darlene Summers said, shrugging her shoulders, "and we don't need a riot here. I would never condone that," Darlene said.

"Trouble's already started at my house," Carol Campbell said. "My husband will hardly talk to me about this."

"Mine either," several women said at once.

Laura smiled. "Whatever it takes, ladies, whatever it takes. The right to vote means everything to us. We will not be denied this basic right."

"I just hope it comes in our lifetime," Carol Campbell said as she walked out the door.

Laura watched the women drive off in their cars, buggies, and wagons. *They're all happy now,* Laura thought, *but that'll change when the trouble hits home. I know.*

CHAPTER 20

BILLY PICKLE'S

Manly walked slowly to town. The sky was as still as the big oil painting in the bank, a picture in itself, but Manly was too preoccupied to notice.

He could have taken the Oldsmobile. He could have taken the wagon, buggy, or horse, but he chose to walk. Walk and think.

Sleepin' on the couch is for losers, he thought. *Daggonit, I'm too old to be hangin' out on the couch like a deadbeat uncle.*

For a moment he wished their old dog Jack was still around. *He was a good dog. He'd keep me company.*

"Hey, Manly, why you walkin'? Your Olds broke down?" Maurice called out.

Manly heard the clump of mules' hoofs and turned. "Oh, hi, Maurice."

"Somethin' happen to your car?"

"Naw," he said, looking away, "I just wanted to walk."

"Uh huh," Maurice said, grinning. "You look like you got the married man's blues."

"It ain't nothin' like that. I just got some things on my mind."

Maurice slapped the wagon bench. "Why don't you hop on up here beside me? We both probably got the same problem."

"We do?" Manly asked, not seeing how that could be.

"Certainly. My Eulla Mae is over at your house for the women's votin' meetin' and she'll come home tonight all fired up about wantin' to vote."

Manly grinned. "Yup, we do have about the same problem."

Maurice laughed. "I knowed it. And I bet you've been eatin' cold food and warmin' the couch like I have."

Manly's jaw dropped. "Not cold food 'cause I fixed my own breakfast."

"And from the looks of your eyes, you slept on the couch, didn't you?"

"It was the first time, and it was terrible," Manly said.

"First time! Why I've been on the couch so many times I call it the Hotel Maurice. Sort of my home away from home," he said, slapping Manly on the back.

As they crossed the Willow Creek bridge, Maurice wondered aloud. "Black man's got enough problems without havin' women problems."

Manly nodded. "I imagine."

"And now my wife is takin' my shotgun money to help put up some statue to an Indian girl. That takes the cake, don't it?"

"I can't understand it myself," Manly said, shaking his head. "Seems they could put up somethin' to Betsy Ross or Martha Washington. Someone who makes sense."

Maurice giddiyapped his mules. "Maybe if they was puttin' up a statue to Harriet Tubman and her underground railroad I wouldn't mind. Or to James Armistead."

"Who?" Manly asked.

"James Armistead. He was the black spy who gave the colonists the information that let us beat the British at Yorktown in 1781."

"I didn't know that," Manly said, scratching his head.

"Lots you don't know. That ain't in no history book. My grand-daddy told me 'bout him."

Manly shrugged. "Never heard of him."

Maurice shook his head. "But a statue to an Indian woman in the middle of Mansfield? Not with my shotgun money," Maurice said in disgust.

"Thought you said Eulla Mae already took your shotgun money." Manly said, trying to suppress a grin.

Maurice nodded. "I'm talkin' 'bout the next shotgun money I save up," he said, chuckling.

Manly got out at Billy Pickle's barber shop and opened the door.

The bell tinkled as he stepped in. The scent of colognes, hair tonics, and rubbing oil assaulted his nose.

Pickle was cutting Lafayette Bedal's hair. "Just a little bit off the top and take the sides down, okay, Lafayette?" It was what he always offered. It was the only haircut he knew how to cut.

Bedal nodded. "That'll be good."

"Okeedokey," Pickle said, combing down the part line.

"Hiya, Billy," Manly said.

"Come on in, Manly," Pickle called out. "Be with you in a moment." He rubbed his fingers through Bedal's hair. "You got a cowlick that could stand up to a tornado, know that?"

Bedal nodded. "Just plaster it down with some of your goo."

"Okeedokey," Pickle said again, as he began to cut.

Manly nodded to the men. As they waited their turns in the barber's chair, the snip-snip of Pickle's scissors mixed with their conversations. Manly sniffed the air. The "never move" bottles of mystery hair tonic and smelling water made him smile. *Pickle uses the stuff on every customer, yet the bottles never seem to go up or down half an inch. That's a mystery to me,* he thought.

Fred and Buddy, two good ol' boys he knew who farmed out near the county line, leaned over. Fred raised his eyebrows. "When you comin' out with us to our secret fishin' hole?"

Buddy grinned and looked around, hoping no one else had heard. "Yeah, ain't no wives around," he said, grinning. "You can fish and cuss and do just 'bout anythin' you want."

"Think I'll pass, boys," Manly said.

"Do you hear what I'm tellin' you? Just guys. No wives allowed," Fred whispered to Manly.

"I heard, I heard. Now let me read this magazine," Manly said, shaking his head.

Snip-snip-snip. Pickle's scissors slowly circled Bedal's left ear. "Hear anymore about this Boyle woman comin' to speak?" Bedal asked Pickle.

Pickle looked at his work, then snipped around the right ear. "Just that she'll probably cause a riot and ruin our Mule Day party." He paused, nodding at his haircut. "You got good hair, Lafayette."

"She ought to locked up and the key thrown away!" Jacob Helling called out. "She and all those jailbirds like Manly's wife."

Pickle looked over, hoping Manly hadn't heard the remark. Manly had, but he pretended he hadn't.

Helling still carried a grudge against Laura. He felt she had humiliated him in front of his wife last winter. Now he poked over at Manly and laughed. "How's it feel to be married to a jailbird?"

Manly didn't look up and said coldly, "You talkin' to me?"

Helling chuckled. "I said, how's it feel—"

Manly looked up and cut him off. "I heard what you said, Jacob. Now, why don't you just mind your own business, hear?"

"Whoa, you're talkin' tough for a man who don't wear the pants in his family," Helling shouted.

Dr. George, the town's only doctor, put down his magazine. He had not forgotten the racist way in which Helling had treated him —a black man—the past winter. Though Helling had apologized to Dr. George, it was clear that not much had changed. Dr. George shook his head. *This leopard hasn't changed his spots.*

"Why ain't you talkin', Manly?" Helling said.

"I think enough's enough, don't you two agree?" Dr. George said.

Helling looked over. "This got nothin' to do with you, Doc. I'm just playin' with Manly here."

Manly wanted to hit Helling but forced himself to cool down. "Everything's okay, Doc. Jacob here was just actin' up, that's all."

Pickle pulled the cloth off Bedal. He quick-brushed the loose hair off Bedal's shirt and collar, then dusted powder around his ears. "This is a barber shop, a man's world. Can't have no bad feelin's in here, boys," he said.

Manly nodded, and went back to reading a magazine. *Slap-slap-slap.* Pickle took some of the mystery smelling tonic and slapped it lightly on Bedal's cheeks and neck.

Jacob Helling shook his head. "If his wife would stop stirrin' up trouble, the whole town would calm down."

"Leave my wife out of this," Manly said, looking up.

"She's the cause of all this, with her writin' trash like this," Helling said, tossing the newspaper onto Manly's lap. "Read that and tell me you agree with it."

Manly handed it back. "Read it yourself," he said, looking down.

Helling stood up. "If anyone in this room agrees with this clap-trap, why I'll shave my head!" He laughed brashly and passed the article around the room.

The Coming Power of Women
By Laura Ingalls Wilder

Ellen Boyle is coming to Mansfield in the interest of women's suffrage. She is part of a movement to bring light into the dark places in the Ozarks and throughout Missouri.

Dark places you ask? Where are they? They are wherever women are denied their equal rights under the law. Whether it takes a year or a decade, women will get the right to vote and help shape the destiny of this country they helped build. However, the ballot is but a small thing in the work before us as women of the nation.

Anybody who thinks that we will accept politics as usual is in for a big surprise. Women will take advantage of the ballot when they get it. If politics are not what they should be, if there is corruption among the people who have taken an oath of office, then we will vote them out.

If the laws are unjust or deny others their due rights, then we will vote to change them. In the process, we may have to vote out a few men.

Do you think I'm claiming too much influence for women? Take a moment and see if you don't agree with me. I hope that everyone will turn out to welcome and listen to what Ellen Boyle has to say. The future is at hand, and the hand is a woman's.

As the men read it, Helling looked around. "If that's not a crock of dung, I don't know what is!" He turned to Manly. "Well?"

"Well what?" Manly said, putting his magazine down.

"Do you agree with it?"

"I feel like tellin' you no, just to shut you up. But my opinion's my opinion, so kindly leave me out of this discussion."

"Kind of hard to leave you out," Pickle said with a grin, "when it's your wife doin' the writin'."

"That's your problem, Billy," Manly said, looking at the page but seeing nothing.

Billy chuckled. "In Hungary, we had an expression that a married man is a caged bird."

"That fits Manly, it sure do." Helling laughed mockingly.

Manly stood up and headed toward the door. Dr. George looked at Helling and said, "You haven't changed much, have you?" Helling didn't know what to say, and watched dumbfounded as Dr. George followed behind Manly.

Pickle called out. "We were only kiddin', Manly, Doc, come on back and let me cut your hair."

Manly exited as Pickle laughed to the men in the room, "He can't take a joke, can he, boys?"

Manly stopped in the street. "I'm gettin' mighty sick of it all."

Dr. George put his hand on Manly's shoulder. "Want to get somethin' to eat? We could go over to the hotel."

Manly shook his head. "Doc, I appreciate your standin' up with me in there. But I shouldn't have let them get to me, that's all. No sense in you gettin' them on your back over this."

"Black man's always got someone on his back," Dr. George said.

Manly looked the doctor in the eyes with new appreciation. "Yeah, I bet you do."

Dr. George paused, looking at Manly. "That Helling is still a closet racist. Imagine him forgettin' that just six months ago, Laura and I—a woman and a black man—saved his two sons. My granddaddy told me a grateful hand without a heart to match is a cold handshake."

There wasn't much Manly could say except try and lighten his friend's mood. "How 'bout we not try to change the world today and get ourselves somethin' to eat instead?"

"If it was afternoon, I'd say we could go to Tippy's and put down a cold beer," the doctor said, wanting to think of better things.

Manly laughed. "That's all I'd need," he said. "Sleep on the couch for the first time and then show up with beer on my breath."

"You slept on the couch?" Dr. George exclaimed. "There's no

medicine in the world that can cure that except time and patience."

They moved aside to let Sarah Bentley and her maid, Martha, walk past. They tipped their hats. "Morning, Mrs. Bentley. Morning, Martha," they both said.

"Gentlemen," Sarah said, half smiling. Martha nodded and trudged past, carrying a load of packages.

"Come on, Martha," Sarah said loudly. "Don't be slowing down on me. Time is money and that's what I pay you for, though sometimes I really wonder why."

"That woman's like two miles of bad road," Manly said, shaking his head.

"I'd hate to be married to her," Dr. George whispered. "She might be pretty but that ain't worth all the aggravation."

"I feel sorry for old Martha," Manly said.

"Too bad her husband's just a barfly," Dr. George said. "She deserves better."

"She deserves somethin'. They all do," Manly said, thinking about Laura. *She deserves somethin'. Maybe somethin' better than I can provide. With her brains, she could have been a doctor or lawyer instead of a farmer's wife. Maybe even a congresswoman, if women could vote.*

He didn't want to think about Laura, Helling, Ellen, or any of it. *I just want to be kept out of it. I don't want to be involved. I just feel like sayin' heck to it all and goin' fishin'.*

He thought about the fishing hole that Fred and Buddy spoke about. *Where men can be men. Where no wives are allowed.* Manly nodded at the thought. *Sounds pretty good to me.*

CHAPTER 21

THE PACKAGE

"Hey, David, there's your wife," one of the bar patrons shouted out.

Cunningham looked up from his beer and saw his wife carrying a load of packages behind Sarah Bentley.

Huleatt had stopped in to pick up the receipts to take to the bank. "Just be glad she's out there and you're in here," he said, laughing. He thought for a moment, then checked his pocket. *If I'm goin' to get back at Ellen, now's the time to start the plan moving.*

He walked over and sat on the stool next to Cunningham. "Glad to see you're workin' hard," he said, mocking the old man.

Cunningham nodded. He knew what Huleatt thought of him but took the abuse for the free drinks. "Just waitin' like you told me."

Huleatt took out a small bottle, about three inches long, filled with a dark liquid. "I want you to put this in your pocket," he said, handing it to Cunningham.

The bottle had no label, so Cunningham asked, "What is it?"

"Just something I want you to mix in with a bottle of Irish whiskey."

Cunningham looked at the bottle and shrugged. "Give me a bottle from behind the bar," he said. "I'll mix it up right here. What is it, flavoring?"

"No, and I don't want you to use one of the bottles from here.

Here's some money," he said, handing him two five-dollar bills. "Buy a bottle of good whiskey from the tavern up on the county road, mix this in with it, and keep the change."

"Thanks," Cunningham said, holding the five-dollar bills as if they were a small fortune. "What should I do with the whiskey after I mix it up?"

"Wait a few days and bring it back to me here."

"And then?" Cunningham asked.

Huleatt grinned. "I'll need you to give it to someone when I tell you."

"Is this part of your funny plan?"

"It sure is, it sure is," Huleatt said, looking around. Then he remembered what else he had in mind. "I've got somethin' I want you to do," Huleatt said, walking back toward the kitchen. He went to the box of cows' tongues that were destined for the afternoon chili.

This ought to liven things up, Huleatt thought, taking a cow's tongue from the ice box. He wrapped it up in a copy of the *Mansfield Monitor* that had Laura's article circled with the words, *For her big mouth,* written above it, and put it in a bag.

"Go leave this against the front door of the *Monitor,*" he said quietly to Cunningham when he sat back down.

"What's in it?" Cunningham asked, opening the bag.

Huleatt took the bag back and twisted the top shut. "Are you workin' or askin' questions?"

"Workin'," the old man answered softly.

"Good. Then go do what I say and make sure nobody sees ya do it."

"Now?" he asked, slipping the small bottle into his pocket.

"Right now," Huleatt said, taking the man by the arm. "Just pretend you're out shoppin'. And don't let that nosy old wife of yours see ya."

Cunningham reluctantly took the package and went out the door. He looked up and down the street, feeling like a criminal. *There's somethin' not right about this,* he thought.

He headed across Main Street, trying not to look anyone in the face. He stopped in front of Bedal's General Store and peered up the street toward the newspaper office.

"Martha, come on, hurry up," Sarah said, barging out the door. She ran head-on into Cunningham, who tripped off the sidewalk, into the dust.

"You should watch where you're goin', old man!" Sarah snapped, adjusting her dress.

"Are you all right, Mrs. Bentley?" Martha asked. She saw her husband. "David! Are you all right, David?"

Cunningham stood up and dusted himself off. "'Scuse me, Mrs. Bentley, but I didn't see ya comin' out."

"You should be more careful," she said, oblivious to the fact that it was her fault.

Martha took her husband's arm and looked into his eyes. "Are you hurt?"

"No, no, I'll be all right," he said, stooping to pick up the package.

"What's in there?" Martha asked.

"Just somethin' I'm doin' for Mr. Huleatt."

Sarah started toward the next store. "Come along, Martha, unless you want to take some unpaid time off."

"Be right there, Mrs. Bentley," she called after her. Turning to her husband, she asked, "David, have you been drinkin' this early in the mornin'?"

"Just a beer, that's all."

"Where you gettin' the money? Sunday's long past and I haven't given you any more spendin' money."

David straightened up. "I got me a job, workin' for Mr. Huleatt."

"Job? What kind of job?" she asked with concern.

"Just a job doin' things. Here," he said, reaching into his pocket. "Here's five dollars. I want you to buy yourself a new dress."

"Five dollars!" she gasped. "What are you doin' for this kind of money?"

"I told you," he said defensively, "just doin' things."

"Doin' things? What kind of things?"

"Come along, Martha," Sarah shouted out. "You're on the clock, you know."

"Yes, ma'am," she called back. "David," she said, eyeing him, "don't be doin' nothin' against the law. Not for money, not for anything."

"You know I wouldn't, Martha," he said, kicking the sidewalk.

"What's in the bag?" she asked, looking at the red spot on the bottom.

"Don't know, don't need to know. It's just my job to deliver it," Cunningham said, feeling embarrassed.

"Deliver it where?" she asked.

Cunningham cleared his throat. "Why won't you let me have some pride, woman? I'm earnin' my own drinkin' money, I gave you five dollars, and I don't need you meddlin' where you shouldn't be meddlin'. Now, I got to go," he said, turning away.

"But, David, aren't you gonna kiss my cheek?" the old woman asked, her lip quivering.

David stopped and turned, then looked away after seeing the pain in his wife's eyes. "Please, Martha, don't cry."

"I only get to see you one day a week. Not like the old days when—"

Sarah came and grabbed the old woman's arm. "If you don't come now, I swear, I'm going to have to leave you behind, old woman!"

Martha tried to squeeze the tears from her eyes and turned, following behind Sarah, carrying more packages than a much younger woman could easily handle. *Oh, David, what are you doin' to yourself?*

Cunningham walked in the other direction and stopped in front of the *Mansfield Monitor's* door. He looked around, saw no one, and left the bag against it. *I better be gettin' to the tavern and buy that Irish whiskey. Might need a drink there. Maybe two. Don't want to be thinkin' 'bout what I'm gettin' myself into.*

Huleatt smiled from the door of his bar, watching Cunningham take off down the street. *Summers won't know what to do,* he chuckled. *He'll pitch a fit for sure.*

For a brief moment he had a burst of conscience about what he was doing, but he shrugged it off. Getting even was the only thing on his mind.

CHAPTER 22

WITH MY EYES CLOSED

After lunch, Huleatt took a stroll through town. He stopped to watch a teenage boy and girl on their horses galloping down the street. The way they smiled and laughed brought back a memory. A memory of riding with Ellen across the green fields of Tipperary, as if they owned the world.

Oh, she was a beauty. He stopped and leaned against a light pole, remembering her face. *She was worth dyin' for. She had a face that could make your heart skip a beat.*

Ellen was ahead of him, racing into the wind. *All I could think about was marrying her. Of having her as mine forever. No one else would ever have her, just me.*

It was the day that changed my life. She had something to tell me. Something that couldn't wait. In his mind he was back there. Back twenty years.

As they rode through the thick grass, he thought, *She's goin' to say she'll marry me. I know that's it. I know that's what she wants to tell me. My ma told everyone that we're going to be moving into the house with them until we build our own place.*

They rode until they reached their special place. A shaded bend in the creek, where no one could see them. They dismounted quickly, as if every moment counted, and headed toward the spot they'd discovered the day before.

"Take my hand, Thomas Huleatt." Ellen Boyle smiled and pulled him along.

"Slow down, slow down," Huleatt laughed, thinking he had the whole world in his hands. The silver locket he'd given Ellen with their photos in it caught the sun's reflections.

Ellen lifted up the curtain of branches and ducked under. "Come on, lad, we've not got all day. My mum will be a-wondering what we're up to."

Huleatt pushed the branches apart and stooped to enter. When he straightened up, he was face to face with this girl—the girl who was prettier than Ireland herself in his mind.

"Kiss me, Thomas, like you've been wantin' to."

"But we've kissed before."

She put her finger to his lips. "No, I mean really kiss me. Like a man should kiss his woman. Isn't that what you've been wanting?"

"No . . . yes . . ." he stammered, then stopped. He put his arms around her and kissed her as he thought a man should kiss a woman. He'd never kissed like that before but it all seemed so natural, so wonderful, so exhilarating.

"I love you. Do you love me?" he asked her, when they stopped to catch their breath.

"Oh, Thomas," she said, with a twinkle in her eye. "Why do you have to go and spoil it now?"

"But I love you. I want to marry you, you know that."

"Love, marriage? This is just a kiss, Thomas, just a kiss."

"Just a kiss?" he said, the hurt showing in his eyes.

Ellen sighed, pushing her fingers through his hair. "I've been trying to tell you but you've not been listening, lad. I like you, maybe even love you. But it won't last, cannot last."

"Why not?" he said, wanting to cry.

She kissed him again and held him in her arms. "Because I don't want to be a servant to any man. I can't tell you why, because I don't know. Something is driving me to show the world that women are not cattle, not property to be—"

Huleatt, who had heard her say all this before, kissed her hard. "Yes, I know, but that doesn't mean we can't get married. You can still—"

Ellen grasped him by the shoulders and looked into his eyes. "If I was to give my heart and body and soul to a man, it would be to you, Thomas, it would be to you. But not now. Maybe later, but not now."

"But when?" he asked hopefully. "I'll wait."

"Aye, I think you would, Thomas Huleatt." Ellen smiled warmly. "I think you would. But there's no future for women in Ireland. It's America I'll be going to."

"You'd leave Ireland?" he asked, astonished.

"In America, women can work and build their own futures. It's not like here where everything's been the same for a thousand years and won't change for another thousand."

"But America? I won't ever see you again." He looked down. "I'll come with you."

She hugged him closely. "I have to make my own way. You don't understand, do you?"

"I love you, Ellen Boyle. I love you," he said, trembling with fear. His whole world was coming apart.

"I'm sorry for hurtin' you, Thomas. Please don't cry," she whispered, smoothing his hair. But the tears just poured down his face.

"I . . . love you," he stammered through his tears.

She couldn't stop her own tears and the two of them clung to one another, knowing that when they broke apart, things would never be the same again.

"I love you too," she whispered. "But my love for you will have to stay as a memory . . . with my eyes closed."

"With your eyes closed?" he asked, not understanding.

"I'll marry you in my dreams, Thomas Huleatt," she said, holding him, trying to squeeze out enough emotion to last a lifetime.

"Marry me today, tonight, please," he cried, burying his face in her shoulder.

"Only in my dreams. But every night I'll love you with my eyes closed. And it'll last forever, until the day I die, just like the pictures in the locket," she said through her tears.

"I'll love you with my eyes closed." That's what she said. Huleatt leaned against the wall, feeling once again the heartache of that moment long ago. *And she left the next week. I never saw her again. And now she's comin' to town, bringin' it all back on me.*

A young boy tapped Huleatt on the leg. "Are you all right, mister?"

Huleatt coughed and tried to wipe the tears with his sleeve. "I'm all right. Just needed to close my eyes for a moment."

She never made fun of me. She never told any of the lads. It's somethin' I've made up in my mind to overcome the hurt.

He walked back to the saloon, unable to understand why he wanted to hurt this woman he had loved so much. *Maybe I should talk with Father Walsh about this,* he thought, though he hadn't been to confession in as long a time as he could remember.

CHAPTER 23

WOMEN SHALL RULE

Summers was fit to be tied. His wife had come home from the Good Government Meeting at Laura's house telling him that women were going to straighten the country out. They argued about women voting and it looked like he'd sleep on the couch again.

Then he received a letter from his daughter saying that when she graduated from college, she wanted eventually to take over the newspaper. That she didn't want to get married just yet. That she wanted a career.

So he left for the office in a bad mood, which was made worse by Laura's latest article. *This has got to stop,* he thought. "Tony, I just read this article by Laura you put on the front page. I don't like it."

Tony Loren looked up from his typesetting and shrugged. "I thought it was pretty good."

"Good? You call this blatant propaganda, this slanted journalism, good?" Summers shouted. He looked again at the galley copy of "Women Shall Rule," and choked. "It's so bad . . . so . . . outrageous!" It angered him so much he read it again.

Woman Shall Rule
By Laura Ingalls Wilder

There is a great deal of speculation, among forward-thinking women, about what things will be like after we get the right to vote. From everyone I've talked to and everything I've read, the consensus is that we will bring on a new order, a new social and industrial revolution.

Men will have to adjust to the fact that in all the democratic nations of the world, power eventually will be in the hands of women, who for too long have been denied their rights. There are more women than men and one day we're going to elect our own leaders. One day a woman shall be President of the United States of America.

Will we be wise and true and strong enough to use this power for the best? While we can't do worse than the "man-made world" we'll inherit, we have to be careful not to make the same mistakes. But since we have not had power, I believe we will be less inclined to misuse it.

It is a fact that, one day, women shall rule side by side with men. I hope we'll be ready for it.

"This is poppycock. Not even worth reading!" Summers exclaimed, tossing the copy into the air.

"So you're not goin' to print it?"

"No, pull it!" Summers shouted.

"Let me figure out what we can put in its place. We don't want a hole on the front page," Tony said stiffly.

"Ask me before you do something like this again. This would have upset the whole town," Summers said. He picked up the receiver on the wall phone and spoke into the mouthpiece on the wall. "Sarah? This is Andrew Summers, Will you please connect me with Laura Wilder?"

While he waited for the lines to be hooked up, he whistled softly. Tony walked to the front door to get some fresh air, his ear cocked to listen to what Summers was going to say.

"Laura? This is Andrew."

Laura was cleaning up in the kitchen, washing the coffee cups from the Good Government Club meeting. "Did you get my article?"

"Yes, yes, that's why I'm calling."

Laura smiled, knowing that her article had upset him. "It'll sell papers, Andrew, and get people talking."

"You've already got people talkin' too much. I'm callin' to tell you that I won't be runnin' this one."

Laura was speechless.

"Did you hear me?" Summers asked.

"You won't be running it? Why not? You've never held back on anything I've written."

"I'm goin' to do it this time. Tellin' people that women are going to rule, that there's goin' to be a woman president of the country. Laura, people are going to think that you're insane for writing it and I'm crazy for runnin' it. I'm just not goin' to do it."

"Is there anything you want me to change?" she asked, suddenly realizing that she had no control over this decision.

"It would take so many changes that you'd just have to rewrite the whole thing."

"I'll do it. You know I will, Andrew."

"Laura, what I'm callin' about is this," he said, taking a deep breath.

Tony Loren stood in the doorway, looking at a pretty girl on the other side of the street. He noticed the bag against the door and picked it up.

Summers coughed, trying to find the words.

"Say what you're going to say," Laura said, overcome by a sinking feeling. *Is he going to fire me?*

"I want you to write about women's things," he blurted out. "Like recipes and quilting parties—that sort of thing."

This was not what Laura expected. "Women's things? That's what I've been writing. The article I gave you is all about women."

"Not women's votin' articles. I mean I want you to write about clothes and sewin'. You know, what women really want to read about."

Laura suddenly felt very alone. She was powerless to do anything about Summers's decision. He owned the newspaper, and that was that.

"Oh no!" Tony cried out, dropping the bag.

Summers turned and saw the expression on Tony's face. "What's wrong?"

"Look!" he said, pointing to the bag. He looked in again and retched.

"Andrew, is there something wrong?" Laura asked loudly.

"Got to go, Laura. I'll get back to you," Summers said, hanging up. "What's wrong, Tony? Are you sick?"

Tony was ashen as he held the bag up for Summers to take, but the bottom fell out and the big, bloody cow's tongue dropped onto the floor.

"This ain't funny," Summers said. "Whoever did this has me to answer to." Then he saw Laura's article circled and the words, *For Her Big Mouth,* written boldly across it.

Looks like it is time to get her to write about somethin' else, Summers thought.

CHAPTER 24

FINGER SIGHT

Laura sat on her thinking rock, trying to sort out her conversation with Summers. His decision made sense and offended her at the same time.

I wonder where Manly is? she thought, then frowned. *I should have told him about guaranteeing the full payment for the statue. He'd have understood and given me his blessing. But I kept it a secret. Went behind his back as if it was none of his business. As if all our money was mine.*

At a loss for what to do and depressed by her guilty conscience, Laura walked down the hill. She went into the kitchen and called Mae Jefferson's number. Patrick Jefferson answered.

"Mr. Jefferson, this is Laura Wilder."

"Hi, Mrs. Wilder," Jefferson said happily. "Mae and I were just talking about you." His British accent still showed through.

"You were?" Laura said, a bit surprised.

"Sure were. I told Mae that you're going to love the statue."

"It's finished?"

"Almost. Mae just got the feeling and has kept right at it for the past few weeks."

"Mr. Jefferson, I—"

"Please, call me Patrick, Mrs. Wilder."

"If you call me Laura."

"All right, Laura. To what do we owe the pleasure of this call?"

Laura hesitated for a moment, then said, "I was just wondering if it'd be all right if I dropped down and visited."

Patrick laughed. "You want to visit or see the statue?"

"Well, I do want to see the statue. You're right about that."

"We'll be here all day," he said.

Laura said it would be a couple of hours and hung up the phone. *A drive will do me good,* she thought. *I wonder what this Mae Jefferson is like? I hear she's a real visionary.*

She got her purse and hat and went to get the Oldsmobile from the barn. Laura took the backroads, winding over the ridge tops. The endless variety of trees in the wooded hills soothed her nerves. The high meadows and meandering valleys seemed to frame the beautiful, almost mystic, foggy horizons ahead.

Ten miles down the road from where Laura had stopped, Mae Jefferson's hands felt along the arms of the statue she had cast. *There's still some rough spots,* she thought, running her fingers along Sacagawea's arms.

Her husband, Patrick, stood back admiring her work. "It's beautiful, Mae, simply beautiful." he said.

Mae turned at the sound of his voice. "Patrick, I didn't know you were standing there," she said, the accents of her heritage coming through.

Patrick smiled. "I've been here for quite a while. I'm always amazed at your talent."

Mae smiled, her sightless eyes looking toward the man she so loved. "I wish I could see you right now, just one more time," she said, sadly shaking her head.

"I think you see everything through those hands of yours," he said softly. He walked to his wife and hugged her.

"It's my finger sight," she said as she ran her hands over Patrick's face, lovingly touching the cleft in his chin, the lobes of his ears, and scratching at his eyebrows.

He was English and she was African—South African. He'd been with a trading company and she was a student in a missionary school. Their love had not been accepted in Cape Town, so they made their way to America, where they thought things would be easier.

They married before Mae lost her sight, and Patrick stayed by her side. Theirs had not been an easy marriage from the beginning —she was black and he was white—and Mae's losing her sight had made things tougher.

Laura pulled into the red dirt drive. She was glad it wasn't raining, because she knew how sticky the ground would be.

The house was not what she expected a famous artist's house to look like. Wood shavings littered the walk. Driftwood hung from the sides of the house and barn. A dilapidated shack stood out back, which she figured must be a kiln.

Mae looked up at the sound of a car approaching. "Are you expecting someone?"

Patrick looked out the window. "That woman from Mansfield called and said she was coming down. Wanted to see how the statue was coming."

Mae put her hand on her face. "But she'll see me and . . . and . . ." she stammered, feeling her way along the wall toward the bedroom.

"Where are you going? Come back here," Patrick said, taking Mae's hand and leading her back to her sitting chair. A half-shaped lump of Ozark brown clay was on the table beside her. Mae's fingers instinctively felt for it, prodding and shaping it.

"There's no sense hiding, is there?" Patrick asked softly.

"But you've never told anyone you sell my works to that I'm black and blind."

"But I tell everyone that I love you. That you're the greatest artist in the Ozarks. In America. Maybe even in the world," he said with a smile.

"Then you must be sillier than I think," she said, "because you've been selling my works as M. Jefferson, like they were done by a man." Her sightless eyes tried to look in his direction.

"You got me there," he said and turned to answer the door.

"But why tell her?" Mae asked.

"Why not?" Patrick said. "She's already paid almost half on the statue, and she's guaranteed the rest."

Mae took three careful steps, picked up a sheet, and covered the statue of Sacagawea, then sat back down.

Patrick opened the door and smiled warmly. "Mrs. Wilder, it's good to see you again. Please come in."

Laura stepped through the doorway. The inside of the house was warm, bright, and cheery, which made Laura feel welcome. "You've got a lovely home," she said, admiring the sunlit rooms, the plants, and the various works of art around the house.

"Thank you," he said, "but my wife did it all." Laura followed behind him to the back room studio. "You want some lemonade?"

Laura nodded. "That would be nice."

Mae took her hands from the clay and folded them in her lap, waiting for them to enter.

"I'll be back in a moment," he said leaving Laura at the doorway of the studio.

She saw Mae sitting and nodded. "Hello," Laura said, looking at the statues against the wall.

Mae smiled, turning her face toward the sound of the voice. "How are you?"

"I'm fine," Laura said, examining the bust of an old man. "I bet you love working around here for Mrs. Jefferson, don't you?" she said absentmindedly, examining the paintings on the wall.

She doesn't know who I am. She thinks I'm hired help. She thinks I'm a maid. But Mae answered, "Yes, I do."

Laura walked to the other side of the room and looked at a clay bird, so lifelike, it took her breath away. "What's she like?"

"Who?" Mae asked.

"Mae Jefferson. I'm dying to meet her."

"I hope you like her," Mae said. *I forgot,* she thought. *I forgot how the world is. Don't bring the world into my house!*

Laura continued her inspection of the various works of art throughout the room. "How long have you been with Mrs. Jefferson?"

"All my life," Mae said, wishing she could just see long enough to look this woman in the eye.

"Really?" Laura said, looking at a picture. "How interesting."

Patrick walked back into the studio, carrying a tray of glasses and a pitcher of lemonade. "So you met my wife. She's amazing, isn't she?"

Laura froze. "Your . . . your wife?"

"Yes," Patrick said, putting the tray down. He walked over and kissed Mae's cheek. "Her works are so perfect that sometimes even I forget she's blind."

"Blind?" Laura said softly, feeling like she was melting. A blush went across her face. She was thankful that the artist couldn't see how she felt.

Laura controlled herself and walked across the room. "Mrs. Jefferson, I'm Laura Wilder, the woman who contracted with you for the statue of Sacagawea."

Mae put her hand out in the air, and Laura took it hesitantly. "It's all right," Mae said softly.

"Am I missing something?" Patrick said.

"Mrs. Wilder didn't know I was your wife. I think she thought I was . . ." Mae stopped and looked down.

"I'm terribly sorry," Laura said sincerely. "I didn't know."

Patrick stepped in to save her more embarrassment. "I guess I forget how things really are. Living off by ourselves in the hills, with no one really coming 'round, lets us forget what the real world is like."

"No, it's my fault," Laura said. "I made assumptions I shouldn't have made."

"It's a fact of life," Mae said. "Just like Patrick selling my work as M. Jefferson so people will think I'm a man. Imagine what they'd think if they knew they were buying art from a blind, black woman married to a white man!" Mae laughed with such intensity that it broke the mood.

Patrick smiled at Laura. "Let's sit down and have some lemonade."

Still embarrassed, Laura sat down and looked around. Beyond Mae was a picture of a black man's face with a crown of thorns. The face was a mixture of agony and ecstasy.

I've never seen a black Jesus before, Laura thought.

Patrick, coughed to get Laura's attention. Laura looked at Mae's sightless eyes. "It must be very hard being a blind artist."

Mae said nothing.

Patrick looked at her. "Mae?"

"She asked is it hard not seeing what I create. I was just think- ing that hard is having to move away from the place where you

were born because you fell in love with someone a different color."
She laughed to herself. "Color. I can't even see colors. It just
seems so silly to me now."

Laura looked up at the picture of the black Jesus and shivered,
with both embarrassment and revelation.

Patrick blushed. "It's all right, Mae, no one's going to hurt you
while I'm around." He put his arms around his wife and soothed
her, kissing off the tears that fell from her sightless eyes.

"Maybe I should leave," Laura said quietly.

"Please. It'll be all right," Patrick whispered. "Just give her a
moment."

"I wish I'd never seen some of the meanness I've seen," Mae
whispered. The tears rolled down her ebony cheeks. Tears of hurt
and rage that were locked in her mind, locked in memories that
had the eyes of her lifetime behind them.

Soon she composed herself. She patted her husband on the
cheek and smiled. "Without Patrick, I wouldn't have been able to
survive all the grief in this world."

"It's okay," Patrick said. "Maybe we should drink our lemonade
and talk about something else."

Mae blew her nose into a handkerchief. "I just wanted this
woman to know that I'm the first one in my family who's been
anything but a poor African. That I made something of myself,
without my eyes and with skin that doesn't get doors opened for
you, even if you're a lady."

Laura was curious. "Have you been blind since birth?"

Mae shook her head. "The doctor told me I was going blind a
year after Patrick and I married in Cape Town. He said there was
nothing he could do."

"That was ten years ago," Patrick said.

"But how do you do it?" Laura asked.

Mae tapped her forehead. "It all comes from up here. I see
everything up here first, then I let my hands shape it. God gave me
the light in my mind."

"She's incredible," Patrick said, looking at his wife with love in
his eyes.

"But for an artist to lose her sight . . . you must have been
devastated," Laura said.

"After I learned I was going blind," Mae said softly, "I spent every waking moment drinking in everything around me. I wanted to stamp it all into my memory."

"She says she burned it all into her memory," Patrick said.

"As long as I had sight, I wanted to use it so that later I could remember everything." Mae looked to where she thought Laura was and said, "I know you didn't mean any harm. You're a good person, I can sense it."

Laura thanked her in relief. "Please tell me what it's been like," Laura said sincerely.

"Tell her about the last day of sight. That's something I'll never forget," Patrick said.

As Mae told the story of the last day she could see, Laura watched her fingers pat and prod the clay. Even as she spoke, Mae began shaping something.

While Mae told about her fears of not being able to do her art, Laura thought about when her sister Mary was suddenly taken by a pain in the head.

I was just twelve years old, but her suffering made my problems seem small, Laura thought. *Mary was delirious with pain. Ma cut off her long, beautiful hair to keep her head cooler. Then we saw that the right side of her face was drawn out of shape. Ma said Mary had suffered a stroke.*

Mary was going blind, the doctor said. Going blind. I don't want to think about it.

"Would you like to see your statue?" Mae asked, handing Laura what she had quickly molded.

"Yes, I would," Laura said. Mae had created a delicate rose with open petals. "This is beautiful. So . . . so real."

"Thank you," Mae said, standing up.

"Did you paint the picture of Sacagawea, Mrs. Jefferson?"

"Patrick painted the picture. He was my eyes on the statue."

"I didn't know you were an artist also," Laura said, looking at the man with new respect.

"I dabble in oils, but Mae's the real artist," he said modestly.

"Why don't you paint more?" Laura asked.

Patrick shrugged. "I guess all the selling and traveling to get Mae's works sold takes up most of my time."

"Did you paint that?" Laura asked, pointing to the picture of the black Jesus.

Patrick hesitated, then nodded vigorously. "It came to me after I came to understand Mae's life and all that has been denied her and her people."

"The black Jesus?" said Mae. "That beautiful face is etched in my mind as clear as day."

Laura watched Mae carefully navigate across the room toward the sheet-draped statue. "I hope you'll like it," she said, pulling it off.

Laura stood up and walked over. Before her was a life-sized statue of Sacagawea, with the baby on her back, pointing the way for Lewis and Clark. "It's just like the picture. Just like the picture," she said.

Laura walked around the statue. "I don't know what to say," Laura said softly, touching the Indian girl's face. "It's so beautiful. You've already finished it."

"I still have some smoothing out to do," Mae said, running her fingers until she stopped on a rough spot. "Now, let's sit back down. I want to hear more about all this statue represents and all about women getting the right to vote."

CHAPTER 25

COLD MOON RISING

"How much does a bottle of good Irish whiskey cost?" Cunningham asked the bartender at the sleazy tavern on the county road.

Cunningham had been eyeing the dusty bottle on the shelf above the bar since he walked in. He'd drunk four nickel beers, which left him with four dollars and eighty cents. Subtract the ten cents for the dinner he wanted to buy, now that he had some real money in his pocket, and he had four seventy to spend.

"Which one?" the bartender asked.

He felt in his pocket for the bottle of strange liquid that Huleatt had given him, then pointed to the dusty bottle. "How 'bout that one? With all the dust."

The bartender peered through the low light then laughed. "You're the first customer in here who's ever had the money to buy good stuff. If you want a shot, it'll be fifteen cents."

"Nope," Cunningham said, shaking his head.

"Nope what?"

"Don't want a shot. I want the whole bottle."

"You know what that'll cost you?" the bartender asked in astonishment. "There's thirty shots in the bottle, which comes to . . ." He paused for a moment, wet his finger, and tried to do the math as he remembered it, in the air.

"I got four sixty," Cunningham said. "That's more than enough."

The bartender verified it by doing the math in the dust on the bar. "That leaves you ten cents."

"No, that leaves *you* ten cents, for a tip," Cunningham said, pushing the money across the bar. *But it does leave me another ten-cent piece in my pocket, for just-in-case money.*

Cunningham took the bottle to the outhouse in the back and opened the cap. *Might as well have a quick nip before I mix in Mr. Huleatt's flavoring,* he thought, tipping the bottle back. Then he poured in the brown liquid from the small bottle and shook the larger bottle. He put the cap back on and dropped the small bottle down the outhouse hole.

Back in Mansfield, the bell tinkled over the newspaper's front door. Summers looked up. James Steadman entered.

"Summers, it's time to put a stop to these inflammatory articles."

"Which ones?" Summers asked.

"You know very well which ones. I want you not to let that Wilder woman stir up any more trouble."

"I've already taken care of the problem. She's goin' to write about women's issues: new babies, fashion, that sort of thing."

Steadman was clearly caught off guard. "She is? Well, that's good. It's time she knew her place in this world."

"I put her in her place," Summers said, not noticing the raised eyebrows of his typesetter.

"Now all we got to do is keep that Ellen Boyle woman from comin' and find a way to keep that Indian statue out of town," Steadman said.

"Mr. Summers, the type's all set," Tony said, still a little nauseated from seeing the tongue in the bag.

"Good, let's run it."

"Do you want to check it first?"

"No, haven't got time. I need to visit with Mr. Steadman. You run it and get the boys to deliver it 'round town."

Tony set the press and locked it down. In all the excitement, he hadn't made the changes that Summers wanted. As the newspaper sheets began printing out, he didn't notice that he had mistakenly left "Women Shall Rule" on the front page.

Laura drove along the backroads to Mansfield, hoping to make it home before dark. But she had left Mae Jefferson's later than she intended.

Driving by herself in the dark scared her. Having to face herself under the cold moon rising made it even harder. *My problems seem so trivial when I compare them to Mae Jefferson's. The love she feels for her husband and the love he feels for her didn't take sight to see. It's a love of the ages that most people will never have.*

For a moment Laura remembered the sickening sensation she used to get, watching her blind sister Mary feeling along the wall. Tapping on the wood planks, tapping her way to everything.

Then she thought about how she assumed Mae Jefferson was a maid. Laura felt deeply humiliated for her own racism. The picture of the black Jesus seemed to hover in front of her. *Life is blind. Am I blind to my own lack of insight?* she asked herself.

As Laura neared Apple Hill Farm, she wondered what Manly was doing. She knew he'd be waiting up for her like he always did, all the lights on, holding the door open for her.

He's so kind, so considerate, she thought. *I'm going to rush up the stairs and hug him. I'll tell him we can't be blind to the love we feel for each other, that each moment we have together is special, because it will never come again. That we shouldn't take things for granted—not our lives, our sight, or our love.*

Manly hung the phone up. It was the fourth call he'd taken about Laura's article. Lafayette Bedal looked at the morning edition left bundled outside his door at sundown, and had told everyone what was on the front page. The phone had been ringing ever since.

The phone rang again. It was Fred and Buddy, daring him to go to the fishing hole with them tomorrow. Fred had said, "We'll have lots of cold beer."

"Count me out, boys. You two go on and have fun."

"Come on, Manly, just come for the afternoon. Or does your wife rule you, Manly?"

Man, oh man, he thought, *they just want to rub my face in it.*

And Laura does too. She won't let up. She's just doin'—just sayin' —what she wants with no mind to what it does to me.

Manly went to the sink and splashed water on his face, trying to calm down. He reread Laura's note about going down to Branson and saw that it was dark outside. Instinctively, he began turning on all the lights in the house, because Laura wasn't home yet.

What am I doin' this for? he wondered, as he turned on the porch light. *Did she bother to warn me that she was lightin' up the anger in the town with this "Women Shall Rule" article?*

He looked at the light cord, then made a decision to do something he'd never done before. He turned off all the lights except the porch light and went up to bed.

Laura pulled into the drive. Except for the porch light, the house was dark. Just like the way she and Manly were treating each other. She stopped the car and stared. It was the loneliest light in the world.

CHAPTER 26

LIFE'S A WONDER, AIN'T IT?

Eulla Mae looked at Maurice. "Take this jar of my garlic dills over to the Younguns. Those boys are always hungry."

Maurice looked at his wife like she'd lost her mind. "Those boys ain't gonna eat no garlic dills. You're just wastin' good pickles," he said, opening up the jar to take one for himself.

Eulla Mae slapped his hand. "These pickles are for Rev. Youngun and his children. You take them over there right now and don't be takin' none along the way."

Maurice grumbled, but took the jar and went out the back door. Eulla Mae came to the screen and called after him, "And don't you be tellin' those Younguns anymore of your tomfoolery!"

"All right, all right," he mumbled, shaking his head. *She don't understand what bein' a child means. She done had all hers preached out years 'fore I married her.* He looked around to see if she was still watching.

"And don't be eatin' none of those pickles!" Eulla Mae shouted from the house.

"You can count on me," he shouted, then said softly, "to eat one the moment I'm behind the barn."

As Maurice walked the back trail eating one of the forbidden dills, he thought about the Younguns, how three white children had so invigorated his life. *I may have taught them a few things, but they sure have given me back the magic. They've shown me what it is to think young again.*

He thought about the moment it came to him, sitting on the hill looking up at the stars. One moment, they were just stars, and the next moment, it was like looking up into the heart of the universe, seeing wonderous things he hadn't thought about since childhood.

He looked down the ridge and saw a stern-faced man and woman riding along, not talking to each other and barely looking at the scenery. *Taking it all for granted they are,* Maurice thought, shaking his head. *People look to find themselves in all the wrong, wrong places. They try to find wonder in the mirror or in a bank book.*

He thought about Eulla Mae, who believed that wonder could only be found in church, birth, and dying. *She don't realize that those things are too powerful, too strong. They take your mind off the moment, off the small things at hand that have the magic in 'em. Like kids. Like the Younguns. Like . . .*

He took out another dill pickle and smiled. *Like this good-eatin' pickle.* He laughed heartily, squirming to unstick his shirt in the humid air.

"I heard that, Maurice!" Eulla Mae's voice echoed through the hills. "You can't fool me!"

He looked around, half expecting her to come flying over the trees, or see her eyes everywhere. But then he laughed again, realizing that she knew him better than he knew himself. *There's wonder in love, in two old people stayin' together in a world always tryin' to pull them apart.*

He crunched into the pickle and skipped a few steps like a schoolboy. *Life's a wonder, ain't it?*

CHAPTER 27

THE SECRET

At the Younguns', while Sherry was off riding again with her father, Larry and Terry decided to get Crabbie ready for the Mule Day contest. Larry had managed to get the bit over Crab Apple's head and was trying to coax him out of the barn.

"Come on, Crabbie, please. You just got to come out and try pullin' the log," he said.

"It's the only way we'll win the ten bucks," Terry said. "We'll buy you a carrot."

Larry nodded. "Buy a lot of carrots with ten bucks."

Terry shook his head. "Don't be tellin' him that," he whispered. "He won't never know if we just buy him one carrot and spend the rest on candy."

"We're talkin' like he's gonna win, when he won't even come out of the stall," Larry said.

Maurice came into the barn eating a dill pickle. "Is your daddy here?" he asked, crunching loudly.

"He's off ridin' with Sherry again," Larry said, frowning.

Maurice handed the jar of big dill pickles to Larry. "My Eulla Mae made these up for you all." He took another crunchy bite of the green pickle in his hand and grinned. "Sure is good. Wanna bite?" he asked, holding out the pickle.

"No, thanks," Larry said, making a gagging face at the smell of garlic.

"Me neither," Terry added, puckering at the thought of the sour pickle.

"One day you'll know better," Maurice said, taking another bite. "Dill pickles give you brains in your head, muscles on your arms, and hair on your chest," he said with a mischievous smile.

Terry looked at Larry. "He's pullin' our leg again."

"You joshin' with us, Mr. Springer?" Larry asked.

Maurice laughed. "Exaggeratin' a bit—maybe."

Larry shook his head and pulled on the mule's reins. "Please, Crabbie. Come on out."

Maurice opened the jar and took out another five-inch pickle. "Crabbie still won't pull, huh?" Maurice asked, licking the juice off the garlic dill.

"No, sir. There's nothin' we ain't tried to get him to move," Larry said, pulling on the bit in Crabbie's mouth.

"You told us you had a secret way of gettin' mules to move," Terry said. "Will you tell us?"

Maurice had forgotten all about the mule-movin' secret he'd joked about knowing. *What have I got myself into now?* he thought, biting into the pickle. *What am I going to tell these two boys? It'd be easier to get swaybacked ponies to talk than get this mule to run.*

"What's the secret?" Terry asked again. "You promised."

"The secret is a secret," Maurice said, playing for time. "And that is that," he said, and turned to go. "See you boys later. Got me some chores to do."

"But you promised to tell us," Larry said. "And you always keep your promises. That's what you taught us."

"We believe everything you say," Terry said softly, hugging his leg.

Lord, forgive me for being such a kidder, he thought, then stopped and turned to Larry. "Did you try everythin' under the sun to get this mule to move?" he asked seriously.

"Yes sir!" Larry said. "We tried everythin'."

Maurice's kidding nature was hard to suppress. He was having a hard time keeping a straight face, looking at the two Youngun boys hanging on his every word. "You try usin' a carrot?"

"Yup," Larry said. "Crabbie just gobbled it down 'fore I could pull it back."

"An apple?"

"Sure did," Larry answered. "He nipped it out of my hand. Almost took my finger off with it."

Maurice covered his smile with his hand. "You try some fresh oats held at arms length?"

"A whole bag," Terry said, "but Crabbie just took the bag from my hands and ate it in the stall."

"You try a glass of milk?" Maurice asked, trying to be serious.

"Ain't tried that," Larry said.

"What else you try?" Maurice asked.

Larry thought for a moment, then said, "Heck, we even tried some of Terry's candy."

"Candy?" Maurice said, surprised.

Larry laughed. "Crabbie gobbled down a whole bag of gum drops, bag and all."

"Yeah, you know I'm desperate when I give my candy away," Terry said.

Maurice sighed. "Well then, maybe there's somethin' else you can do. I don't want to be givin' my granddaddy's mule-movin' secret away for no reason."

"But . . . but," Larry pleaded.

"But nothin'. Secret like this is handed down in the family only. Worth its weight in gold to mule skinners, but us Springers have kept it to ourselves since ol' Pharaoh ran us out of Egypt."

"Your granddaddy was with Moses?" Larry asked in awe.

"That was my great-great-great-great-granddaddy, Adam Moses Springer," Maurice said, thinking that he had taken this tall tale one step too far.

"Adam Moses?" Larry said in awe. "You're related to both of them?"

"I guess we all are," Maurice said. "Now I got to go."

The Younguns didn't want to change the subject. They took what he said as gospel truth. "Maybe Pa could have you tell the Sunday school class about your great-great-great-great—"

Maurice interrupted him. "No, now don't be mentionin' what I'm tellin' you to nobody," Maurice said, looking for a way to change the conversation. Crabbie came to the rescue, hee-hawing loudly.

"But we got to get him to move," Terry said. "We need ten bucks real bad."

"What you boys need that kind of money for anyhow?" Maurice asked.

"We'll split it with you," Terry said.

"I could never make money off my granddaddy's secret. That's against the way things ought to be."

"Tell us the secret, please," Larry pleaded.

Maurice swallowed another piece of pickle trying to think of something to say. He had boxed himself into a corner.

I like to kid—no, I love to kid with these children. I wish they knew when I'm funnin' 'em. Lord, forgive me, but I can't help lovin' to kid with 'em as much as I love 'em. I ain't tryin' to do no harm, no sir.

"Please, Mr. Springer," Terry said one more time.

"I'm thinkin', I'm thinkin'," Maurice said, tosseling Terry's hair. He finished off the pickle and took out another, shaking his head at the mule. "Mr. Crabbie," he said, tapping the pickle on the mule's nose for emphasis, "guess I'm gonna have to tell them my secret."

Crabbie sniffed the pickle, shook his head, spun around and stepped backward two steps.

"He moved!" Larry shouted. "You made him move!"

"I did? I did!" Maurice laughed.

Terry took the pickle from Maurice's hand and waved it under Crab Apple's nose. "Move your tail, Crabbie!"

Crabbie shook his head at the smell. "Watch out!" Larry screamed, ducking for cover.

Crabbie jumped backward, trying to get away from the pickle. He knocked the boys over as he charged from the barn. Maurice was amazed and followed behind the mule, watching him prance around the barnyard.

The boys followed Maurice and came to stand beside their friend. "Thanks," Larry said.

"For what?" Maurice asked.

"For tellin' us the secret," Larry said, watching Crabbie move around.

"How'd your granddaddy figure out that dill pickles would make a mule move backward?" Terry asked.

Maurice looked at the smiling boys. *I don't want to be fibbin' to 'em, but what do I do?*

So he did what he thought best. "My granddaddy was one smart man. He taught me a lot of things that don't come in school books."

"Yeah, like the power of smelly pickles." Terry smiled, then frowned. "How do you get him to go forward?"

Maurice took the pickle back from Terry and walked over to the mule. He was trying to come up with an answer. "Let me think for a moment," he said, putting the pickle to his mouth. He crunched loudly next to Crab Apple's ear and the mule jumped forward.

"Larry can do that," Terry said.

"Do what?" Maurice asked, crunching again to make the mule move.

"I'll wave the pickle under his nose. Larry's got to crunch it by his ear, 'cause I don't like pickles."

"I don't either," Larry said, souring at the thought.

"You both got to eat 'em, that's only fair," Maurice said, eating the last bite of pickle in his hand.

"But we don't got any pickles," Larry said.

Maurice smiled. "You got a nice, full jar of garlic dills that Eulla Mae made up. Come on, boys, you've got some mule pickle movin' to learn."

For the rest of the afternoon, they crunched pickles in Crabbie's ear and waved them under his nose. They had him going in mad circles, back and forth.

Maurice laughed. "They should show this at the movie show."

But the Younguns had the secret down pat and a bunch of pickles in their tummies. That evening, their father thought it strange that they weren't hungry for dinner and wondered why they went to bed early.

After Larry turned out the lights, he said to his brother, "I'm sick of pickles. Never want to see another one in my life."

Terry burped loudly in the dark. "You can't quit now."

"Wish I was a judge of the cookie and cake contest instead of a mule pickle mover," Larry said.

"Who picks the judges?" Terry asked, ears perked to the thought of eating cookies and cake.

"Mrs. Bentley picks the kid judges."

Terry moaned. "Furget it. She blames us for somethin' everytime we get around her fool kid, Silly Willy."

"Willy's a judge," Larry said.

"Figures! He's so spoiled, he gets everything he wants." Terry slipped his hand into the candy stash hidden behind the wall board and snuck out a gumdrop. "There ought to be a law against her pickin' her own son. That's not American."

"Sweet's a judge too," Larry said.

"Sweet!" Terry exclaimed. "After he gets through judgin' the cakes and cookies, there won't be nothin' left for the rest of us!" The news was so upsetting, that he had to eat another gumdrop. "Wish Sweet would let me take his place. Now *that* would be great."

"No way he's goin' to let you do that."

"You never know. Maybe he can be persuaded," Terry whispered.

"Don't go doin' somethin' that will get you in trouble. Eatin' stinky ol' garlic dill pickles is bad enough without gettin' any more punishment."

CHAPTER 28

BAD DREAMS

Time had slowed down. Laura could hear Manly breathing in the dark. She could almost sense what he was thinking.

Where am I? she wondered. *What's happening to me?* Her ears perked up at the sound of Manly's voice. *Where is he? I don't see him.*

"Come over here," Manly said, appearing out of nowhere. He patted the chair next to him at the kitchen table. "Sit here. It's time we talked."

Laura had never seen him look so intense. She sat in the chair and put her hands together. "Yes, I think we need to try and work things out between us."

Manly shook his head. "I'm not talkin' about workin' things out. I think we need to talk about my goin' away for a while."

"Away? To where?"

Manly shrugged. "I just sort of feel like ridin' and campin'. Off by myself. So I can figure things out."

"What are you talking about? I don't want you to go off alone!" Laura said.

"It's what I want, Laura. I'm tired of you leadin' me around by the nose. Maybe if I go off for a while, I'll come up with some answers about makin' my life with you better."

"When are you thinking of going?" she asked.

He stood up and pushed in his chair. "I'm leavin' now."

"Please don't go, Manly."

"You won't miss me," he said, and he closed the door behind him.

Laura sat up in the bed. She gulped for air, trying to orient herself in the dark of her bedroom. Manly was next to her, sleeping as far away in their bed as he could without falling off.

It was a dream, just a bad dream. I don't want to lose Manly. I love him. She turned and lightly touched his shoulder. "I love you, Manly. I love you," she whispered in the dark.

Manly grunted and moved perilously closer to the edge. Though he was awake, he didn't say a word. He stared off in the dark, pretending to be asleep.

His friends and neighbors in Mansfield were still making fun of him. *Everyone's taunting me, calling me a whipped dog, telling me I should be wearing a skirt. And Fred and Buddy calling me chicken again because I won't even go to the fishin' hole with them.*

Laura put her head back down on the pillow as Manly's thoughts drifted back to DeSmet, the Dakotas, and a girl back there he'd liked before Laura. A simple farm girl who had eyes for him.

She'd have been content being married to a farmer. She wouldn't have wanted to write for no newspaper, stirrin' up trouble, upsettin' the town—upsettin' her husband. I'd have been the boss, no questions asked. The boss. That's what a man's supposed to be, ain't it? So why am I lettin' Laura push me around? Ain't she suppposed to love and obey? Ain't that what our vows were all about?

Then he remembered that Laura had excluded the word "obey" from their wedding vows. *She knew what she was doin' even then, yes she did. I was just love-struck dumb. I should have listened more carefully. My friends warned me that she was a headstrong woman, bound to want her own way. But I didn't listen, no sir, I just was struck by the love tree. The whole durned tree fell on my head and now I'm so covered over I can't see daylight.*

"Manly, are you awake?" Laura asked quietly.

"No, but I am now." He looked at the clock, purposely not looking toward Laura. "Land's sake, woman, it's three in the morning. This ain't no time to talk!"

"But I just had a bad dream. I want to talk about it."

"Save it 'till the morning. Ain't nothin' goin' to change before daylight no-how."

A tear fell down Laura's cheek. *But we've got to talk sometime. We've got to tear down this wall between us!*

She snuggled up against him, wanting to squeeze out all the hostility and forget her bad dream.

"I said I wanted to sleep, okay?" Manly said, in an irritated tone. *I'm not a whipped dog,* he thought angrily.

"But I just wanted to hug you. You're my husband. I love you."

"That's all fine and dandy, but right now I'm a tired man who's got to face another day of ribbin' in town."

"Ribbing?"

Manly sat up. "Laura, you can have all the pleasant dreams in the world about women rulin' the world, about you thinkin' you're the ruler of Apple Hill—"

"Oh, Manly, that's absurd. I don't think that way."

Manly stared at her, then said very slowly, "Well, what I'm thinkin' or what I'm dreamin' is probably the one area that you can't do nothin' 'bout." He turned and snuggled back down under the covers. "I'm goin' to sleep."

"But I want to talk," she said, feeling the tears well up again.

"Then talk to yourself. That's what you've been doin' in our house anyway."

Laura sat in the dark, feeling lost and hopeless. There was a black cloud over her head. Never in their married life had they slept back to back, not talking or touching. It was as if the wall between them was growing taller, covered with barbed wire and embedded with broken glass.

What's happening to us? Why can't we talk it out? Can't he understand that what I write is what I feel? That it's my soul coming out in words?

She looked at Manly. *I don't ever want to lose you, Manly Wilder. For better or worse, that's what we said. Those were our vows. To love and obey—* Then she remembered taking out the word "obey". *He knew I was independent. He knew that before he married me. He's got to accept me the way I am.*

She lay back down, feeling like a lost soul trying to fight against the wind. *Am I right? Why do I feel that I'm always right? Does Manly want something else out of life that I'm not seeing? Is there a simple side of two people in love that I'm missing? Am I taking him for granted?*

There was no sleep ahead for Laura. She tossed and turned, trying to see the light, looking for the path to straighten things out between them. But the first light she saw was dawn. Another beautiful day for the world but the start of another troubled day for Laura.

The day began with a call from Summers about the tongue. It was all downhill from there.

CHAPTER 29

HAPPY DAZE

Rev. Youngun was in a happy daze. He had gone to sleep with Carla on his mind and had awakened still thinking about her.

When should I give Carla the ring? he wondered over and over. *Probably at the station. Yes, that's the best place. Right when she gets off the train from Cape Girardeau. She'll be so excited that we'll have the whole rest of the visit to make plans about her selling her house and moving in with me and the children.*

"Pa, can Larry and I go ridin' with you and Sherry this afternoon?" Terry asked, tapping his father's shoulder.

"Yeah, Pa, we feel left out," Larry said.

Rev. Youngun blinked. "What? What did you say?"

Terry shook his head. "What's wrong with you, Pa? You ain't been hearin' nothin' I've been sayin' all day."

Larry nodded. "You sick or somethin', Pa?"

"No, boys, I've just got things on my mind."

Sherry skipped into the room, singing a rhyme.

Pa and Carla, sittin' in a tree
K-I-S-S-I-N-G,
First comes love, then comes marriage,
Then comes Terry in the baby carriage.

Terry jumped across the room and grabbed her pigtails. "Pa ain't gettin' married!"

"Is too, is too!" she shouted. Terry yanked her head down and she screamed, "Pa, make him stop!"

Rev. Youngun stood up. "Children, children, stop this! Stop it right now!"

Terry's eyes welled up. "Are you thinkin' of gettin' married?"

"Are you, Pa?" Larry asked, his lip beginning to quiver.

"Well, I have been thinkin' about it, and I know you like Carla."

Sherry skipped around again. "Pa bought a ring, Pa bought a ring!"

Rev. Youngun felt his pocket then looked around the top of his desk. "Sherry have you been snoopin' in my things?"

"Did you buy that widow Pobst a ring?" Terry asked.

"Sherry," Rev. Youngun asked, "do you know where my ring is?"

Sherry held out her hand. She had the engagement ring on her thumb. "You mean this, Pa?"

Rev. Youngun reached for Sherry, but not before Terry had piled on top of her. Larry tried to pull them apart, but it was a regular catfight in full swing.

Finally, after Rev. Youngun restored order, he looked at Sherry and said, "You are not allowed to snoop around my desk." Terry stood behind him and stuck his tongue out, which made Sherry cry.

Rev. Youngun turned around. "Terry, what did you do?"

"Just licked my lips, Pa. That's all." When Rev. Youngun turned his back, Terry stuck his tongue out again.

"Give me the ring back," Rev. Youngun said.

Sherry held out her hand but the ring was gone! "I dropped it," she said looking down for it.

Rev. Youngun went into a panic. "Carla's arriving in less than two hours, and I need the ring."

"For what, Pa?" Terry asked softly.

"You gonna give her that ring, Pa?" Larry asked.

"What I'm gonna do is my business," Rev. Youngun said defensively.

"But it's our business too, Pa," Sherry said, tears falling down her cheeks.

"Please don't get married, Pa," Larry cried. "We don't want to leave you."

"Yeah, don't take us to the orphanage," Terry said, whimpering.

Rev. Youngun looked at his three crying children. *They think if I marry Carla I'll get rid of them?* He kneeled down and hugged his children together.

"I'll never leave you, never," he said, trying to soothe their fears. "Whatever gave you that impression?"

"We just thought that gettin' remarried meant you started over. That's what we heard the kids say at school," Larry said.

"Well, I guess getting married again is sort of like starting over," Rev. Youngun said.

"But if you start over, what happens to us?" Terry asked. "You gonna start over and have more children?"

"Yeah, we heard that some parents leave their children in an orphanage so they can have more," Larry said.

"Don't leave us!" Sherry cried.

"Larry, Terry, Sherry. You three are always going to be with me. If I was to get married again, you three would be with me."

"Are you goin' to marry Carla?" Sherry asked.

"Is that what the ring's for?" Larry asked.

Rev. Youngun sighed. "I haven't asked Carla to marry me, but I intend to ask her. If she accepts, then I'll give her the ring. It's an engagement ring. Sort of a symbol that she is for me and no one else."

"I'll marry you, Pa," Sherry said softly, squeezing onto his leg.

"I know you would, Sherry, but you're my daughter and daughter's don't marry their fathers. One day you'll understand."

Terry looked around, scratching his head. "If you marry Carla, where's she gonna sleep? Sherry's bedroom?"

"Please don't let her take my bedroom, Pa," Sherry said.

"We got room in our bedroom, Pa," Larry said, trying to be helpful.

"Room?" Rev. Youngun laughed.

"For a third bed," Terry nodded. "She could sleep in there with us."

"Kids, kids, if Carla does marry me, she'll sleep in my room."

"With you, Pa?" Sherry said, shocked.

"A husband and wife sleep together. That's the way it is," Rev. Youngun said.

"But that's where Ma slept!" Larry exclaimed.

"That's right,"said Rev. Youngun.

"Ma wouldn't like that," Terry said softly.

"I think your mother would understand," Rev. Youngun said gently. Then he brightened with an idea. "Maybe we'll even move into a bigger house. What would you all think of that?"

The three Youngun children stared at each other. They didn't know what to say.

"Well," Rev. Youngun asked, "would you like to move into another house?"

"No!" they all exclaimed in unison.

"We like livin' here," Sherry said.

"Our animals are here," Larry said.

Rev. Youngun grinned. "It was just an idea."

"A bad idea," Terry said, snuggling against his father. Rev. Youngun snuggled the three children, making them feel safe from the changes that were coming to their world.

CHAPTER 30

THE RING

They couldn't have hugged any tighter, but it was time for Rev. Youngun to go. He looked at his pocket watch. "Carla's train is due soon," he said, standing up. "Now, where's the ring?"

They all began looking underfoot. None of them noticed Beezer the parrot walking out of the room with the engagement ring hanging from his mouth. After a futile twenty-minute search, Rev. Youngun was beside himself.

"You kids keep looking while I go pick up Carla."

"Can't we come, Pa?" Sherry asked.

"You come with me, Sherry." He put his hand on Larry's shoulder. "I'm countin' on you and Terry to find that ring. It's very important to me, you understand?"

Both boys nodded, then Larry asked, "When you come back, will you take us horseback ridin' with you and Sherry? Will ya, Pa?"

"I won't have time for that today, but maybe after the father-daughter campout, the three of us will go riding together. How'd you boys like that?"

Larry's feelings were hurt, but he hid his emotions. "Fine, Pa. That sounds great," he said quietly.

"Why's she comin' anyhow?" Terry asked. "She was just here 'bout a month ago."

"She's gonna stay with you boys while Sherry and I go on the father-daughter campout."

"You mean she's comin' to babysit us?" Terry exclaimed.

"We can go stay at the Springers'," Larry said. "That'd be better."

"I've already invited her and that's that." He took his hat off the rack in the hall and put on his coat. "Got to go," Rev. Youngun said, checking his watch again. "You boys find that ring now."

They watched in silence as their father carried Sherry down the stairs, swung her on his back, and trotted off to the barn to get the buggy.

"You want a stepmomma?" Larry asked, watching them ride off.

"I'd rather have the chicken pox and never eat candy again," Terry said.

"We better find that ring," Larry said.

"What happens if we don't?"

Larry was stumped. "I don't know. Maybe it means he can't ask her to marry him."

"Then you look for it," Terry said, walking off toward the kitchen. "No sense helpin' along somethin' you don't want to happen."

He didn't notice Beezer sitting on his perch with the ring in his beak. "You're pathetic!" Beezer squawked. "Say your prayers."

"I'm prayin'. I'm prayin'," Terry said under his breath, "that we don't get a new stepmomma." He opened the ice box and took out the last piece of pie left from dinner. Then he looked around to see if Larry was watching and gobbled it down.

Why do boys gotta like girls anyway? he thought, chewing as fast as he could. *What can they do that we can't do?*

Sherry snuggled up against her father as they crossed the Willow Creek bridge. "Pa, I love you just the way you are."

"That's nice," he said, clicking the reins.

"I can cook."

Rev. Youngun smiled at his daughter. "Sherry, are you trying to tell me something?"

She burrowed her face against his coat. "If you don't want to get married, you don't got to."

"Have to," he corrected her.

"No, you don't!" she misunderstood. "We're a family just like we are, ain't we?"

"Aren't we," he corrected again.

"I think we are," she said, answering what she thought was a question.

"Sherry, if I never got married again, we'd do just fine as a family. But there's something about Carla, something that I feel." He looked at his daughter. "It's hard to explain to a child, but I . . . I . . ."

"You love her, Pa?"

"Yes," he said, finally able to say it to at least one of his children. "Yes, I do."

"And you want to marry her too, Pa?" Sherry asked, looking intently at her father's face.

"If she'll have me."

Sherry reached over and hugged his waist. "Well, if she won't have you, you've always got me."

At the train station, Rev. Youngun parked the buggy and carried Sherry in. The sound of the approaching train whistle echoed down the tracks. The hustle-bustle of the train station matched his mood. He shifted from foot to foot, trying to shake off the goose bumps.

I think I'll give her the ring the moment she gets off, he thought. He reached into his pocket, feeling around for the ring, but then remembered it wasn't there.

He frowned. "I hope your brothers find that ring."

"If they don't, you can just tell Carla about it. It's the thought that counts, that's what you always tell us," Sherry said, not understanding the importance of the ring to her father.

"This is a little different," he said. "You need to have the ring when you ask someone to marry you."

"Is she gonna sleep in your bed tonight?" Sherry asked innocently.

Two elderly spinster sisters, members of his congregation, walked by with shocked expressions on their faces. "What did she say?" Beatrice, the older of the two asked, cupping her hand to her ear.

"Expecting someone, Rev. Youngun?" Ida asked.

Sherry piped up, proudly. "We're waitin' on the widow Pobst from Cape Geronimo who's comin' to sleep in my Pa's bed!"

"Sherry, she is not. She's just coming to . . . I've got a friend visiting, who's staying at the Mansfield Hotel. Everything's proper, you can trust me." The train whistled again, interrupting him.

Beatrice chuckled. "Have a nice time." Rev. Youngun watched the sisters walk off with their canes.

Sherry shrugged. "But I thought you said that Carla was going to sleep in your room and not the boys' room."

"I did," he said, taking off his hat and wiping his brow. "But that's after we're married."

A flutter of nervousness went through him as the train pulled into the station. *I hope she says yes. She's just got to.* Sherry noticed that his fingers were crossed behind his back.

On the train, Carla Pobst watched the now-familiar buildings of Mansfield come into view. She straightened out her long dress, adjusted the waist, and discreetly moved her bodice back into place. She quick-brushed her hair, then dabbed perfume behind her ears.

I hope he asks me to marry him, she thought. *I've already told him that I would if the time was right. And now it's right.*

Since meeting Thomas Youngun, she'd gotten over the hurt of losing her husband at sea. Thomas brought sunshine back into her life.

She closed her eyes and sighed. *If he gives me a ring, why, I'll jump into his arms and kiss him in broad daylight. I want to get married again. I do.*

A baby cooed to its mother in the seat behind her. Carla turned and felt an urge to be a mother. *And I want to have his baby too. Maybe three babies. That would make six children.* She smiled. *That would be a houseful. I just hope his children want me as much as I want to be a part of their lives.*

The clackety-clack of the train slowed down. Carla heard and felt the brakes as the train came to a stop. Then Carla carried her bag to the door and took a deep breath. *What if he doesn't ask me?*

Not even wanting to think about that, Carla stood at the exit, looking for Thomas Youngun. She didn't notice that he was right below her.

"Are you going to stand there all day?" Rev. Youngun asked.

"Oh, Thomas, I didn't see you," she said, stepping off into his arms.

He spun her around, lost in happiness, then realized that he was a minister, out in public, with his daughter and half his congregation watching him.

"Oh, Carla, I'm so glad you came," he whispered into her ear, as he set her down.

Carla smiled. "You asked me and I'm here," she said, pecking him on the cheek. A dozen eyebrows raised around them.

"There's so much I want to tell you, so much I want to say," Rev. Youngun exclaimed, lost in her eyes.

"Me too," she said, feeling like a teenage girl.

Sherry had never seen her father like this before. She coughed loudly. Carla looked down. "Oh, Sherry, I didn't see you. What a surprise!"

"Pa made me come," she said, hiding behind her father's legs.

Carla pulled her around and lifted her up. "You remembered how to put pigtails in, didn't you?"

Sherry blushed, shaking her pigtails loose from Carla's hands. "I like wearin' 'em, that's all."

"Where are the boys? Carla asked.

"They're home lookin' for the—"

Rev. Youngun clapped his hand over Sherry's mouth. "I left them at home. They had some things to do."

Sherry pulled her mouth free. "Yeah, they're lookin' for it."

"It?" Carla asked, looking into Rev. Youngun's eyes.

"It's nothing. Just something we lost around the house," he said. "Now, let's get you checked into the Mansfield Hotel so you can freshen up. Then we'll go out to the house and have dinner."

"That sounds wonderful," Carla said, taking his hand. "I want you to talk about whatever's on your mind. I think this will be a special trip," she said.

Sherry watched from behind them. *Oh brother,* she thought, *I think Pa needs to see the doctor.*

When they got back to the house, Rev. Youngun called out for his sons. "Boys, Carla's here, come on out."

Larry and Terry peeked out through the screen, then came out, holding their hands behind their backs. "Good to see you, Miss Carla," Larry said.

Carla smiled and went up the stairs. "You two are sure growing up," she said, putting a hand on each boy.

"Can't change much in a month," Terry said.

Carla laughed. "The whole world can change in a month," she said, looking at Rev. Youngun.

"Sherry, why don't you take Carla into the house and get her something cold to drink," Rev. Youngun said. Sherry skipped up and took Carla by the hand into the kitchen.

Rev. Youngun looked at his sons. "Did you find the ring?"

"Found a napkin ring," Terry beamed. "Why don't you give her that?"

Rev. Youngun closed his eyes and calmed down. *Lord, please give me strength and patience.* He looked at Larry. "Did you look everywhere?"

"We looked everywhere, Pa."

Carla opened the door and looked out. "Thomas, Sherry said you lost a ring of some sort. Want me to help you look?" she asked coquettishly.

"No, everything's okay," he said.

Terry shrugged. "We couldn't find the ring."

"A ring, Thomas?" she asked, enjoying his discomfort.

"What's that in your hand, Terry?" she asked.

"A napkin ring."

Carla was crestfallen. "That was the ring?" she said, closing the door behind her.

When she was out of hearing range, Larry said, "Pa, that wasn't the ring we were looking for."

"I know it," Rev. Youngun said.

"But you fibbed," Larry said.

"No, I didn't. I didn't say anything," Rev. Youngun said, squirming a bit.

"But you let her think a fib," Terry said, really enjoying his father being on the hotseat.

Sherry sipped her lemonade and came up with an idea. "I'll be right back," she told Carla, and raced up to her father's bedroom. "I know it's here someplace."

She knew she wasn't supposed to rummage through his closet, but she remembered the box of her mother's things. *Pa always said the box was for me when I got older,* she thought.

Then she found it. Opening it carefully, she saw the picture of her mother, who had died when Sherry was barely more than an infant. Wrapped in tissue paper, at the bottom of the box, were her mother's engagement and wedding rings.

She took the rings and the picture of her mother and went into the kitchen. Her father and Carla were sitting at the table, talking quietly.

"Here are some rings for you," Sherry said proudly, handing Carla her mother's rings.

Rev. Youngun coughed, feeling a rush of helplessness overtake him. Carla eye's brightened. "Oh, Thomas, they're beautiful. Thank you so much. I love them," she said, slipping the engagement ring on, then hugging him.

Sherry was so happy, she took the picture of her mother from behind her back. Carla's arms were wrapped around her father, who was speechless and unable to grab the picture away.

"They belonged to my momma," Sherry said proudly.

"What? What did?" Carla asked, feeling a shiver run up her spine.

"The rings. Here's her picture. I thought you'd like to see her since you'll be sleepin' in her bed."

Carla looked at the picture, then slipped the engagement ring off and handed it back to Rev. Youngun. "I don't think this is funny."

"It's not a joke. It's just an accident," he said weakly.

"Yeah, 'cause we lost your ring, so I thought . . ." Sherry stopped, sensing she had done something wrong.

Carla felt her forehead. She felt lightheaded. "I think I need to go back to the hotel and rest, Thomas. I feel faint."

"Just come sit down on the couch. You can rest until dinner," Rev. Youngun said nervously.

"No, please take me back," Carla said, walking by him.

Sherry began to whimper and Rev. Youngun looked at the picture of his wife. "Sherry, take your mother's pictures and rings back up to my closet."

"Sorry, Pa," she sniffled. "I was only tryin' to help."

"I know. I know," he said, putting his arm around her.

"I'm ready to leave now, Thomas," Carla called out from the front porch.

"What's wrong, Pa?" Larry asked, stepping in through the back kitchen door. Terry stood behind him.

"Nothing. Nothing, boys. Carla's not feeling well and wants to go back to the hotel."

Beezer sat on his perch in the dining room, with the missing ring clutched in his claws. "Say your prayers!" he squawked loudly.

Rev. Youngun looked at Larry. "Serve dinner to your brother and sister. I'll be back in a while."

Carla was waiting on the porch, tears streaming down her face. She turned away when he stepped out onto the porch, not wanting him to see her cry.

"Carla, I'm so sorry. I would never want to hurt you."

"Seeing the picture of your wife made me think about my husband, wondering what he was thinking about when his ship went down . . ."

Rev. Youngun put his arms around her. "Let's not talk about the past. Let's talk about the future."

Carla lightly pushed him back. "But the picture brought back the past. Oh, the memories you have in this house, in your bed. Norma is everywhere. It's as if she were sitting next to me now, wondering what I'm doing in her house."

Rev. Youngun didn't think, and looked around for a moment, then took Carla's hand. "I'll get you back to the hotel, and we'll talk about it all in the morning."

"I can't live with the ghosts, Thomas. I never thought about it until this moment. I don't want to walk in your wife's footsteps. It's not healthy."

"We'll move. We'll buy another house. I'll do whatever you want," he said.

Carla turned away, looking out over the hills. "Maybe moving away would give us both a fresh start. A chance to start again. To establish our own life together." She spun around. "Yes, that would be best," she said, stepping into his arms.

As they hugged, they didn't notice the six eyes with tears, watching through the screen. When the buggy was out of sight, Larry said, "I don't want to move. I don't want to leave Mansfield."

"Me neither," Terry and Sherry chorused together.

As Carla and Rev. Youngun crossed the Willow Creek Bridge, Carla kissed him lightly on the cheek. "But I haven't even been given a ring yet. You haven't even asked me to marry you. I think I'll wait for that," she said, smiling mischievously.

"Tomorrow night. We'll make it a special night," Rev. Youngun said.

Back at the house, Beezer twirled the ring on the end of his beak, tried chewing on it, then swallowed it.

CHAPTER 31

WOMEN'S WORK?

Laura spent the early afternoon working on "women's articles" for Summers. He called twice, wanting to know when she'd have one ready. But no matter how hard she tried, her heart just wasn't in it.

The phone rang in the kitchen. "I'll get it," Manly shouted out. He picked up the receiver. It was Fred and Buddy. They were daring him to go with them to the fishing hole.

"Just come look. I swear you'll think it's heaven," Fred said.

"Yeah," Buddy said, "and a couple of ol' boys from Mountain Grove are coming down with some beer and a side of beef and—"

Fred butted in. "And we're gonna stuff ourselves like pigs, eat with our fingers, and burp, belch, and—"

"I get the picture," Manly said.

"Cause there ain't no wives around!" Buddy howled into the phone.

Laura had no idea what they were talking about. She began a piece about what happened when the men enlisted in the army for the Spanish-American War.

Women took their places, doing men's jobs, and when the men returned from war, they wanted their jobs back. Was that fair? I say not.

Laura put her pencil down. *That's not what Summers wants.* She remembered the conversation she'd had with one of her neighbors about farm work, and picked the pencil back up.

> *One of my neighbors is managing the farm this summer during the absence of her husband, who is off working in the city to earn extra money. She planted and cultivated and plans to tend to the harvesting, threshing, and haying. She and the children care for the horses and cows, the pigs and chickens. She buys and sells and hires and fires. In short, she does all the work and business that her husband would do if he were there. And keeps up her own work besides. Who ever said that women were the inferior sex?*

Laura nodded, quite pleased with herself, but knew that it wouldn't please Summers. She heard Manly's footsteps going up the stairs. "Everything okay, Manly? Who was that on the phone?"

"Nothing, just a couple of guys from the feed store. Got something they want me to come see."

Laura shrugged. *What do men see in a feed store? Who wants to look at old sacks of seed anyway? Think they'd have more exciting things to talk about.*

She needed some help coming up with a suitable story for the paper, so she picked up the phone and called Summers. "Andrew, this is Laura."

"What do you want? I'm in the middle of proofing."

"I'm having trouble coming up with something to write."

Summers chuckled. "Why don't you write about Gibson girls going out of fashion or maybe about . . ." He thought for a moment. "I've got it! Why don't you write about beauty parlors?"

"Beauty parlors? Mansfield doesn't even have one," she said.

"That's the point," Summers said loudly. "Write about the home beauty parlor treatments that you women are always givin' to yourselves. That's something every woman would want to read about."

Laura shook her head. *Home beauty parlors? That's a far cry from demanding the right to vote.* "I'll try, Andrew," she said.

"Good, that's my girl," he said condescendingly. "Now get me some good copy and I'll save a space for you. Gotta go. Bye," he said, and hung up.

That's my girl? Laura frowned, putting down the phone. *He's acting like the rooster of the henhouse. It doesn't seem fair that I have to write this silly stuff and he gets to write as he feels.*

Laura went back to her desk and began writing what she didn't want to write about.

The Home Beauty Parlor
By Laura Ingalls Wilder

Beauty is only skin deep, says the old adage. We all admire beauty of character, but the possession of it is no excuse for neglecting our personal appearance. Indeed, it seems to me there must be a fault in the character when one is satisfied with anything less than the best she can make of herself.

Though every country town has a barber shop, the lack of beauty shops for country women is another example of what we have been denied.

Laura stopped and erased the last sentence. She replaced it with:

Until we get a beauty parlor in Mansfield, I want to tell you about what you can do at your own home beauty parlor.

Laura finished the article, telling about all the beauty tricks she'd learned over the years. Manly walked through the room, reading the *Farmer's Almanac.*

"Want to read what I've written?" she asked.

"No thanks, I guess I'll just hear about it 'round town," he said, not looking at her.

"But this is different." she said, handing him the copy.

"I told you," he said, looking at her, "I don't want to be involved. You and I will smooth things out, but we just need some time. I got some things to think about." He shrugged. "I got to go into town. See you later."

"But, Manly, I'm writing what Summers wanted."

"Summers just likes to sell newspapers. I'm sure your articles are doin' that," he said, walking off.

"What are you in such a hurry for? You're only going to the feed store," she called after him.

"I'm goin' down to do some things with the guys," he said, letting the door bang behind him. "They got somethin' they want to show me."

With the guys. Show him? She shook her head, confused. *Manly's never really done anything with the guys. He likes being by himself, puttering around the farm, or being with me. But with the guys? This doesn't make sense.*

She watched him ride off like a teenager on his horse, then bounded from her chair and went out to the porch. She called after him, but it was too late. He had already ridden out of sight. *Oh, Manly, please don't do something foolish. I love you. I'll show you. I'll make it all up to you.*

Dr. George pulled up the driveway to Apple Hill Farm to say hello. He was making house calls in the area and thought he'd have a cup of coffee with Laura.

He saw her leaning against the porch door, with tears in her eyes. "What's wrong?"

"Oh . . . oh, hi, Dr. George," she said, wiping her eyes.

He turned off his engine and came up the steps. "What are you crying for?"

"I've just got a lot on my mind."

"Where's Manly?" he asked.

"I don't know," she said glumly.

"Is that what's on your mind?" he asked, concerned.

"Oh, Dr. George, things just seem to be going wrong. Ever since I got arrested, Manly and I . . . Manly and I . . ." She couldn't control her emotions and broke down on his shoulder.

Dr. George put his arm around her shoulders and said softly, "Why don't you and I go sit in the kitchen and have a cup of coffee? Let's talk this thing out, make you feel better," he said, walking her along.

Laura kept her head down, letting him lead her on, wanting only to feel good about her life again.

At that moment, Manly stopped his horse on the crest of the ridge and looked around. *Why am I goin' to the fishin' hole? What do I need there?*

Manly had never been one to hang out and fish with the men who were looking for excuses to escape from their wives. *Why'd I do it? Why'd I accept their dare? Thought I wanted to feel good about myself, but this is makin' me feel worse.*

Why did I come? Why didn't I turn them down when they called me? So what if they'd called me chicken?

As Fred and Buddy approached, Manly made a decision. He shouted to them, "I've changed my mind."

"What do you mean, you changed your mind?" Fred asked. "We're almost there."

"Don't chicken out now, Manly," Buddy sneered. "We're gonna drink all afternoon."

"Sorry, boys," Manly said, "but I'm goin' home."

"You're what?" Fred said, scratching his head.

Buddy laughed. "Scared of your wife, Manly?"

"No, I'd rather go spend some time with her."

"With your wife?" Fred exclaimed.

"Yeah, my wife," he said, and he turned his horse toward home.

CHAPTER 32

ON TO MANSFIELD!

homas Huleatt paced back and forth outside the church. He'd been up all night, trying to come to grips with his emotions as he remembered Ellen.

Father Walsh walked toward Thomas. "Do you need to talk, Thomas?"

He sighed. "Father, I think I do."

Father Walsh was surprised. He hadn't heard a confession from Huleatt in ages. "Well, come in, come in. Let me get my collar on and I'll meet you in the confessional."

Neither man knew that Cunningham had fallen asleep in the confessional next to Huleatt's. He'd come into the church earlier, waiting for a priest.

He woke up when Huleatt entered, and he started to leave, but recognized Huleatt's voice as he started to pray out loud.

Huleatt was on his knees praying when Father Walsh opened the slat. Huleatt poured out his heart and soul. About his love for Ellen and the urge to strike back at her, which he felt he couldn't stop. He told about the plan he had in mind to stop her. He told it all, because he knew that his confessor would never reveal his confession to anyone. What he didn't know was that Cunningham had heard it all too.

When Huleatt left, Father Walsh stayed in the booth, praying that Huleatt would come to reason.

In St. Louis, Ellen was released from jail with much fanfare. Her supporters cheered as she came out onto the street, holding her hands aloft like a victorious prizefighter.

"You got something to say to the press?" several reporters called out.

Ellen shook her head. "What I'd like to say you couldn't print," she said. "But if you want a headline, say that I just finished reading an article written by a woman named Laura Ingalls Wilder, and it expresses my thoughts exactly."

"What's it called?" a burly reporter asked.

"What paper's it in?" another said, jostling for position.

"It's in the *Mansfield Monitor,* and it's titled 'Women Shall Rule.' "

The reporters looked among themselves. "That's a small town rag, isn't it?" the burly man asked one of the others.

Ellen shook her head. "It's better copy than you've been printing in the *St. Louis Post-Dispatch,*" she said, handing the article to them. "Read it." She pushed through the throng.

"Where you going?" a reporter called out.

"On to Mansfield!" she shouted, like she was heading to a meeting with the president of the country.

Ellen got into the automobile that was waiting for her, and her assistant climbed into the back seat. Ellen waved to her admirers as they drove away.

She looked at the latest copy of the *Mansfield Monitor* that was waiting for her, and as she leafed through the front section, she stopped cold. There was a picture of Thomas Huleatt, standing in front of his saloon. Under the picture was written,

Thomas Huleatt Planning to Expand Tippy's Saloon

It can't be. It's just someone with the same name, she thought. She put the paper down, then looked at it again. *It is! It is Thomas!*

Here I've been thinking about him ever since I left Ireland, wondering where he is, what he's been doing, and he's in the town I'm heading toward.

Ellen closed her eyes, remembering how much she had loved him. How he had wanted to marry her. How she sometimes wished she'd taken his hand, become his wife, had his children, and lived the life in the Ireland she now missed so much.

No girl in her right mind would have turned him down, she thought. *He was handsome, he was sweet, and he had a family job awaiting him.*

Oh, Thomas, I've loved you with my eyes closed since we last kissed. I've been with you in my dreams every night since we parted. I'm driven by my mission, but I sometimes wish that someone else would take the torch and let me enjoy the rest of my life. Maybe go back to Ireland. Yes, to Ireland.

Opening the locket, she looked at the face of the boy-man she loved twenty years ago and compared it to the newspaper photo. She smiled. *You're still a handsome devil. I bet your wife keeps a close watch on you.*

She drifted to sleep, knowing that when she left him in Ireland, she had left her heart behind. *And now's he's here, in America, in Mansfield. Where I'm headed.*

In her dream she was standing with Huleatt in their secret place again. In Ireland. Surrounded by the bushes. Just the two of them, alone. Lips locked together with the intensity that only young love, first love, brings.

The driver turned, "To the train station?"

Page put her finger to her lips. "She's asleep. Let's take her back to the hotel so she can get a good night's rest."

CHAPTER 33

DOCTOR'S ORDERS

It had taken Rev. Youngun two buggy rides, but he finally made Carla feel good again. They avoided going back to his house, satisfied just to be together again.

The ring was still not to be found, though the Younguns turned the downstairs upside down. Beezer didn't have much of an appetite, but worrying about the parrot was the last thing on anyone's mind.

Sherry had come along on this buggy ride, so she could sit with Carla at the fashion show given by Sarah Bentley. That was the last place Larry and Terry wanted to go be, so they stayed home, working with Crabbie for the Mule Day contest.

At the hotel, while her father waited in the lobby for Carla to come down, Sherry worried about the way her father was acting. When she saw Dr. George, she climbed down from the buggy and ran over.

"Dr. George."

He looked down and smiled. "Yes, Sherry?"

"I think my Pa's sick."

"You do?" Dr. George asked, with a look of concern.

"Uh huh, I do. He ain't eatin' much, he don't seem to hear what you're sayin', and his mind seems lost. He just ain't his own self."

Dr. George looked over and saw Rev. Youngun step out of the hotel with Carla on his arm. It appeared that Carla had forgotten something and they went back inside.

Dr. George leaned over and whispered into Sherry's ear. "I think your Pa's been bit by the love bug."

"The love bug?" she said. "Is he going to die?"

Dr. George laughed and picked her up. "Ain't nothin' to worry 'bout. It'll all calm down after a while."

"But what's wrong with him?" she asked.

Dr. George struggled for words. "Well, your Pa's kinda feelin' his oats. Like the way the horses get in the spring. Your Pa's feelin' things he hasn't felt in years. It's good for him."

"But he's actin' funny."

"Just bear with him and my doctor's orders are to give him a lot of love, hugs, and understanding. You hear?" he asked, putting his face close to hers.

She nodded and kissed him on the cheek.

CHAPTER 34

SWEET NOTHINGS

School let out early after the big math test. Terry didn't feel much like hanging around with the kids after school. The test had been hard. Terry was pretty sure he'd flunked, so he headed home to console himself. His candy stash was hidden behind his bed. It was so big, he had enough candy to last a year if Bedal's General Store went out of business in the morning. He sat with his mouth stuffed, gooey-chewy gumdrop juice running down his chin. He looked at the clouds and thought about how he'd like to be eating cotton candy at the fair.

"Wanna go practice Crabbie?" Larry asked, coming out onto the porch.

"Don't feel like it," Terry mumbled, his teeth stuck together by the chewy mess.

"What'd you say?"

"Leave me alone. I'm eatin' gumdrops."

Larry could only figure out the last word. "Gumdrops? Gimme some."

Terry was reluctant to share, but he also didn't want his brother to tell his father, so he pulled two out of his pocket and handed them over. Normally, it would have only been half of a half of a gumdrop, but with all the candy he had upstairs, Terry was in a generous mood. He didn't know what was going to happen when the grades came out, so he just decided to forget it all for the time being and enjoy the moment.

When Terry was able to talk, he asked, "What say we go see Sweet?"

"What for?"

"I want to see if I can trick him . . . er, ask him if he'll let me be a cookie judge."

"Fat chance," Larry said, shaking his head.

"Come on, we'll ride Crabbie over."

"I'll come if you bite the pickle," Larry said, thinking quickly.

Terry pondered it for a moment, then agreed. "Come on, let's go," Larry said.

"I'll be down in a moment," Terry said, and went to the box of junk he kept next to his bed. "It's in here someplace," he mumbled to himself. "Ah ha," he said, pulling out some string.

In the barn, Larry had a box set up next to Crabbie so they could climb on his back. "What's the string for?" Larry asked.

"You'll see." Terry tied the string onto a stick and the other end onto a pickle. "This is for goin' backward," he winked.

They climbed on the box and mounted Crabbie. Dangit yipped to come, but Larry got down and tied him to the barn door.

When he got back on, Terry looked at the pickle and closed his eyes. "Okay, Crabbie," he said, "let's head out." He crunched down on the pickle next to the mule's ear. When the mule stepped forward, Terry slipped and dropped the stick with the pickle between Crabbie's ears.

Crabbie sniffed the dangling pickle and pulled backward. "Whoa, go forward!" Terry screamed, crunching down on the pickle again, but it was too late. Crabbie backed into the barn and dumped them onto the ground.

"Dummy," Larry said, dusting himself off. "You dropped the backward pickle stick in front of his nose."

"Sorry," Terry said.

They got back up and Terry crunched down again on the dill in Crabbie's ear. The mule took off at a fast clip. "Hold on!" Terry laughed and soon he was crunching Crabbie along the trail to the other side of town where Sweet lived. They found him sitting on his porch, eating a pie.

"Hi, Sweet," Terry said innocently.

"What do you want?" Sweet asked.

"We just came to see our buddy."

"I'll bet," Sweet said, taking a big bite of pie.

"Is that good?" Larry asked.

"Sure is. Mom made it all for me," Sweet said, eating faster now, worried that the Younguns would want a bite.

Terry had a different tactic in mind. "You just take your time eatin' that big ol' pie. And when you finish, I've got some dessert for you."

Sweet smiled, a ring of strawberries around his face. "This is my dessert," he said.

"No, this is your dessert." Terry grinned, and held up the bag of gumdrops. He took one out and popped it into his mouth. "I know you love these."

Sweet did love gumdrops. He loved all candy, but gumdrops were at the top of his list. "For real?"

"For real," Terry said.

"Ask him," Larry whispered.

"Hold on. I'll get to it," Terry said impatiently.

After Sweet had finished the pie and half the bag of gumdrops, Terry asked the big question. "Sweet, what would it take to get you to let me take your place at the pie judgin' contest?"

"More money than you'll ever have," Sweet said, popping another gumdrop into his mouth.

"Ah, come on, Sweet. I'm your best friend."

Sweet brought out the lucky penny that Terry had traded him. "I still can't get that to work. I want my money back."

"A deal's a deal," Larry said, coming to his brother's defense.

"I've almost rubbed the face off the coin. Can't get nothin' I'm wishin' for," Sweet said, rubbing the coin and shaking his head.

"You just don't know what you've been wishin' for, that's all," Terry said.

"That's not so," Sweet said.

"Uh huh, sure is," Terry said. "You can't help it that your mind ain't tellin' your mouth what you've been wishin' for, that's all."

Sweet scratched his head and ate another gumdrop. Terry took the bag away. "Hey, give that back!" Sweet shouted.

"Say I wish."

"I wish," Sweet repeated.

"For the bag," Terry said slowly.

"For the bag," Sweet parroted.

"Back."

"Back," Sweet said. "Now give it to me!"

Terry handed him the bag. "Now don't ever say that the lucky penny didn't make one of your wishes come true."

Larry knew that things were going nowhere fast. "Come on, let's get outta here."

"You think about lettin' me take your place as a judge," Terry said, "and I'll give you something you've always wanted."

"What is it?" Sweet asked.

"I ain't tellin'. But if you let me take your place, it'll make you happier than you've ever been."

He took a bite of the dill pickle and crunched into Crabbie's ear. The mule turned around and trotted away. "I'm gettin' sick of garlic," he said to Larry.

Larry frowned. "Don't breathe on me," he said, holding his nose.

"Bye, guys," Sweet called out.

"See ya later, Sweet," Terry shouted.

Larry held the reins. "What do you have to give him?"

"Don't know," Terry said, hanging his tongue out to get the dill pickle smell off of it. "When I figure it out, I'll tell you." He shook his head. "All I know is that a few minutes ago I had a big bag of gumdrops and now I got a bag of sweet nothings."

They came upon Maurice Springer at the Willow Creek Bridge. He stopped his wagon as they came by. "See you got Mr. Crabbie movin' like a race horse," he said.

"Maybe not like a race horse," Larry said, "but he does what we tell him."

Maurice looked at the pickle on a stick. "What's that? You goin' fishin' or somethin'?"

"Naw," Terry said, "it's just our backward pickle stick for movin' Crabbie around."

Maurice shook his head. *These boys are crazy.* "Well, just keep my granddaddy's secret a secret."

"We will," both said together.

"Mr. Springer?" Terry said.

"Yes, son?"

"You know any way to get Mrs. Bentley to let us judge the cookie contest?" Terry asked.

"You might as well think 'bout eatin' the green cheese on the moon."

"Why's that?" Larry asked.

"'Cause you got about as much chance," Maurice said. He clicked the reins. "See ya, boys. I gotta go into town now."

Terry dangled the pickle stick in front of Crabbie's nose. The mule stepped backward in front of Maurice's wagon.

"Get that fool mule outta my way. You moved him in the wrong direction."

Terry smiled. "No, I didn't. You crunch forward and pickle stick backward,"

"We know what we're doin'," Larry said.

Maurice closed his eyes and shook his head. *Give me strength to survive these fool kids.*

"Isn't there anything you can tell us?" Terry asked. "Didn't your granddaddy tell you something 'bout gettin' women to change their minds?"

"No, boys, I ain't been told no secrets 'bout that."

"But you know her, don't you?" Larry asked.

"I only know from the talk I hear 'round town that the way to get to Mrs. Bentley is through her cat, Cuddles."

"Through her cat?" Terry asked.

Maurice nodded. "I hear if her cat likes you, she'll like you. Now get on outta my way. I got some business to attend to."

Terry smiled, put the pickle between his teeth and crunched loudly. The mule took off trotting toward the hills.

"Where we goin'?" Larry asked, holding on for dear life.

"We're goin' to Josie's."

"Josie's?" Larry exclaimed. "Why we goin' way up there?"

"To ask her about pleasin' cats," Terry said. "She knows somethin' 'bout everythin'."

They rode through the hills, following the path along the ridge, and found the old herb woman of the hills working in her garden. Her old place had changed since Susan Ponder and her kids moved in, after escaping from a dangerous cult a while back.

Terry looked at Josie's shoe tree and shook his head. *I still think she's crazier than a coot.* He smiled thinking about the shoes she took in payment for her herb advice and how she threw them up onto the branches so poor people could pick shoes from her tree to wear.

Josie looked up and grinned. "Well, if it ain't the Younguns. Is this a social call or are you here to give me your shoes?"

Terry pulled his feet back. "Don't be thinkin' 'bout takin' our shoes."

"Yeah," Larry said, "your tree's got enough shoes already."

Josie shook her head. "There's never enough shoes for my tree 'cause there are more poor people 'round here than shoes."

Larry looked at the tree and said, "Josie, we got somethin' to ask you."

"It'll cost you," she said.

"How much?" Terry asked, not liking the way Josie was eyeing his shoes.

Josie dusted off her dress. "Depends."

"Depends on what?" Terry said.

Josie walked over and stood next to Crab Apple. "Depends on what you need and if I got it." She got a whiff of Terry's breath. "Phew-wee, you smell worse than a dead 'possum on the road."

Terry covered his mouth and spoke through his fingers. "Sorry."

"He's been eatin' dill pickles," Larry said.

"Garlic dill pickles," Josie said, sniffing the air.

"Got to," Terry said through his fingers.

"Why?" Josie asked. "Why's anyone got to eat somethin' that bad?"

"'Cause it's the secret way to get Crabbie to move," Larry volunteered.

"Secret way?" Josie exclaimed. "Who's secret way?"

"Can't tell you." Terry said through his thumb and forefinger. "It's a secret."

Josie threw her hands up into the air. "First you tell me that eatin' garlic dills is the secret way to get Crabbie to move, then you tell me that you can't tell me who told you the secret 'cause it's a secret." She put her hands on her hips and sighed. "A secret's a secret, not the person who told you the secret," she said, and turned and walked away. She didn't want them to see the smile on her face.

"But we promised!" Larry said.

"Then promise your way outta here. You've done got me so curious that I'll never be able to sleep."

"But Mr. Springer told us—" Terry stopped. He knew he had given it away.

Josie smiled and walked back. "Now, ain't that better to tell ol' Josie what she wants to hear?"

"I guess," Terry said.

Josie smiled. "Means you get to keep your shoes," she said. "Now what you want to ask me?"

"We want to know how to get cats to like you," Terry blurted out.

She laughed. "Is that all you want to know?"

"You know what to do?" Larry asked.

"Sure. Just hold some catnip in your hand and a cat will love you."

"Catnip?" Larry asked. "You got any?"

"How much you need?" Josie asked.

"Just enough for one cat," Larry said.

"Well, boys," Josie said, "I promised Susan and the kids that I'd meet them in town for this fashion show. See that bag hanging over on the shed wall?" The boys nodded. "Well, inside that is a bunch of dried catnip I use in some of my fixins. Take yourselves what you need."

"How much?" Terry asked, as she walked back toward her cabin.

"How much what?" she asked, turning around.

"How much the catnip cost?" Larry asked.

"You already paid for it," she said.

"We did?" Larry said.

"Sure. I got the secret of the secret out of you. Curiosity killed the cat and I would have probably died curious in my sleep if you hadn't told me Maurice's secret." She smiled and shrugged. "So you boys saved my life. Take some catnip, take all you need," she said. And she walked off, whistling a shrill tune.

Terry got down from Crabbie and got the whole bag off the wall. "Hey!" Larry exclaimed. "You're takin' the whole bag!"

"She said take all you need," he said. "I wanna make sure this cat likes us."

Halfway up the ridge, the scream of a wildcat echoed through the hills. Larry got scared. "What if that wildcat smells the catnip?"

"Here," Terry said, pulling out a wad of catnip and stuffing it into the back of Larry's britches, "you take care of him."

"Hey!" Larry shouted, "Cut that out!"

They wrestled on the back of the mule and again the backward pickle stick dropped in front of Crabbie's nose. The mule backed up like a freight train out of control.

"Stop, Crabbie, stop!" Larry shouted, looking at the cliff they were heading toward.

Terry lifted the stick and crunched down on the pickle. Crabbie stopped, spun around in a circle, then moved forward. At the top of the ridge, Terry stopped the mule.

"What's wrong?" Larry asked, looking around for the wildcat.

"I'm tired of driving," Terry said. "It's your turn to do the crunchin'."

After they switched places, they heard a wildcat's growl echo through the hollow. Larry grabbed a pickle from Terry's sack.

"What you doin'?" Terry said, looking around as the wildcat roared again.

Larry was eating the dill with one hand and trying to pull the catnip out of his britches with the other. He crunched as loud as he could. "Let's get outta here!" he shouted.

Crabbie shot forward and Larry didn't notice that Terry had tied the bag of catnip on his back belt loop. *Don't want no wildcat followin' me if we fall off,* Terry thought.

Neither of them saw the wildcat standing on the ledge above them, weaving back and forth, burning with fever.

CHAPTER 35

CATNIP

Larry and Terry rode Crabbie through the hills, taking the shortcut to town. Behind the livery, they tied him up and opened the catnip sack.

Larry looked in and frowned. "This is just a bunch of dried sticks and leaves."

"Josie said cats like it," Terry said, sniffing a handful. "Not much to it."

Larry sniffed it. "Smells more like an old attic."

"Well, let's get to it," Terry said.

"What are you doin'?" Larry asked. Terry was stuffing the catnip in his socks, pockets, and underpants.

"I just want to make sure the cat likes me." He handed the sack to Larry. "Make yourself cat-nice too."

Larry shook his head, thinking this was another dumb thing that his younger brother had gotten him into. When the sack was empty, the boys started toward the Bentleys' house. They hadn't gotten more than five feet when the first alley cat came running out.

"Hey, get off me!" Terry protested, but the cat was jumping and pawing at his pants.

Another alley cat came running out, then another and another, and soon they were surrounded.

"What do we do?" Larry shouted.

Terry reached into his underpants and pulled out a bunch of

catnip. "When I give the word, we run," he said. He nodded to Larry, then dropped the catnip on the ground. "Let's go!" he shouted.

They ran down the alley, leaving a dozen cats lying around in the dirt, happy with life for the moment.

Sarah Bentley had her gramophone playing one of the newest songs. Thinking no one would see her, she picked up her skirts and danced around the room with gay abandon. Cuddles watched for a moment, then slipped from the room.

Sarah kicked up her heels and swished her skirt as she spun around the room. *This was the rage back in New York.* She remembered the night she teased her husband-to-be with her dancing.

She remembered her father coming into the room, just as William made his first advance. *Poppa almost tossed him out on his ear.*

Sarah suddenly felt as if she was in her twenties again and not the grand old age of thirty-five. She skipped from the parlor and headed into her husband's study and found him sitting at his desk, working on papers.

Sarah used her most seductive moves and twirled around the room. Bentley watched, amused for a moment. *What's she doing now?* he wondered.

"Don't you remember this dance?" she asked, in a breathless voice she'd once heard an actress use on stage.

"It looks familiar."

She danced around him. *I know he loves this,* she thought. *He'll be jumping up to dance with me any moment.* She touched her hands above her head, and slid down onto the couch in front of him. *This is the part where he goes crazy.* She smiled and batted her eyes.

She must have lost her mind, Bentley thought. "You feeling all right?"

Sarah fluttered her eyes and pouted her lower lip. "Never felt better, sweetheart."

"Is there something in your eyes?" he asked.

"William!" she said, standing up. "I thought you'd remember

the dance I did for you back in New York when you could hardly keep your hands off me."

He did remember and knew he'd pay for this slip. "I'm sorry, Sarah. Of course I remember it. You just danced me speechless, that's all."

Just then Martha appeared in the doorway.

"Yes, what do you want?" Sarah asked, frustrated.

"Sorry, mum, but there's two boys here to see you."

"Two boys? Who are they?" Sarah asked, straightening her skirt, thinking they were some of Willy's friends.

"The Youngun boys," Martha said.

"Oh," Sarah said, her mood changing. "Those horrid trouble-makers."

"What do they want?" Bentley asked.

"How in heavens do I know?" she asked.

"Shall I bring them in?" Martha asked.

"Bring them into the parlor and tell them I'll be right in."

Martha went back to the front door and opened it. Larry and Terry stood there, with their hands behind their backs. "The missus will see you in the parlor."

"Thanks," they said, stepping in.

"Not so fast," Martha said, pushing them back.

"What's wrong?" Larry asked.

"Take your shoes off."

"Take our shoes off?" Terry exclaimed. "Does she have a shoe tree too?"

"A what?" Martha said, perplexed.

"A shoe tree. Where you keep shoes for poor people," Terry said, as if Josie's shoe tree was the most normal thing in the world.

Martha shrugged. "The missus makes everyone take their shoes off. Keeps dirt out of the house."

The two boys looked at each other, then sat down. "Could you give us a minute?" Larry asked.

"I'll be standin' in the kitchen. Don't come in until they're off," Martha said, and walked off.

When she was out of sight, Larry and Terry quickly took off their shoes. They removed the catnip they'd hidden in the bottom, and pushed it into their socks. When Martha came back, they stood quietly, innocent as angels.

Larry smiled. "We're ready," he said.

"You should get your mom to darn your socks," Martha said, looking down. Four big toes wiggled back up at her.

Terry's head dropped. "Don't got a mom."

"Everyone's got a mom," Martha said, thinking they were fibbing.

"Our mom's dead," Larry said.

"Oh dear," Martha whispered. "Would you two lads like some milk and cookies while you're waiting?"

"That would be nice," they both said, as they walked into the parlor.

They spent the next ten minutes eating fresh-baked cookies and examining the expensive things scattered around the room. "Don't touch anything," Larry whispered.

"I won't," Terry said, feeling the arms of an ancient Chinese vase.

"Hey, look at this!" Larry said loudly, pointing to a framed sword on the wall. Terry turned and knocked the vase. Larry's mouth dropped in horror. "Watch out! Catch it!"

Terry tried to catch the vase, but it fell on its side and broke in half.

"Now you've done it," Larry said, looking at the broken treasure.

"What are we going to do?" Terry asked.

"Not we, *you.* I didn't break it."

"I'll say you did," Terry said. "So you better help me or we're both in trouble."

"What are we going to do?" Larry asked.

Terry pulled a wad of gum from the foil in his pocket. "Start chewin'," he said, putting some into his mouth and handing Larry the rest.

"But it's already been chewed," Larry said.

"It's either chew it or explain how you broke the vase," Terry said, chewing as fast as he could.

Larry continued to protest. "But I didn't break it!" he said.

"My word against yours," Terry mumbled through the wad of gum in his mouth.

Larry took the gum and began chewing. When it was soft enough, they carefully spread it around the edges of the cracked vase and set the vase back in place.

"Think it'll hold?" Larry asked.

"It's just got to hold until we get outta here. Then maybe she'll blame it on Willy."

"What do you boys want?" Sarah asked from behind them.

They both turned, nervous as worms in a bait box. "Oh, hi, Mrs. Bentley," Larry said. "We just came to visit and—"

"Visit? I'm a very busy woman. I have a fashion show this afternoon and—"

"And we won't take much of your time," Terry said, getting to the point.

Sarah stood there with her arms crossed. "Well?"

"Well," Larry stammered, "we was wonderin' if—"

"Get to the point, young man."

Terry gave him the sign that he'd take over. "Like my brother said, we was wonderin' if you'd let us be the next-in-line judges for the bakin' contest."

"Next-in-line judges? I don't understand," Sarah said.

Cuddles came running into the room and reared back at the entranceway, arching his back. Sarah reached down and picked him up. "Cuddles doesn't like many people. You boys seem to upset her, so if you'd kindly leave."

Cuddles pushed out of her arms and ran up to Larry. She sniffed his legs, his feet, his socks.

"Cuddles, what are you doing?" Sarah shook her head in amazement. "I've never seen you act this way, Cuddles."

Terry smiled. "Cuddles likes us. That's good, ain't it, Mrs. Bentley?"

"I think so. Maybe I've been wrong about you boys." She walked to the couch and signaled for the boys to sit down. "Now, you boys want to be alternate judges, in case William Junior or Sweet get sick. Is that right?"

The boys nodded. Cuddles jumped up onto Larry's lap and purred contentedly.

"I'll tell you what," she said, shaking her head and smiling. "If they don't get sick, I'll personally make sure that you get first pick of the Mule Day pie winners. How's that sound?"

"Delicious," Terry grinned.

Willy came into the room. "What are you two doing here?"

"William, is that any way to talk to our guests?" Sarah asked.

"Guests? I thought you said they were—"

Sarah cut him off. "Bring up a chair and talk with us. You'll be amazed at Cuddles. She loves them."

Willy made a face, and Terry stuck his tongue out behind Sarah's back. When Sarah turned, he was smiling like an angel. Cuddles lay on his back in Larry's lap, feet up in the air, purring like a freight train coming full blast down the tracks.

"What's wrong with Cuddles?" Willy asked.

Sarah smiled. "Nothing. He really likes these boys."

Willy stood next to the table with the vase on it and thought he noticed something wrong. He peered closer. *There's a crack!* he realized. But when he reached to examine it, it just fell apart, breaking into a hundred pieces on the hardwood floor. Sarah's mouth opened.

"William! That was from the Ming Dynasty!"

"But Mom, I didn't do nothin'. I . . ."

"Go to your room, William." When he had left, she turned to the boys. "I've decided that we need three judges for the baking contest."

"That's great!" the Younguns exclaimed.

"Which one of you will be the judge?" she asked.

"I will!" they both said in unison.

"Oh, we can't have four, we can only have three," she said with a smile.

"How 'bout we be half judges?" Terry asked.

"Half judges? Whatever do you mean?"

"Well," Terry said, "Larry could judge the cookies, 'cause he likes them best, and I could judge the pies, 'cause I like them best. We'll each judge half the contest."

Sarah laughed. Cuddles was now moaning with delight, rubbing around on Larry's face and neck. "Cuddles, is that okay with you? Should we let them be half judges?"

Meow, meow, Cuddles screeched, then fell on his back, purring in ecstasy.

Sarah stood up. "I'll see you boys at the contest. Now, you better run along, because I have a fashion show to go to and a vase to clean up."

"What a mess," Terry said, pretending to examine the piece, but actually removing the two long strings of gum.

"Martha will get to it. Now you boys run along."

The Younguns took off down the front walk and ran back to where they'd left Crabbie. They pulled all the catnip from their pants and socks and put it back in the sack. Leonard Harvey came walking down the alley, carrying a bag of books from the library.

"Hey, Leonard," Terry called out. "Can I see what you're reading?"

Leonard was suspicious. "What for?"

"'Cause I've been thinkin' that maybe I should be a bookworm like you so I could be smart."

Leonard handed up his bag and didn't notice Terry dumping the catnip in the bottom of it. Larry rolled his eyes.

"Good books. Good heavy books," Terry said, hoisting one in the air. "These are the best books for growin' brains, ain't they?"

Leonard didn't know what to say, so he just nodded.

"Well, thanks for lettin' me see what bookworms read," Terry said, handing him back the bag. "See ya," Terry said, crunching the soggy pickle he'd kept wrapped in his pocket into Crabbie's ear.

Leonard scratched his head as he watched them ride off. He didn't notice the fifteen or twenty alley cats headed his way.

CHAPTER 36

CHANGE OF HEART

Sherry sat close to Carla as they rode in the buggy to the fashion show. Rev. Youngun kept his back straight, tipping his hat to everyone he passed—even the wooden Indian at the front of the barber shop.

Carla smiled at Sherry, who said, "Pa, that was a statue you just nodded to."

Rev. Youngun looked at Carla and blushed. "Guess I'm just so excited, showing you off to the town and all, I didn't notice."

He waved to Father Walsh who was heading down the sidewalk at a fast clip. "Good to see you, Father."

"Top of the day to ya, Reverend," Father Walsh said, as he headed into Tippy's Saloon. The men inside bantered back and forth around the bar. They stopped when they saw the priest. "Care for a drink, Father?" the bartender asked.

"No. I want to see Mr. Huleatt," Father Walsh said, giving a stern look to several of his parishoners who had strayed.

"He's in the back. I'll go get him," the bartender said.

Huleatt appeared from the office door at the end of the bar. "Father Walsh? This is a surprise."

"Just need a moment of your time, Thomas," he said, and he walked around the bar and into the office without being invited.

Huleatt noticed the raised eyebrows of the bartender and just shrugged it off. He closed the door behind him and looked at the priest. "Well, what can I do for you?" he asked in his best Irish brogue.

"You can cut out the malarkey, for starters, and then you can tell me that you thought about what we discussed."

Huleatt's face darkened. "You mean in the confessional?"

"That's what I'm talking about. I asked you to pray for some common sense."

"You told me to pray for guidance."

"Guidance, common sense, it's the same thing. Well?"

"Well what?"

"Did you get some common sense?" the priest asked impatiently. "What you're plannin' to do to the woman you once loved is wrong."

Huleatt laughed heartily. "Father, I did what you said and changed my mind."

"You what?" Father Walsh asked in astonishment. He knew what a hard-headed reputation Huleatt had and couldn't believe his ears.

"Just what I said. I changed my mind. That's what you wanted, isn't it? I'm not going to give her the sleepin' medicine to keep her from speaking."

Father Walsh smiled. "By the bells of heaven, that's wonderful."

"I thought about what you said and decided to remember things as they used to be," he said, taking a bottle of whiskey out from the drawer of his desk. "Want a pick-me-up?"

"No, no," the priest said. "I can't tell you how proud, how pleased, I am that you came to your—" Father Walsh stopped, looking for words.

Huleatt laughed. "You mean, that I came to my senses? That's the truth and it doesn't bother me." Huleatt pulled a picture of Ellen and him from his desk drawer. They looked happy and in love. "We were a good bit younger then, but this is the way I want to leave things between us."

Father Walsh took the picture, then gave it back. "You're going to see her when she comes to town, aren't you?"

Huleatt looked at the picture and shook his head. "I want to remember her as she was. She's probably changed now. Maybe even married."

"You don't know that for a fact."

"The fact is, Father, that I was a boy who loved her twenty years ago. She probably never thinks a moment about me."

Father Walsh put on his hat. "You never know what the heart will do, lad, you never know." He stopped at the doorway. "You're doing the right thing, Thomas. I'm proud of you."

Huleatt closed his eyes and was back riding across the green of Ireland. Ellen was on the horse in front of him, her hair flying in the wind. They were laughing. They were happy. They were in love.

Cunningham tipped his hat to Father Walsh at the front door of the saloon, fearing that the priest could read his mind.

Father Walsh looked at him. "See you in church Sunday, David?"

"I'll be there, Father." He nodded, then went to the bar. He placed the sack carefully on the bar, then sat at the stool and signaled the bartender. "A cold one."

"Coming right up," the bartender said, wiping down a mug and drawing a draft. He set it down in front of Cunningham. "You hear about the rabid wildcat that was spotted outside of town?"

"Nope," Cunningham said, shaking his head. "I hope someone shoots it."

"They've been looking for it," the bartender said. "What's in the bag?"

Cunningham sipped. "Just something that Mr. Huleatt wanted. Is he here?"

"Yeah, but he's busy," he said, picking up the sack.

"Hey, hey," Cunningham said, reaching to grab it back, "that's for Mr. Huleatt."

Inside the bag was the bottle of Irish whiskey he mixed up with the sleeping liquid Huleatt had given him. He'd hidden it for several days, troubled by the knowledge of what he'd heard and what the bottle was for.

"We've already got enough of this," the bartender said, shaking his head.

"This is special," Cunningham grinned.

The bartender looked around. "Want a quick tipple?" he asked, taking the cap off.

"No, no!" Cunningham said, grabbing his arm. "Don't be drinkin' none of that!"

"Okay, okay," he said, putting the cap back on. "What do you want me to do with it?"

"Could you put it behind the bar and give it to Mr. Huleatt for me?"

"Sure thing, Cunningham," the bartender said, putting it with the rest of the stock.

Cunningham sat and, nursed his beer. *If I try to get Mr. Huleatt to change his mind, he'll know I heard the confession. If I go to Father Walsh, he'll know I've sinned. If I go to Martha, she'll know that I've been hired to hurt somebody. And if I tell Ellen when she comes to town, Huleatt will find out and fire me.*

Then he thought about the five-dollar bill he'd given to his wife and imagined the fine dress she'd buy for herself. At that moment his decision was made. He'd say nothing.

After Cunningham finished his beer, he left. The bartender knocked on the office door. "Mr. Huleatt?"

"Yes, yes?" Huleatt said, blinking his eyes.

"Cunningham brought you a bottle of Irish. Said you wanted it."

"Just put it on the side," he said, not really paying attention.

"Yes, sir."

Huleatt looked at the picture of Ellen. *I almost did the wrong thing to you, Ellen. Whoever has your heart is the luckiest man on earth.*

CHAPTER 37

GUILTY CONSCIENCE

"Oh, Manly," Laura said, "please come to the fashion show with me. It'll give us a chance to talk."

Manly shook his head. "You know I don't like those things." He glanced at Laura's face, then turned away. He'd been deep in thought since he'd decided to not go to the fishing hole. He rode aimlessly through the ridges and tried to think things out, to come up with a way of straightening things out between Laura and him.

They had talked, but the conversation was strained, and they slept again on opposite edges of the bed.

Manly looked at Laura from the corner of his eye. He was embarrassed for even thinking of escaping to the fishing hole with the other men. *I don't need to get away from my wife,* he thought, *I need to talk to her, to get things back to the way they were. She's my best friend. She's my partner.* The worry had kept him awake all night.

"Manly," Laura asked softly, "what's bothering you?"

"Nothing," he said, finishing his milk. "I got to go tend to the cows."

"But we've got to talk," she said, taking his arm. "I want to apologize for any pain I've caused you."

Manly turned. "You don't have to say nothin', but there's somethin' I got to tell you," he said, looking down. He wanted to tell her the truth about heading out to the fishing hole, to get it off his conscience.

Laura took his chin in her hands and looked into his eyes. "What is it?" she asked, worried now that something had happened.

The phone on the kitchen wall beside them rang loudly, breaking into the moment. Manly picked it up. "Hello, what do you want?" he asked, still not used to answering a phone.

"Mr. Wilder, this is Patrick Jefferson, Mae Jefferson's husband."

"Yes?" Manly said, smiling at Laura. He liked the British accent.

"Would you please give your wife a message. Tell her that Mae's goin' to have the statue finished by the Fourth of July."

"Good, she'll be glad to hear that," he said, then put his hand over the phone and said to Laura, "Statue will be ready for Ellen Boyle's Mule Day speech."

Laura smiled and Manly went back to what Patrick was saying. ". . . would you also tell her that?"

"Tell her what? I missed what you were saying," Manly said.

"Tell her that we'll wait payment for the rest of the money so they can have time to raise it. We'll deliver before we're paid because her guarantee is good enough for us."

"Guarantee? What are you talking about?" Manly asked.

Laura's ears perked up at the word "guarantee" and her heart dropped. "Give me the phone, Manly."

He turned away, holding the phone and listening to Patrick. "Your wife guaranteed us payment for the balance if the funds weren't raised by her club. Just give her that message, will you please?"

"I sure will," Manly said, and he hung up the phone.

He turned to Laura who began to speak, "Manly, let me explain. I—"

"You guaranteed payment without tellin' me?" he said with quiet intensity.

"I just didn't get around to it," she said lamely.

"Didn't get around to it? Like it was no big deal guaranteeing us paying for the statue with *our* money. Not *your* money, but *our* money."

Manly was fuming. Laura tried to hug him. "I wanted to tell you, but things just slipped my mind."

"You sort of took out a mortgage, didn't you? Like I did back in the Dakotas. Like you've been hounding me about for fifteen years."

He was about to scream at her, then took a deep breath to control himself. When he spoke, the words came out slowly, like sentences in themselves. "You. Should. Be. Ashamed. Of. Yourself."

Manly turned to leave. "Manly," Laura said, "come back. Let's talk about it. You said you had something you wanted to tell me."

"Not anymore," he said. The screen door slammed the point home.

CHAPTER 38

HIGH FASHION, LOW BLOW

By the time Laura arrived at the fashion show, almost everyone else was there, so she had to park behind the church. She nodded to the other ladies and the few men in the room.

Laura was not in a good mood. She was angry at herself for not telling Manly about the guarantee, and she was saddenned that he'd found out just at the moment he had wanted to talk.

On the small stage, Sarah Bentley was giving a speech titled "Cookies, Fashion, and Life," which was being received with polite applause. Laura looked at the beautiful dress that Sarah was wearing and then down at her own.

Though the dress was clean and nice, it was several years old. She looked around the room. The other ladies had worn their finest, taking the fashion show opportunity to show themselves off. A wave of insecurity washed over Laura.

She smiled to Rev. Youngun who was snuggled close to the widow Pobst. *You can tell they're in love. Just like Manly and I were . . . are,* she thought.

After Sarah's speech, some of the young women of Mansfield modeled the latest fashions that had been sent in from New York. Snakelike jewelry was the rage, and the serpentine shapes made from beads, gold filigree, and pins were on every outfit.

Sarah said to the women from the side of the stage, "Notice how the serpents are not definite. They're there but not so obvious as to be repulsive." The ladies in the room looked more intensely. "If you look carefully, you'll notice that some are even wearing snake rings, combs, and hair pins."

The women in the room applauded and the models in front curtsied slightly. Laura wasn't feeling very stylish. Suddenly, she wanted to tell the room that if women were only to be admired and covered with ornaments, their right to vote would never be taken seriously.

Laura went to the ladies' room to wash her face. She smiled at Martha Cunningham, who was waiting outside the rest room door. Laura didn't notice Martha's husband, David, coming down the hall.

In the rest room, Sarah was primping in front of the mirror. "Well, if it isn't Miss Know-It-All," Sarah said, looking at Laura's reflection.

"Hello, Mrs. Bentley," Laura said, looking into the mirror, then turning her back to Sarah.

Sarah chuckled. "Don't like what you see?"

Laura spun around, livid with built-up frustration. "Sarah Bentley! Just because you're rude doesn't mean that we can't be civil to each other!"

Sarah started to snap back, but half-turned and took a deep breath. She had gotten to Laura and knew it. "I agree," she said, smiling as she turned back to Laura. "That's why I was going to offer you some tips on how to put on make-up."

Laura was rattled by her comment and clearly showed it. "Tips? Why would I want tips from you?"

"I hear you're an expert on home beauty parlors, but from what I see, you need some help."

"Sarah Bentley, you're pathetic!" Laura said angrily.

Sarah smiled. "I may be a pathetic creature, but you wear your make-up like a circus clown." Sarah turned back to the mirror. "But I guess that comes from learning to put make-up on in a bumpy wagon." She turned and half-closed her eyes, looking closely at Laura. "Or did they even *have* make-up on the prairie?"

Laura ignored her and turned to the mirror. She fiddled awkwardly with her hair, trying to calm down. "That's a nice feathered dress, Sarah. Are those vulture feathers?"

Sarah turned, and grinned like a cat. "No, they're not from your

flock. These are peacock feathers, since you don't seem to know."
Sarah turned back to the mirror and licked her lips to smooth the
lipstick. "I guess the only birds you saw on the prairie were crows
and vultures eating dead animals."

Laura looked back in the mirror and said coldly, "I knew what
the feathers were."

"I guess a Fifth Avenue dress would make you uncomfortable,"
Sarah said. She sighed loudly. "I'd have worn my buckskins to
make you feel more comfortable, if I had any."

Laura licked her lips and brought out the remains of some lip
color she rarely used. "I'm going to pretend you don't exist."

Sarah clapped. "Good! And if you'd move away, it would almost
be a reality!"

"I said I'm ignoring you," Laura said again. "There's nothing
you can say that will bother me."

Sarah was enjoying the game. "I could teach you how to fix that
rat's nest on your head. You have such pretty hair for an older
woman."

Laura tried to ignore her.

Sarah was on a roll. "You know, if you'd lose a few pounds, you
wouldn't look like such a pollywog."

Laura started to say something, but closed up her purse instead.

Sarah couldn't stop herself. "That's a nice dress. Did you make
it yourself or did you get it from the church poor box?"

Laura was unable to take any more of it. "You're a hateful
woman, Sarah Bentley!" she said coldly.

"From you, that's a compliment." Sarah smiled, staring at
Laura.

Laura turned to go, and said, "I feel sorry for your husband,
having to wake up with you every morning."

Sarah set her feet and said loudly, "At least he wakes up next to
me, or has your husband stopped sleeping on the couch?"

It was like an ice-cold bullet in her heart. Laura staggered for a
moment, but didn't turn. She pulled herself together and walked
out of the rest room.

She walked past Martha and David. She walked past Rev.
Youngun and Carla. She walked past her friends in town without
saying anything.

All she could think about was getting into her car and getting outside of town. Getting away from everybody before she broke down in tears.

Sarah came out of the bathroom, satisifed that she had won the mean-spirited battle. She looked at Martha and David. "Are you ready, Martha, or do you want to take some time off?"

"I'm ready, ma'am," Martha said.

"I'll see you, Martha," David said, and kissed her on the cheek. "Thanks for listening to me."

Martha watched him walk off. He'd told her about hearing the confession, about what Huleatt's plans were for drugging Ellen. She'd told him to go to Father Walsh.

"Are you coming, Martha?" Sarah asked, standing impatiently with her hands on her hips.

Martha hesitated, then said, "I want to tell you what my husband said."

"What is it?"

Martha walked up and whispered, "He said that Huleatt is planning to drug Ellen Boyle so she can't speak."

"I think that's just booze talk."

"Ma'am? Don't you want to tell someone and stop it?"

"Martha, first of all, I don't like Ellen Boyle and all she stands for. And second, your husband's a drunk—a drunk, do you understand?" Sarah turned and walked away. "I wouldn't believe a word he says. Next thing you know is he'll be seeing pink raccoons and elephants flying around Mansfield."

You're wrong! Martha thought, smarting at the hurtful words.

CHAPTER 39

TIME TO TALK

When Laura got back to Apple Hill Farm, she found Manly sitting on the front steps. He was so down, he looked like an old basset hound.

"Manly," Laura said, trudging up the stairs, "this hasn't been a good day. If you want to fight with me about that guarantee—"

"Nope, I've thought about it. You just made a mistake, that's all."

"That's all?" she asked, surprised.

"I've made plenty of mistakes. Can't be blamin' you for somethin' you did that just happened."

She sat beside him on the stairs, holding her purse in her lap. "Oh, Manly, I was wrong. The money in the bank is our money, not my money."

Manly nodded and stared off toward the orchards. "What are you thinking about?" Laura asked.

"About you and me."

"Come to any startling revelations?" she asked. *If he's got something bad to tell me, it's coming now,* she worried.

Manly looked into her eyes. "Laura, I've been worried that you didn't love me anymore. That you were just tired of me."

"No, Manly. I love you." She hugged him, crying happily. "I was worried that you didn't love me anymore. That we had drifted too far apart to come back together."

Manly turned and took Laura's hands. "You mean more to me

than anything on earth. I don't want to ever do nothin' to lose you and . . . and . . ." He broke down in tears, holding her close to him.

For a moment there was no one else in the world except the two of them, hugging tightly, letting their hearts pour out over the common bond of their marriage. Strengthening them. Pulling them together.

Without saying a word, Manly took Laura's hand and walked her through the doors and into the house that would once again be a loving home.

CHAPTER 40

MULE DAY

Sherry got into her long pants. It was the first pair her father had ever bought her. He didn't like her wearing pants—he wanted her to dress like a little lady like all the other little girls in Mansfield—but he told her that riding a horse in a dress western-style was not the thing to do.

This was the day they were to ride out on the father-daughter campout. While her father packed their bedrolls and food, Sherry packed the essentials: her blankey and her dolly, Carrie Nation.

"Are you ready yet, Sherry?" Rev. Youngun called out. He had their horses saddled and tied to the front steps.

"Coming, Pa."

At the top of the stairs, she saw Terry and Larry staring at her. "Have fun," Larry said, without much enthusiasm in his voice.

"I will," she said, then went over and hugged him. "I wish you could go."

"What about me?" said Terry from the boy's bedroom.

Sherry made a face, but Larry frowned. "Oh, all right," said Sherry. "I wish you were coming along too."

"Fibber," Terry said, putting his candy stash away. "I bet Larry made you say that."

Sherry took the stairs two at a time and went out onto the porch. "Ready to go, Pa."

"Good. Just go make sure the ice box door is closed, and then we're off," Rev. Youngun said.

"Who's gonna watch the boys this morning?"

"They'll be fine until Maurice gets here to take them to the parade. Then tonight Carla will watch them."

Sherry checked the ice box then stopped to look at Beezer. He hadn't eaten in several days and didn't look well at all. "What's wrong, Beez? I don't want you to die."

As she stroked the nape on the back of Beezer's head, the parrot began gagging. Sherry panicked. "Beez! Beez, are you sick?"

It happened so fast that she didn't realize at first what she was staring at in the mess that came up. *That's Pa's ring*, she finally realized. *That's Pa's ring!*

"Come on, Sherry, we've got to get going for the roundup meeting at the church," Rev. Youngun called out.

Sherry made a face, picked the ring out of the mess and ran into the kitchen and washed it off. When they were halfway to town, she handed her father the ring. Even Sherry, as little as she was, could comprehend the sheer joy that showed on his face.

Maurice got into his new jeans and pressed work shirt and headed over to the Younguns. He'd promised Rev. Youngun that he'd help the boys get Crabbie to the Mule Day events.

He whistled along the trail. *I must be livin' right.* He smiled, looking around. *Couldn't ask for a more perfect day. Got my tummy full of biscuits and ham, drank two cups of hot coffee, and got a kiss from Eulla Mae.*

He came up to the back of their barn and called out, "You boys ready?"

"We're in here," Larry answered.

"Day's a-wastin'," Maurice said, opening the barn door. He stopped dead in his tracks. "Lawd-a-Moses, what in tarnation is that?"

The Youngun boys were standing next to Crabbie, whose ears seemed to have grown ten inches over night. "What is that?" he asked, staring at the mule.

Terry beamed. "It's Crabbie."

"I know that. I mean, what are those things on his ears?"

Larry smiled and patted Crabbie. It had taken Terry and him

almost an hour to put the long pointed ears they'd made from old cloth and wire on Crabbie's head. "You like his ears?"

"Think he'll win the prettiest mule contest?" Terry asked.

Maurice walked around the mule. "Looks like a bat from the moon," he said, shaking his head.

"Don't you think he's pretty?" Terry asked.

Maurice grinned. "You boys think you're pretty smart, hookin' up this rig, don't ya?"

"We might win both contests," Larry said.

"Both contests?" Maurice asked.

"The prettiest mule and the pullin' contest," Terry said. "Ten bucks each. That's twenty bucks we're goin' to come home with."

Maurice knew that their mule ear disguise would never work, but he had to give the boys credit for trying. "You know, it took a lot of smarts to come up with this idea."

"Thanks," Larry beamed.

"But listen to me first," Maurice said. "This ain't Halloween. Them judges will see through these fake ears like a hot knife through butter."

The boys were crestfallen. "You think so?" Larry asked, looking at the ears through different eyes.

Maurice nodded. "'Fraid so. You see, boys, you were just gettin' a little greedy, tryin' to win both contests. Odds are that if you try to win both, you'll lose both."

"Then what should we do?" Terry asked.

"I think you should just enter one. My advice is to enter Crabbie in the pullin' contest."

"For sure?" Terry asked.

"For sure," Maurice answered. "Now, come on, we're gonna miss the parade. Where's Sherry and your Pa?"

Larry shook his head. "Pa took her to town early. They're leavin' for the father-daughter campout right after the events this afternoon."

"And he's leavin' us with Carla to babysat us," Terry said.

"He means babysit," Larry said, correcting his brother.

"Well, things could be worse," Maurice said.

"And things could be better," Larry said. "We could be stayin' with you."

"Well, be that as it may, you have someone to watch over you, which is more than a lot of children have. So come on, let's get into town before we can't find a place to sit down."

With a jar of pickles and Dangit in the back of the wagon, Terry, Larry, and Maurice led Crabbie behind them into town. They only had to stop twice so Terry could crunch him forward, which gave them plenty of time to get a good seat before the parade.

Mule Day was about the biggest event in Mansfield each year. It had begun as an informal get-together before the turn of the century, when owners of mules and horses brought their stock to Mansfield to show off what they had.

By nine in the morning, the streets of Mansfield were lined with people. There were floats and marching girls from the farm clubs, and the county council waving from a big Oldsmobile.

The highlight of the parade was a twenty-mule team driven by Oscar Erickson, the blacksmith from over in Norwood and the best mule trader around. He rode through town like America's version of the old Roman chariot parades, waving to the crowds.

Flags and banners flew all over town announcing the many events. There was a checkers contest in the town square, a craft show, and a baked goods sale—not to be confused with the cookie and pie contest to be held around noon at the Methodist church hall.

Maurice left the boys alone while he checked out the knives and guns display on tables in front of the sheriff's office. "Don't be little troublemakers while I'm gone," he said as he walked away.

Terry pulled some firecrackers out of his pocket. "What are you doin'?" Larry asked. "Mr. Springer said we shouldn't get into trouble."

"No," Terry said, walking away. "He said we shouldn't be little troublemakers."

"Then what do you got in mind?"

"Simple. We're gonna be big troublemakers and not get caught!"

Larry shook his head but followed Terry anyway. Terry dropped a firecracker in the town square outhouse, managed to toss one inside the big tuba as the band marched by, and even let one loose where the old men were playing checkers.

Larry just watched, feeling half guilty and half innocent, but enjoying every moment of it. He was fascinated by his brother, who at times, seemed like a one-boy havoc squad.

Terry ran through the crowds, putting lemon in the water cups for the whistling contest, pulling as many pigtails as he could find, and moving the cakes around in the cake walk contest until only a paper-thin five year old could get through without stepping on them.

By the time Maurice got back, Terry was tired out. "This is good sweet corn. You boys want me to buy you some?"

"I'd rather have cotton candy," Terry said.

"I'm not hungry," Larry replied, hoping that Maurice hadn't heard about Terry's antics.

"You boys been good?" Maurice asked, biting on the ear of corn.

"I have," Larry grinned.

"What 'bout you, Terry?" Maurice asked.

"Right as rain I've been good. I wasn't no little troublemaker, you can count on that."

Maurice finished the corn and dropped it into the trash barrel on the sidewalk. "Sure you boys don't want some corn?" They shook their heads no. "You boys heard the news?"

"What news?" Larry asked.

"'Bout Sweet."

"What about Sweet?" Terry asked. "Did he explode from eatin' or somethin'?"

"No sir," Maurice said, "he's come down with the chicken pox."

"Chicken pox?" the boys exclaimed.

"And he can't be the judge of the pie and cookie contest." Terry jumped up. "Where you goin'?" Maurice asked.

"Got to find Mrs. Bentley."

"Yeah," said Larry running behind him, "we're the next-in-line judges."

They found Sarah Bentley with a group of women at the craft sale. "We're ready to eat!" Terry shouted as they ran into the roped-off area.

"Don't be sayin' that!" Larry whispered, bopping him. "Sweet's sick, Mrs. Bentley."

"He is?" she asked, concerned. "What's wrong?"

"Got the chicken pox," Terry said. "It's too bad for him but good for us."

"It is?" she said. Then she remembered what she'd promised the boys.

"We're here to help judge," Larry said.

"Point us the way to the pies," Terry said, shaking with excitment.

"Oh, dear," Sarah said, shaking her head.

As the Younguns tried to figure out which pies they wanted to eat and judge, Rev. Youngun held Carla's hands in his church office. He'd left Sherry with the other girls who were tending their horses.

"Carla," he said, "I've got something for you."

"What is it, Thomas?"

Without any fanfare, he took out the ring and put it on her finger. "This is the ring I bought you. Sherry found it. We can get married whenever you want."

Carla's eyes brightened. "But you haven't even officially asked me yet."

"Will you marry me?"

Carla hesitated for a moment and turned to the window. His face registered concern, but all she was doing was trying to compose herself. "Yes," she said, slowly turning around. "I will marry you. I will be Mrs. Thomas Youngun."

Rev. Youngun hugged and kissed her, then danced a jig around the room. Carla laughed and clapped. Rev. Youngun grinned. "Let's elope!"

"We can't," she said.

"Come on," he said, still dancing around. "We can slip off in the buggy up to Norcross and get married. No one will be the wiser."

"But you've got Sherry waiting for you outside."

He stopped dancing. "I know, I know. It just seems that it's something we should do right now, that we shouldn't wait." He took her in his arms. "I just have the feeling that something's gonna happen, that's all."

Carla covered his face with kisses. "Thomas, Thomas," she cooed between kisses, "we've got the rest of our lives awaiting us.

Nothing's going to come between us or happen to us. I love you. I love you."

Outside, Julia Steadman was giving Sherry a hard way to go. "You're wearing pants," she sneered.

"Pa said it's all right," Sherry said, grooming her horse.

"Why don't you just become a boy. You ride like a boy and fight like a boy."

Sherry turned. "Why don't you get outta here 'fore I think about actin' like a boy and knockin' you down?"

"I'm goin' to the craft show. My father says it's not right for girls to learn how to camp. That's boy stuff." Julia stuck her tongue out. "You're just snips and snails and I'm sugar and spice, and that's all there is to it." She took off before Sherry could react.

Across the town square, under the tent, the pie and cookie judging was about to begin. Sarah Bentley whispered to her son Willy, "Don't let them bother you."

Willy looked at Terry and Larry, who were wearing aprons. Though the judging hadn't even begun yet, Larry already had half of a cookie in his hand and Terry had a strawberry pie ring around his mouth.

"Mother," Willy said, shaking his head, "I don't think this is going to work out."

"Time to eat!" Terry shouted out.

Sarah handed them each a pencil and note pad to list the results. "And I want you to take this very seriously. The young ladies of the county have baked their hearts out for this event."

"And how do we decide who the winner is?" Larry asked, slipping Dangit a cookie under the table.

"You decide by the taste," Sarah said.

Terry grinned. "They all look like winners to me," he said, sticking his finger in a blackberry pie. From the corner of his eye he noticed two freckled fingers creeping along the edge of the table toward the cookie plate. Then the freckled arm attached to the fingers appeared, and a handful of cookies disappeared. A brown hand snuck up on the other side and grabbed a handful from another contestant's plate.

Terry looked around to see if anyone else had noticed, and casually walked over, acting as if he was examining the cookies.

He looked under the table and saw his friends Little James and Frenchie smiling back with cookie crumbs on their faces. He leaned over, pretending to tie his shoe, and lifted up the table skirt. "What are you guys doin'?"

"Eatin'," Little James said.

Terry frowned. "I know that, but I'm the judge, not you guys."

"We're just helpin' you out," Frenchie said.

"Get out of the way," a man came screaming through the baking contest tent, "an animal's gone crazy over at the mule stalls."

Maurice ran up behind the man. "You boys better get over there," he said, breathing hard.

"What's wrong?" the boys asked in unison.

"Crabbie's goin' crazy. I told 'em to wait, but they didn't pay me no mind."

"What?" Larry asked.

"I told 'em to wait for you boys to come back. But the pullin' contest is about to begin and they wanted to get your mule over with. Crabbie done kicked the judge in the behind and is knockin' the stuffin' out of everythin'."

Larry followed Maurice. Terry was hesitant. He looked around at the cookies and pies. *This is what heaven must be like,* he thought.

"Come on!" Larry shouted. "You got the pickles."

Terry felt the soggy dill in his pocket and sighed. "Can we start judgin' now?" he asked Sarah.

Sarah, who had heard everything Maurice had said, just shrugged. "Sure. Why, just go right ahead."

"Great!" Terry shouted, grabbing his judge's box. He ran up and down between the tables, filling it full of cookies and pies, shouting, "Winner! Winner! Winner!"

"What are you doing?" Sarah shouted, running behind him.

"I'm gonna judge and run at the same time," he shouted, carrying the box as carefully as he could. He only had to stop twice to fill his mouth full of cookies. Sarah didn't notice the hands reaching up behind her, clearing the cookies and pies off the table.

By the time Larry and Maurice got there, a circle of men and mule traders had gathered. "That's the kickingest mule I done ever seen!" one of the men shouted out.

A burly mule trainer from Springfield stepped in front of Crab Apple with a two-by-four in his hand. "Move away, boys," he said, circling around the mule. "You got to hit a mule between the eyes to get his attention."

Larry ran into the circle. "Stop it! Leave Crab Apple alone!"

The mule trainer turned to look at Larry and didn't see Crab Apple rear back. He kicked the board from the man's hands, sending it flying over the crowd.

"Dangit," the mule trainer shouted out, "that mule's dangerous!"

Dangit the dog, who had followed behind Terry, rushed through the circle of legs and grabbed the man's pants. They got so tangled up, he fell in the horse trough.

Larry climbed on Crab Apple's back. "Time to go, Crabbie." But the mule didn't move.

Terry came running up, jumped onto a box, and bounded up onto Crab Apple's back. "Listen up, Crabbie," he shouted, crunching down on the pickle.

The mule trainer pulled himself out of the horse trough and stood there dripping wet. "Gimme my board. I'm gonna whack that mule!"

But at the crunch of the pickle, Crab Apple bolted forward, knocking the man back into the horse trough. Maurice shook his head as the boys held on for dear life. *This is turning out to be a Mule Day to remember.*

CHAPTER 41

HIT THE TRAIL

Rev. Youngun waved good-bye to Carla as he and Sherry rode off from behind the church. The line of horses headed toward the north hills. No one noticed the wildcat that was following them along the top of the ridge.

The wildcat opened his mouth to growl out the anger over the burning madness in his rabid brain. But the riders didn't hear it. His cry was drowned out by the whistle of the St. Louis train approaching.

Ellen Boyle and Page O'Mally watched Mansfield come into view. To Page, it was just another whistle stop, but to Ellen, it was as if time had stopped. All she could think about was Thomas Huleatt and what might have been.

Laura and her Good Government Committee welcomed them at the station. Manly waited on the side, uncomfortable with meeting Boyle, but trying to meet Laura halfway.

Laura smiled. "Welcome to Mansfield," she said.

"You think this will be as wild as St. Louis?" Ellen asked, looking around, nervous about seeing Huleatt.

"They speak their minds here, but the difference is they let you say your piece. Usually."

Page held up Laura's article on home beauty parlors. "This is quite a switch from 'Women Shall Rule,' isn't it?"

"Just a temporary change in tactics," Laura said.

Josie the herbalist was in town for the parade and had stopped in to watch the train arrive. She never traveled much, but she enjoyed looking at other people coming and going places. She listened to the stranger speak.

"Well, I hope you've got me a spoon for my collection," said Ellen.

Laura looked down, then into her face. "Mansfield's not big enough to have a commemorative spoon."

Ellen sighed. "I should have thought as much. Oh well, now if someone could find me the Salem black cat and witch spoon, that'd please me to no end."

Black cat and witch spoon? Josie thought. *I got one of those at home.* Josie stood there a moment, trying to decide what to do. Should she give it to Ellen Boyle or keep it for herself?

Steadman had heard that Boyle was arriving on the train, and charged through the assembled women at the station. "Mrs. Boyle, my name is—"

Ellen sensed trouble and interrupted him. "That's Miss Boyle."

Steadman laughed nervously. "Oh, I guess I should have known that." For a moment, they locked eyes, eyes that couldn't hide the resentment that each felt for the other.

"Miss Boyle, my name is James Steadman, and I'd like to challenge you to a debate."

"A debate on what?" Ellen asked. "I'm here to raise funds for the building of a statue."

Steadman turned to Laura. "Would you mind if she and I debated the women's voting issue? I'm sure it would draw a better crowd."

"It's not up to me," Laura said, "it's up to Miss Boyle."

Ellen laughed. "If you want to debate, then you can have a go at me. There aren't two sides on this issue."

Steadman smiled. "Then it's a deal. Shake." He held out his hand and Ellen hesitated, then shook it vigorously. "You shake like a man," Steadman said with smiling venom.

"And you shake like a snake," she snapped, then stopped.

"What's wrong?" Page asked trying to see what had caught Ellen's attention.

Standing on the side was Thomas Huleatt. He and Ellen had locked eyes. First he smiled, then she smiled, and soon they were walking toward each other like they were the only people on earth.

It was like they were back in Ireland. Twenty years younger. With no one around. Huleatt felt faint, dizzy. Boyle almost couldn't breathe. It was something that each thought would never come again. That feeling of love, wanting, needing each other.

"What's gotten into her?" Page asked Laura.

Steadman saw Ellen walking toward Huleatt. When they hugged, he didn't know what to think. "Huleatt? What are you doin' man? I thought you dropped her?"

Manly laughed. "You ever been in love with anyone beside yourself, Steadman?"

Ellen and Huleatt were oblivious to it all. *I love you,* Huleatt mouthed, tears rimming his eyes. *I love you,* Ellen mouthed, her throat catching on her own tears.

They were virtually nose to nose, but neither could find the words to express their feelings. Huleatt closed his eyes, but Ellen gently opened them with her fingertips.

"Don't close 'em, Thomas Huleatt. I want to love you with my eyes open."

"You remembered," he whispered.

"I never forgot, not for a moment," she said, taking his face and kissing him lightly.

When he reached out and hugged her, and kissed her like his life depended on it, the crowd was so surprised they all began to clap. Everyone was cheering. Everyone, except Steadman.

"I read that you own a pub," she said, after their lips unlocked.

"In America they call 'em saloons," Huleatt said.

"I'd like to see it," she whispered.

"Come on," Huleatt said, taking her hand. "Let's go have one for the green. We've got twenty years and a whole ocean to catch up on."

Ellen took his hand and laughed at the shocked expression on her assistant's face. "I'll meet you at the hotel in an hour."

As they walked away, Page asked Laura, "Where is this hotel?"

Manly picked up their bags. "It's this way," he said, walking toward the street.

"Come on," Laura said, taking her arm, "we'll wait for Ellen with you."

CHAPTER 42

HELPLESS LITTLE GIRL

Several miles outside of town, the line of father-daughter riders rode along the ridges. They headed to a spot near Mountain Grove where they could safely camp beside a stream.

Sherry's old horse just plodded along, but Rev. Youngun's filly was skittish. The filly's head turned from side to side, as if looking for something.

"What's wrong with your horse, Pa?" Sherry asked.

"I don't know," he said, rubbing the horse's neck, "something's bothering her."

They followed the old logging road until the trail ended, then cut across a cold stream and up through a split in the rock ridge. They'd been riding for an hour and were about five miles from Mansfield.

It was a hot, humid June day, and before long the horses were bathed in sweat. Rev. Youngun's horse bucked up. She didn't want to stay in line.

No one saw the rabid wildcat following them on the boulder above. It tracked them with its filmy eyes, dripping saliva, foam on its lips.

Suddenly, the other horses began to spook. The wildcat screamed loudly. Some of the girls screamed as their fathers looked around, trying to calm the horses.

"Pa, look!" Sherry screamed, pointing to the wildcat. It looked ready to jump at him.

Suddenly the wildcat jumped at Rev. Youngun. But the filly reared up in time and the wildcat missed. Rev. Youngun held on as best he could, but his horse bucked up, then went in circles.

"Whoa, stop, stop!" he said.

"Look at that cat's mouth," Mr. Bedal shouted.

"It's rabid!" several men said at the same time.

Everyone saw the foam coming from its lips. Rev. Youngun's horse backed against the rocks and spun around. He slipped halfway from the saddle and smashed the left side of his head against a sharp outcrop.

"Oh, no," he said, trying to hold on. His vision was blurred. He reached up and felt the blood. He was dizzy and couldn't see out of his left eye, but he managed to hold onto his saddle.

"Pa!" Sherry screamed, but he was dazed and slumped forward on his horse.

The other horses reared up around them, and took off back down the trail. The wildcat spun around in circles, then charged toward Rev. Youngun's horse.

Sherry froze, not knowing what to do. Her father was slumped on his horse.

"Ride off, Sherry," her father cried weakly. "Get outta here. That wildcat's rabid."

Rabid! The word hit her like an arrow. She'd heard what rabid animals can do. If they bite you, you'll die. She looked at her father's bleeding face and then at the animal who was stalking him.

Without thinking, she charged her horse between them. "Leave us alone!" she screamed at the dangerous animal. The wildcat moved forward, swiping at her with his paw.

"Sherry, ride away. He'll kill you," her father moaned. Blood ran down the side of his face. His shirt was streaked with crimson.

The wildcat jumped forward and Sherry charged her horse toward it. She backed her horse up and took the filly's reins. "Hold on, Pa!" she screamed, kicking her horse, who didn't need much prodding to race away.

Sherry didn't know where they were headed. All she knew was that she had to get her Pa to safety and away from that rabid animal.

The gun shot she heard behind her didn't register. All she could think about was the wound on her father's face.

"Good shot," Bedal said to Campbell, who put down his rifle.

"Is everyone all right?" asked Scales, the telegraph operator.

A little girl with tears in her eyes whimpered, "Rev. Youngun was hurt bad."

"Where is he?" the men asked, looking around.

"Look here," Bedal said, pointing. "Look at the blood on this rock."

"And on the ground here," Campbell said.

The men looked at the dead wildcat and then at the blood. "If he got bit, he's gonna die," Bedal said.

"Maybe he just bumped his head," Scales said.

Campbell shook his head. "He must be losin' blood fast. No matter what happened, if we don't get him to Dr. George, he's gonna die."

"And he's got the little girl with him," Scales said.

"A hurt man and a helpless girl. That's bad news," Bedal said. "Come on, let's try to find them."

CHAPTER 43

FOR THE GREEN

"There's so much I want to say," Huleatt said, looking into Ellen's eyes.

"We've got some time," Ellen smiled.

"But what about the debate? Can't you skip it?"

"I came here to speak, and that I've got to do," Ellen said. "But I've thought about you for so long that it seems I've never left you."

"But you did," Huleatt said, looking down.

Ellen found it hard to explain how she felt. Something inside told her to reach out and start again. To take this man and tell him all she'd been through, all she'd learned.

She smiled. "Hey, Thomas," she said. "This is supposed to be a happy reunion."

"I . . . I'm just overwhelmed," he said, taking a deep breath.

"Well, we're in your saloon. What do you say we have one for the green? For old times."

Huleatt signaled to the bartender. "Bring us two shots of Irish whiskey."

"Coming right up, boss," the bartender said. He watched them go into the office, then he took the bottle out from under the bar that Cunningham had left and poured two drinks.

The bartender took the drinks into Huleatt's office, set them down, and left without saying anything. Huleatt looked into Ellen's eyes. "I still love you," he whispered, "with all my heart and soul."

"I'll toast to that," she whispered.

They drank the toast and he said, "There's somethin' I want to show you." He took out the picture of them he saved.

"Oh, Thomas!" she said, "look how young we were!"

He smiled. "You haven't aged a day. Let's sit on the couch for a moment. I'm feeling kind of dizzy."

"So am I," she said, suddenly feeling the world slip away. Within moments they were asleep on his couch. The picture of the two of them back in Ireland sat on Ellen's lap.

Laura and Manly waited in the lobby of the Mansfield Hotel for Ellen to check in. Page had begged off, supposedly to get some air. But she really wanted to snoop around the saloon to see what Ellen was up to.

The bartender found Huleatt and Boyle passed out and called Dr. George, thinking they were dying. Cunningham came in and sat at the bar, wondering what all the commotion was about. He looked into the office and knew immediately what had happened.

"They ain't gonna wake up for a long while," he blurted out.

"What, what'd you say?" Dr. George asked.

"I said, they ain't gonna wake up for a long while. They're drugged asleep."

"Drugged?" Dr. George exclaimed, putting down his probe. "How do you know?"

"'Cause I did what Mr. Huleatt asked me. I put the sleeping medicine in the bottle of Irish," Cunningham said. "It's a long story," he sighed.

The bartender looked at him. "Was it in that bottle you brought here a few days back?" Cunningham nodded. "Oh, Lord," the bartender said, shaking his head. "That's what I poured the two of them."

When Page heard what happened, she raced back over to the Mansfield Hotel and told Laura and Manly. "What are we going to do?" she asked frantically. "Who's goin' to debate that lout?"

"I don't know." Laura said, frowning. "I wish we had someone else to take Steadman on."

Manly put his hands on Laura's shoulders. "You gotta do it, honeybee."

"Me? I've done enough to upset you."

Manly put his finger to her lips. "It's somethin' you gotta do. Ain't no one else in this small town got the power of your mind."

"But Manly, I—"

"No ifs, ands, or buts, girl. You go give him your best and that's it. That's the way I want it."

Laura hugged her husband as tightly as she possibly could.

CHAPTER 44

PLEASE DON'T DIE, PA!

Sherry found what she thought was a safe spot by a stream, and managed to get her father off his horse. Blood streamed down his face, and he couldn't see clearly through his left eye.

"You're hurt bad, Pa."

"I know. Where are we?" he asked, half dazed.

"I think we're between Mountain Grove and Mansfield." She knew his wound needed to be bandaged. Sherry opened up her trail pack and took out the only dress she'd brought along.

"What are you doing?" he asked, as she ripped it into strips.

"I got to bandage up your head."

What happened to me? Rev. Youngun wondered as she wrapped the dress strips around his head. His mind was blank. He remembered the wildcat, his horse bucking, but after that it was a foggy blank.

The blood seeped through the bandages. Sherry felt like crying. *Please don't die, Pa!*

Rev. Youngun couldn't keep his head up. "Got to . . . lie down," he managed to get out.

She put her trail pack under his head. "I've got to get you help, Pa." But her father didn't answer. *Should I stay with him? How do you stop blood? I need Dr. George.*

As the bandages she had tied turned a dark red, Sherry knew she couldn't wait much longer. She listened to the voice of strength inside her and mounted her horse.

I've got to save my Pa! I've got to!

"I'll be back soon, with help," she said, but he didn't answer.

She rode off, slapping the horse's flanks to make him go faster. "Hurry! Pa's dying!" she cried out.

Halfway up the ridge she turned and looked back. *What if I get lost? What if I can't find my way back? If I can just get Pa onto his horse, I can pull him behind me. I can get him to the doctor faster.*

Sherry rode back down and lifted her father's head up. "Pa," she said softly, sickened by the sight of so much blood. "You're comin' with me."

There was no one else to help her. She was all alone. She struggled to lift him up, but he was too heavy. "Stand up Pa. Wake up and stand, Pa. We've got to get to the doctor."

Her father retched and moaned. Sherry closed her eyes and prayed like she'd never prayed before. Her father rose to his knees, then to his feet. He staggered to the horse by draping his arms over Sherry's shoulders and stumbling behind his little daughter. He gripped the saddle horn.

"You can do it, Pa. You can do it," she said, pushing his leg up.

Rev. Youngun squeezed the saddle horn and pulled, but fell down on his knees.

"Get up, Pa," Sherry begged. "You got to get up on the horse."

She struggled to pull her father up, not noticing that her blouse and pants were covered with blood. "Grab the saddle, Pa," Sherry whispered. "Pull hard."

CHAPTER 45

THE GREAT DEBATE

Word hadn't gotten back to Mansfield about the wildcat and the search for Rev. Youngun and his daughter. The other Younguns were back at the festivities.

Maurice managed to smooth things over with the mule trainers so that Crabbie could enter the log-pulling contest. Terry crunched and moved the pickle on a stick like levers on a machine. To everyone's surprise but Maurice's, Crabbie managed to pull the log the farthest.

Carla was proud of her future step-sons and took them for ice cream at the stand set up next to city hall. Little by little, the boys were beginning to accept her.

By sunset, a crowd gathered at the flag-draped podium that had been set up for Ellen's speech. Steadman had spread the word that their debate was sure to be a battle royale, and only a few knew that Ellen was not going to be there.

Steadman's supporters were gathered in the streets and some ladies from the Good Government Club had shown up in red, white, and blue outfits. Taking Laura's hand, Manly walked her out of the hotel. They hadn't gone more than a few steps when he stopped. "Laura, I got to tell you something."

"What Manly? I've got to go debate Steadman."

"That's what it's about," he said. "I just want to tell you that I've been jealous of how you can speak your mind, 'bout how you can write so good, 'bout how you seem to know so much."

"Oh, Manly."

"No, listen. I wish I had your brains. I wish I could do what you do, but I can't," he said, looking down.

She squeezed his hand and whispered, "I wish I had your courage, your strength, and the ability you have to take other people's feelings into consideration. I wish I didn't fly off my own way without thinking first. I . . ."

Ellen's assistant called out from down the street. "The debate's about to start. Are you coming?" Page asked.

Manly smiled. "She's comin'. And I'm comin' with her."

They kissed on the street, under the gas lamp. It was a new beginning. When Laura stepped up onto the platform, she had the world in the palm of her hand. She had everything she needed. She and Manly were together.

In the woods north of town, Sherry gripped the reins of her father's horse. "Hold on, Pa, we're almost there."

She tried to sound reassuring, but inside she was anything but sure. As the darkness closed in around her, the little bit of trail she'd found disappeared. All her fears of the dark came out but she fought them back. *I've got to save Pa,* she told herself over and over.

Rev. Youngun knew that his life was in his daughter's hands. For some reason, all he could think was, *I'm in the hands of Adam's rib.* He smiled for a moment, then grimaced with a pain that ripped through his head. He vomited down the side of his horse, feeling like he was dying.

She's a brave girl, he thought, holding on to the mane of the horse. *She's saving my life. She's as brave as any man.* He nodded, then shook his head, even though it pained him. *No, she's a brave person. A very brave little person.*

Back in Mansfield, Laura ignored the catcalls as she took her place next to Steadman. Objectivity had gone out the window. The crowd was divided along gender lines. Summers watched from the back, covering the story, standing in the middle.

The debate began along the debating rules that Steadman insisted upon, but soon broke down into a verbal free-for-all. The men in the crowd were on Steadman's side. "Let's take a vote on women having the right to vote," he shouted smugly. "All those in favor, say aye."

The hands from the women's side of the room went up. Steadman laughed. "Your votes don't count."

"That's the point," Laura said. "We helped build this country but we can't vote."

"The law's the law," Steadman said condescendingly.

"Women can no longer hide behind their husbands and their opinions," Laura said to the crowd.

Steadman stopped her. "You should be home taking care of your husband and not here taking the place of that Irish old maid, Ellen Boyle."

Martha and David Cunningham waited for Laura to speak. Sarah Bentley nodded approval at Steadman's comments.

Laura shook her head. "Mr. Steadman calls Ellen Boyle an old maid, but there are no more old maids anywhere in the world. Once women were placed in one of two classes and labeled accordingly. She was either 'Mrs. So-and-so' or she was an old maid."

"Pity the ones who aren't happily married," Steadman said mocking Laura. "They're missing out on their one true career."

"You're wrong, so wrong," Laura said. "Women are successful lumber dealers, livestock breeders, caterers, doctors. Why, they've entered every ordinary profession."

Steadman interrupted her. "God help us if women take control. We'll be having beauty parlor wars in every town." The men in the crowd laughed and cheered him on.

Laura held up her hands for silence. "Women will one day be serving in Congress. Mr. Steadman doesn't realize it, but our sheer numbers mean that one day we shall rule side by side with men."

"Not in my lifetime, God forbid," Steadman said, shaking his head.

"Mark my words, women are not helpless. With the ballot in our hands, we're going to be making decisions in the democratic world."

Steadman banged the podium. "Women are needed to rock the cradle, where they belong. Women are not ready to rule this country, or any country. They are ignorant about government and too uncontrolled in their emotions."

Laura stayed calm. "More and more women and men are coming to stand together on terms of equality. We want to bring politics out into the open." Laura looked across the faces in the crowd. "We deserve the right to vote. That fact is not open to debate."

"Any man who believes that women can handle voting is no man at all," Steadman shouted, looking around the room. "Is there a man in the house who will stand up for this nonsense?"

Heads turned throughout the room. Laura looked. No one stood up. Laura saw some of the women grumbling and held up her hands. "Look into your souls. It is you men who have to answer the sound of this silence."

From the back of the room, a solitary clapping was heard. Manly came walking down the center of the room, clapping loudly. Laura thought her heart was going to burst with love.

From the side of the room, Summers clapped, then Maurice. Martha pinched her husband and he stood up and began to clap. Laura wanted to cry but didn't want to give Steadman the edge. Sarah looked at the men around her, feeling betrayed.

"Did you know about the plan to drug Boyle?" Dr. George called out as he entered the room.

Steadman was caught off guard. Bentley motioned him over and whispered what had happened. Steadman came back and said, "Though I will defend my right to disagree to Mrs. Wilder, I want to state that I had nothing to do with what happened to Miss Boyle."

"Good," Laura said. "Now I'd like to pass the hat so we can build the statue that we're supposed to be talking about. We're still almost sixteen hundred dollars short."

"Hold up the picture so we all can see what it will look like," Maurice called out.

"I'll do better than that," said a man's voice with a British accent.

All eyes turned as Patrick Jefferson pushed the covered statue in on the small wheeled base. At the door of the hall stood Mae, holding on, searching with her sightless eyes.

Laura walked through the crowd and took Mae's hand. "Mrs. Jefferson, it's me, Laura Wilder."

"I stood outside and heard what you said," Mae said. "Those were powerful words."

"The truth will set us both free," Laura said. "Now come on, I want to introduce the gifted artist who made the beautiful statue of Sacagawea."

"Did you already uncover it?" Mae asked, taking a hesitant step forward.

"No, you're going to," Laura said, walking with her toward the podium.

CHAPTER 46

BLACK CAT SPOON

"Hold on, Pa!" Sherry said, gripping the reins of her father's horse. "I can see lanterns up ahead."

Sherry rode toward the lights and emerged through the brush to find a group of men who'd been tracking them in the dark.

"Who's that," Lafayette Bedal called out as Sherry rode toward them.

"It's me, Sherry," she answered. "Come on, Pa," she whispered, "not too much longer."

Some of the men helped Rev. Youngun from his horse. "He's bleeding bad," Campbell said.

The sheriff looked at the blood seeping out from the bandage. "Who put this bandage on?" he asked loudly.

Sherry sat on her horse, suddenly worried she'd done something wrong. "I did," she said weakly.

Sheriff Peterson turned and paused. "You did a good job. You saved your daddy's life, little girl." He turned to Bedal, "You ride to town and let the doc know we're comin'." As Bedal mounted his horse, the sheriff shouted out, "Let's make a stretcher so we can move Rev. Youngun safely."

Bedal rode hard through the woods and didn't slow down until he came down Main Street. He went to Dr. George's office, but he wasn't there. A neighbor said he was down at the debate, so Bedal rode his sweat-drenched horse to the town hall and hopped off.

He ran into the room, panting. "Is Dr. George here?" he shouted.

All heads turned in the room. "I'm right here," Dr. George said.

"You got to come quick," Bedal said excitedly. "Rev. Youngun's been hurt bad." Carla closed her eyes. Larry looked at Terry, whose eyes were rimmed with tears.

"Where is he?" Dr. George said, walking toward Bedal.

"His daughter saved him. The little girl saved him. His head's cut bad and—"

"Take me to him," Dr. George said.

"They're bringin' him to your office," Bedal said. "Come on."

Carla and the two boys followed them to the doctor's office. Rev. Youngun's head was bandaged up and he lay on the office couch.

"Oh, Thomas, are you all right?" Carla said, grasping his hand.

Rev. Youngun looked up. "I hurt, but the doctor says I'm going to live."

Larry stood at the end of the couch. "Pa, how'd you manage to save yourself?"

Terry looked over and saw his sister in her blood-soaked clothes curled up in the corner. "Is Sherry okay?" he asked.

"Nothin' some sleep and a good, warm bath won't cure," Dr. George said, smiling.

Sherry lay in the corner, fast asleep, sucking her finger and holding her blanket and dolly. Rev. Youngun said, "Your sister saved my life. She's a hero. A real little hero."

Across town at Tippy's, Ellen and Huleatt were coming around. Their heads felt weighted down and they didn't know what had happened to them.

"Thomas, one moment I was talking with you and the next moment . . ."

Huleatt figured out what happened and shook his head. "Just rewards," he said, laughing.

Ellen rubbed her eyes. "What's this?" she asked, looking at the spoon in her lap.

"What is it?" Huleatt said, blinking and trying to focus.

"Why, it's the black cat and witch spoon!" she exclaimed. "Now my collection is complete!"

"How'd it get here?" Huleatt asked.

"It's what I've been wishing for," Ellen said.

"I don't believe in magic, do you?" he asked.

"It was magic that brought us together," she said. Neither of them noticed Josie watching outside the window, smiling.

Ellen snuggled against Huleatt's shoulder. "I had a wonderful dream."

"What'd you dream about?" Huleatt whispered, hugging her.

"I was back in Ireland."

He smiled. "So was I," he said.

"At our secret—"

"Place by the creek. Behind the bushes where we . . ."

She smiled and touched his lips with her fingers. "Where we first kissed and I didn't listen to my heart," she said, looking down.

"It's never too late to try again," he said, kissing her chin.

"Here? Right here?" she whispered.

"How 'bout back in Ireland, where it all began?" he said.

Ellen's assistant came into the room, "Ellen? Ellen, are you—" Page stopped when she saw them kissing and closed the door. *She's changed. I've never seen her this way.*

CHAPTER 47

TOGETHER AGAIN

The next day, Bentley pulled his car into the dirt drive of a small house. Martha and David Cunningham looked at one another.

"But you said you were driving us home, Mr. Bentley," Martha said.

"That's right, to your new home," said Bentley.

Tears came to Martha's eyes. "But we rent down the lane."

"You deserve this. You've put in a lot of years for my family. I'm giving you this house to live in for the rest of your lives on this earth. And David," he said, turning to the old man, "I'm going to pay you a salary each month to take care of Martha and buy all the necessities. But there'll be no money for drinking. Is that understood?"

The old man nodded. "Yes, Mr. Bentley."

"Good. I've got some of my crew carrying over all your possessions from the old house and your clothes from our house."

"But what about the missus?" Martha asked.

"What about her?" said Bentley.

"Who'll do the cleanin'?"

"She'll get by," he said, handing them the keys. "Now go on inside. You've earned the rest."

They got out and stood by the car. Bentley started to back up, then stopped. "And Martha, there's one other thing."

"Yes, Mr. Bentley."

A loud *meow,* echoed from the front porch.

"Cuddles comes with the house. See ya," he said, pulling away.

At the Younguns' home, Rev. Youngun was recovering nicely under the care of Carla Pobst. While she nursed him, they made plans for their marriage. She wanted a big wedding and he wanted a small one. But they both wanted the same thing—to be married to each other.

Sherry seemed to walk taller. She would forever have the knowledge that she'd saved her father's life. Summers wrote a nice article about what a little hero Sherry was.

Over at Apple Hill Farm, Laura, Manly, Ellen, and Huleatt sat on the front porch. Huleatt had come to tell them that he and Ellen were going to Ireland.

Laura smiled at Ellen. "I'm happy for you. Happy for you both."

Ellen squeezed Huleatt's hand. "Not many people in life get a second chance."

"And I don't intend to let her go this time," Huleatt said.

Manly stood on the corner of the front porch looking out over the orchards of Apple Hill Farm. He coughed to get attention. "Can I ask a silly question?"

They all turned. "Yes?" said Laura.

He looked at Ellen. "If you're goin' back to Ireland, who's goin' to take your place while you're gone?"

"I don't understand what you mean," Ellen said.

"What I mean is, who's goin' to speak at all the rallies and such?" asked Manly.

Laura nodded. "I was wondering about that myself. We've got so much work to do before we can vote."

"My assistant, Page O'Mally, is a good speaker and committed to the cause. She, along with Susan B. Anthony and the other ladies, will have to carry on without me for a while."

"For how long?" Laura asked. "You've given your heart to the movement here in America."

Ellen paused, looking at Huleatt, then said. "I have given my heart to getting women the right to vote, but it's time to do something for my self. Something for my own heart."

She looked at Laura and smiled. "You've got your husband, your daughter, and this wonderful farm. It's taken you how long to do all this?"

"About twenty years," Manly answered.

"Well, it's been twenty years since I thought I lost Thomas. It's time for me to have a life of my own."

"But you just can't drop it. You've been too committed to the women of America," Laura said.

Huleatt started to answer but Ellen nodded once that she would handle it. "Thomas and I are going back to Ireland to try and recapture something we left behind a long time ago."

"But we've almost got the right to vote. I can feel it coming," said Laura. "The women of America need you."

"The Irish women need her also," Huleatt said. "Ellen won't be givin' up her convictions, she's just goin' to see if she wants to marry an old saloon keeper like me."

"Oh, Thomas," she said, laughing.

"Though I hope we'll be gettin' married at my mum's old house in Tipperary, I don't care if we get married on horseback." He took Ellen's face in one hand and turned her chin. "I don't want to ever lose you again."

He kissed her lips lightly, which ended all discussion of what their plans were.

After Ellen and Huleatt left for town, Summers called on the phone. "Laura, got something here for you."

"What is it?" she asked, curiously.

"Got here a check for one thousand five hundred and forty-two dollars."

"What?" Laura exclaimed. "That's exactly what we owe on the statue."

"Yup, made out to the Good Government Club's statue fund."

"Where . . . where did it come from?"

"It's a secret," he said.

"A secret? Come on, Andrew, tell me."

"Well, seems that last night me, Steadman, and Bentley got together down at Tippy's and agreed to fund the statue on two conditions."

"What are the conditions?" Laura asked suspiciously.

"Hold your horses," he said, enjoying the suspense. "Let me read 'em here." Laura could hear the rustling of paper over the phone. "Condition number one, is that you don't reveal who put the money up."

"All right. That's okay with me," said Laura.

"And condition number two is . . ." Summers paused.

"What is it, Andrew?"

"I put a couple bucks into the fund, and I want you to write the things that you feel. No sense having you write things that aren't from your heart."

"Oh, Andrew, you don't know how happy that makes me."

Later that evening, after the covers were turned down, Laura looked at Manly. "You're on my side of the bed," she said.

"I know," he said, grinning. "No sense sleepin' so far apart any more."

"Manly, you're the most handsome man in the world. I love you," she said, kissing his cheek.

Manly knew that he wasn't the most dashing man, but it didn't matter. Their marriage had changed for the better. They were together again, stronger in their renewed love and affection for one another.

Though women still didn't have the right to vote, what had happened in Mansfield was a bit of the small miracle that was happening all across the country. Opinions were changing. Reason was prevailing and in a few more years, women would have the right to vote.

But the real magic, the real miracle, took place a few weeks later in Ireland. On a mid-summer's day, a middle-aged man and woman rode across the green fields of Ireland. Her auburn hair flying free, his body alive with excitement, both their hearts pounding with joy.

Thomas Huleatt and Ellen Boyle found their secret place beside the creek. They returned to same spot where their hearts had stayed behind, waiting for them to return. Nothing had changed except for the twenty years of lost time that showed on their faces.

As they stood swearing never to part again, it was a simple act of love. The twenty years of loving the memory of what could have been with their eyes closed, made them appreciate the time they had left and the vows they planned to exchange.

Though it wouldn't change the world, it would change *their* world and the children they planned that would follow them.

ABOUT THE AUTHOR

T. L. Tedrow is a bestselling author, screenwriter, and film producer. His books include the eight-book "Days of Laura Ingalls Wilder Series": *Missouri Homestead, Children of Promise, Good Neighbors, Home to the Prairie, The World's Fair, Mountain Miracle, The Great Debate* and *Land of Promise,* which are the basis of a new television series. His eight-book series "The Younguns", to be released in 1993, has also been sold as a television series. He lives with his wife, Carla, and four children in Winter Park, Florida.